Christie Barlow is the num author of nineteen roma iconic Love Heart Lane Se *Farm* and *Kitty's Countryside D* cottage in a quaint village in the four children and two dogs.

Her writing career came as a lovely surprise when Christie decided to write a book to teach her children a valuable life lesson and show them that they are capable of achieving their dreams.

Christie writes about love, life, friendships and the importance of community spirit. She loves to hear from her readers and you can get in touch via Twitter, Facebook and Instagram.

f facebook.com/ChristieJBarlow
X x.com/ChristieJBarlow
BB bookbub.com/authors/christie-barlow
instagram.com/christie_barlow

Also by Christie Barlow

THE VINTAGE FLOWER VAN ON LOVE HEART LANE

CHRISTIE BARLOW

One More Chapter
a division of HarperCollins*Publishers* Ltd
1 London Bridge Street
London SE1 9GF
www.harpercollins.co.uk
HarperCollins*Publishers*
Macken House, 39/40 Mayor Street Upper,
Dublin 1, D01 C9W8, Ireland

This paperback edition 2024
1
First published in Great Britain in ebook format
by HarperCollins*Publishers* 2024
Copyright © Christie Barlow 2024
Christie Barlow asserts the moral right to
be identified as the author of this work
A catalogue record of this book is available from the British Library

ISBN: 978-0-00-841325-5

Printed and bound in the UK using 100% Renewable Electricity
by CPI Group (UK) Ltd

For Anita Redfern,

You're my absolute best friend. You're without a doubt the person I can trust with anything. Thank you for always being there for me when I need it most and making my life so much fun when we are together.

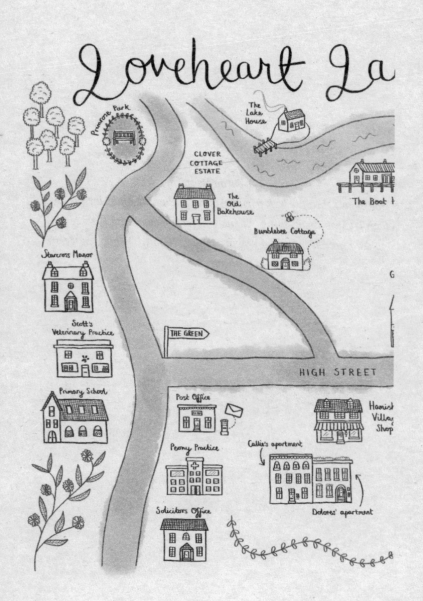

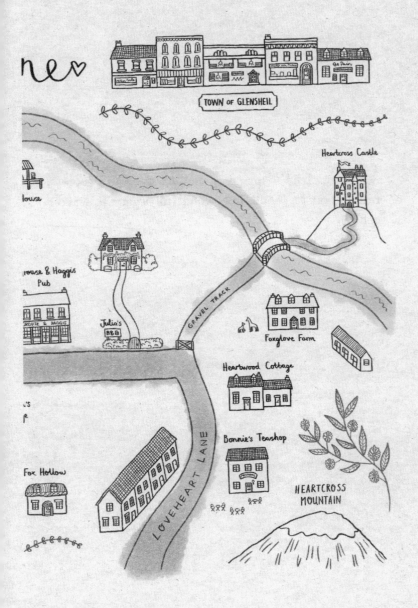

ne ♥

TOWN OF GLENSHEIL

Heartcross Castle

...ouse

...rouse & Haggis Pub

GROUSE & HAGGIS

Julia's
B&B

GRAVEL TRACK

Foxglove Farm

...'s
...

Heartwood Cottage

Fox Hollow

Bonnie's Teashop

LOVEHEART LANE

HEARTCROSS MOUNTAIN

No matter what happens in life, be good to people. Being good to people is a wonderful legacy to leave behind.

Taylor Swift.

Chapter One

'Dear friends and family, as we gather here today to remember and honour the beautiful journey of Ada Jones, we also come together to celebrate the legacy of love, kindness and joy that Ada has left behind in the village of Heartcross. Ada was a huge part of our community for over eighty years and the well-known face of The Vintage Flower Van, where she shared with us on a daily basis her joyous smile and beautiful blooms for over sixty years. We will begin today's service with Ada's favourite song, "All Things Bright and Beautiful". The first verse will be sung by Ada's great-niece, Florrie, along with Ada's lifelong friend Dolores Henderson.' With a nod, the vicar gestured for them to move to the front of the church and face the congregation.

With their arms linked, Florrie could feel herself lightly trembling. Aunt Dolores looked at her, her expression tender as she whispered, 'I've got you.'

Florrie's heart melted. Ninety-nine years old and Dolores was still looking out for her. Dolores wasn't her real auntie, but a friend who'd earned the title of family through her friendship with Ada. Together, they stepped forward and stood in front of the casket before turning to face the mourners. Florrie was thankful to have Dolores by her side. She wasn't used to being in the limelight, unlike Dolores, who was world famous – an international singing superstar whose career spanned too many decades to remember. Swallowing a lump in her throat, Florrie hoped her voice would hold out as the organist looked towards them and began to play.

From behind her sunglasses, Florrie's watery eyes glanced out over the sea of faces. All of Aunt Ada's friends and the community of Heartcross were standing in front of her, each of them remembering Ada and each of them wearing a flower, handpicked only this morning from Ada's garden, pinned to their clothes in memory of her.

By the end of the second verse the whole church was in full song. It was one Aunt Ada would sing often throughout the different seasons whilst she worked away in the gardens of her home, Rose Cottage, which she loved with all her heart. Some of her prize roses were displayed in the floral arrangements around the church. Ada had been eighty-four years old when she passed away, and had been a florist for all of her life. Following in Ada's footsteps, Florrie too had become a florist and now had her own shop, Buttercup Barn, situated just off Love Heart Lane, in the Heart of the Village shopping complex.

Ada's whole life had been all about blooms and not a single corner of the courtyard and garden in the grounds of Rose Cottage was without a flowerbed. The cottage stood on the outskirts of Heartcross, in the Scottish Highlands, where the main village was lined with traditional whitewashed houses and the prettiest gardens, all set against the spectacular backdrop of Heartcross Mountain. Ada's pastel pink vintage flower van with its duck-egg blue awning had been standing outside Rose Cottage for as long as anyone could remember. What Ada didn't know about flowers wasn't worth knowing and Florrie's fondest memories were working alongside her during every school holiday. They were days full of wonderful colours and so much laughter. According to Aunt Ada, 'Flowers are like friends, they bring colour to your world', and she had even had that quote carved into a wooden plaque that hung above the door of The Vintage Flower Van, along with a photograph of Ada's father (and Florrie's great-grandfather), Willem Hughes. Aunt Ada had been Florrie's favourite person in the whole wide world and such an inspiration in every part of her life.

As soon as the song came to an end, Martha, another of Ada's closest friends, stepped forward and stood behind the microphone to share a couple of funny stories from the past, her voice faltering at times as emotion got the better of her. She told the story of Ada's obsession with flowers, which had started when she was a teenager.

'She'd been encouraged at school to seek a career in admin' – Martha rolled her eyes and the congregation laughed – 'because of her teacher's perception that there was never any money in flowers. Of course, Ada didn't listen. No, she was savvy right from the start and erected rows of glasshouses on the land of Rose Cottage so she could cultivate her own stock. By staggering their growth and providing them with warmth and artificial light throughout the seasons, Ada proved everyone wrong. Her business pulled in a good income right from the start, and there are not many professions that smell as nice as having your own flower van with only a short commute to work!'

Even though Florrie owned her own florist business, she'd made a promise to Aunt Ada that the iconic flower van would always remain in business. It was now her main priority; a means to keep Aunt Ada's legacy alive.

As the service came to an end, Florrie blotted her tears with a tissue and put on a pair of sunglasses. She stood up, shook the hand of the vicar and thanked him for a beautiful service before she turned and headed slowly towards the doors at the back of the church. The close-knit community sharing her grief touched her arms as she walked past, offering their condolences. She was followed by her good friend Isla, who had been her rock ever since Ada's passing. Florrie knew she couldn't have gotten through the last couple of weeks without her.

'So sorry for your loss,' Rona said from where she and her daughter Felicity were standing at the end of a pew halfway down the aisle.

'Thank you. It's difficult for all of us.' Her gaze spanned the pews, acknowledging those standing at the back of the church, and her eyes caught on a handsome man in the very back row. He wore an exquisitely cut suit with a black tie and as he held her gaze, the look of adoration on his suntanned face had Florrie's heart beating fast and her stomach beginning to churn.

It couldn't be him. Not on today of all days?

Surely not.

After lifting her sunglasses to take a better look she lowered them promptly.

It was him.

A face she hadn't seen for over eight years and one she'd never expected to see again in this lifetime, if she was honest with herself. What the hell was Tom Houston doing at her great-aunt's funeral? Why would he come here? And why now? Maybe to apologise? If so, it was eight years too late.

Mulling over her options in her mind, Florrie wondered if she should acknowledge him, but knowing everyone was watching her from the sidelines, she paused. She needed to stay dignified; she couldn't go causing a scene at Aunt Ada's funeral.

Isla touched her arm. 'Are you okay? You've gone very pale.'

'I just need some air,' she replied.

'That's understandable,' Isla said kindly.

Florrie looked over in Tom's direction again. He'd disappeared. She quickly scanned the church, trying to catch sight of him, but he'd slipped away, as though he'd never been there at all.

Chapter Two

Outside the church, Florrie led the mourners to the graveside. After the vicar said one last prayer Aunt Ada was lowered into the ground and laid to rest. Florrie was restless, her eyes constantly flitting between the various mourners, trying to spot whether Tom was part of the group, but she couldn't see him. She began to question whether her mind was playing tricks on her. Had it actually been him? She hadn't seen a recent photo of him – hadn't seen *any* photo of him for a very long time, after distancing herself and blocking every channel of communication between them all those years ago, determined to never give him the chance to humiliate her a second time.

Suddenly, Florrie became aware she was surrounded by silence and all eyes were on her. The vicar's gaze was also fixed in her direction. Immediately, she realised that the vicar had requested something from her, but she'd been too distracted looking for Tom to hear what it was. She glanced towards Isla, who thankfully rescued her by nodding towards the flowers that were in the buckets at the side of the grave. Quickly picking up a couple of stems and a small mound of soil, Florrie threw them on top of the coffin and the rest of the mourners followed suit.

After more condolences were offered the crowd began to disperse, heading for the wake at the Grouse and Haggis. Florrie stayed where she was, wanting to take a moment to say her last goodbye. Isla, Martha and Dolores stayed with her.

Removing her sunglasses, she wiped the tears away again with a tissue before putting them back on. 'I'm glad I decided not to wear any mascara today,' she said with a small chuckle, trying to lighten the mood. She pointed to the graves either side. To the right was Ada's husband, Great-Uncle Ewart, and to the left were Ada's parents and grandparents. 'All back together,' murmured Florrie. 'I bet Aunt Ada insisted they were all waiting at the pearly gates with a glass of port to greet her.'

'And I think that's exactly what we're going to do now, raise a glass of Ada's favourite tipple at the wake.' Dolores pointed her walking stick towards the wrought-iron gates of the cemetery.

Florrie nodded, swallowing another lump in her throat. Waves of emotion kept washing over her and she had to do her very best to keep her composure when all she wanted to do was crumple in a heap under her duvet and sob her heart out. At least the saddest part of the day was now over. This afternoon she was relying on Dolores and Martha to lift everyone's spirits, which would include imbibing some of the alcoholic kind. They both loved an audience, and were both natural storytellers with perfect comedic timing when it came to a punchline. They would be in their element as the stars of the show, allowing Florrie to blend into the background as she processed her grief.

After one last teary bow of the head towards the grave, she walked away with the other women.

'It was a beautiful service. You've done brilliantly to get through the week, and especially today,' said Isla.

'And just look at the glorious sunshine. Ada is shining down on all us,' shared Martha, who slowed down and pointed to a poster tied around the wooden post with string. 'By the way, what are you going to do about that?' she asked Florrie.

They all stared at the poster, which was for Flowers in Bloom, the annual Heartcross competition that attracted garden enthusiasts from far and wide.

'Aunt Ada loved that day of the year. And everyone loved to see what she had created,' said Florrie.

The competition was so popular that it had been televised on numerous occasions, with the competing Heartcross residents eager to showcase their gardens and win the coveted first prize. But it had been very difficult to compete with Ada, who had won every single year for the past three decades.

'But as for this year ... I'm really not sure. Maybe it's time to pass the baton on,' added Florrie thoughtfully.

'Or maybe you should enter the gardens at Rose Cottage in memory of Ada,' suggested Dolores. 'Those blooms meant the world to her. She grew those gardens from bare, uneven land, which took a lot of blood, sweat and tears. And Ada always loved seeing the joy and appreciation on the faces of the community and tourists as they walked through the gates.'

'And, of course, the love of gardening was how she met her wonderful husband.' Martha chuckled. 'I was there that day.

They were competing against each other in a floral competition. Ewart was the clear favourite, Ada the underdog. He thought he had it in the bag, but little did he know who he was up against! Ada won, Ewart walked over to congratulate her, and the rest is history. They created the gardens together at Rose Cottage and Ewart often worked in The Vintage Flower Van. That pair were made for each other and grew together. I think you'll meet the man of your dreams through your own love of flowers,' Martha said sagely.

'The only men who ever come into Buttercup Barn to buy flowers are already in a relationship. They buy for their wife, or their girlfriend, they send roses on Valentine's Day or anniversaries. Failing that, they're there for wedding flowers or funeral flowers, so the chances are pretty slim.' Florrie smiled.

'You mark my words, the love of your life has something to do with flowers, and possibly The Vintage Flower Van. I can feel it,' argued Martha.

'As much as I love you and your psychic powers, I've been a florist for a very long time now, and I haven't met anyone.'

Martha looked her straight in the eye, the intense gaze unnerving Florrie for a second. 'That's because your heart hasn't been open to love.'

Martha's words resonated with Florrie and she felt a tiny shiver ricochet through her body. There was no denying she'd guarded her heart in recent years. Why wouldn't she? It had taken her a long time to piece her broken heart back together after what happened … after Tom's betrayal.

She remembered the very afternoon that they'd first met like it was only yesterday…

It was the last day of her uni term before the summer break and Florrie was sprawled out on a picnic blanket up in the sand dunes on Castle Sands Beach, which was the best spot to overlook the turquoise sea. As usual, the waves were breaking around the rocks in the shallows, causing a blue-white lace to foam over the shore. The sun was high in the sky and the beach busier than usual, with holidaymakers dotted up and down the golden sand and surfers catching the big breakers out in the water. She glanced at her watch and then looked up to find that he was right on cue. Tom Houston walked onto the beach and towards the usual rock where he peeled off his shirt, put on his goggles and strolled straight into the sea without flinching. The rest of the university swim team were right behind him but her gaze was fixed on Tom, who was as powerful as the waves and moved through the water effortlessly. His shoulders were broad and his tanned skin glistened. Florrie couldn't take her eyes off him. There was something about Tom Houston that she'd always found captivating. He was perfect.

It wasn't long before Tom waded from the water. He must have sensed someone was watching him because he glanced up towards the sand dunes. He was looking straight at her and though she was looking straight back at him, she knew, thanks to her sunglasses, that he couldn't be a hundred per cent sure she was staring in his direction.

It was the perfect way to spend the morning before her last lecture.

A couple of hours later, Florrie was standing in front of the vending machine outside the lecture theatre looking in dismay at the bottle of water stuck between the glass and the coil. She was about to walk away when out of the corner of her eye she saw a sudden movement. She jumped at the sound of a fist hitting the glass.

Thud!

The bottle dropped and Florrie looked sidewards then upwards straight into eyes of Tom Houston. He bent down, retrieved the bottle and held it towards her, and she took it from him, his touch sending an unexpected shiver down her spine.

He was standing close to her, making her heart beat faster. Up close, he was everything she'd imagined him to be. His skin was tanned and smooth, his hazel eyes mesmerising, and the aroma of his aftershave caused an eruption of goosebumps over her entire body.

'Thank you,' she said, hoping her voice sounded relatively normal.

'You're welcome. I can't have anyone dying of dehydration with only one lecture to go.' His eyes were fixed on hers and he didn't break her gaze.

He made her nervous.

With a rapid heartbeat Florrie twisted the lid off the bottle and went to take a drink, completely missing her mouth. Feeling like a fool, she looked down at the wet patch on her T-shirt, then wiped the water from her chin with the back of her hand.

Tom didn't try to hide his smile. 'Were you watching me this morning, Red?' he asked in his posh Scottish twang.

She avoided the question, unwilling to admit that she'd been watching him, even if he already knew. 'Red?' she quizzed.

He pointed to her long red hair. It fell to the middle of her back and was dotted with beads. Embracing university life, Florrie had her own style going on. In addition to the beads, she was also wearing all the colours of the rainbow. Her jeans were baggy and rolled up at the ankles and had coloured flowers embroidered down the side of each leg. Her feet sported bright yellow Crocs, her T-shirt was orange and her cardigan crimson.

Tom, on the other hand, looked like he'd just walked off a catwalk. He fitted perfectly into his navy suit, which screamed designer, his pink tie complemented his shirt and his brogues were polished to within an inch of their life.

'My name is Florrie.'

'Florrie, derived from the Latin "florens", which means "flourishing" or "blooming" and evokes the image of thriving flowers.' He looked towards her jeans. 'I'm guessing you like flowers.'

'I do,' she replied, smiling. 'And you are very knowledgeable about Latin phrases.'

There was a glint in his eye. 'Thanks, I still think the name "Red" suits you more.'

'And you are?' she asked.

'Tom,' he replied.

Of course, Florrie already knew everything about him.

———

She tried to push thoughts of Tom from her mind, determined not to let anything spoil the day. There was still an undercurrent of hurt and confusion in her feelings about him, small bouts of anger bubbling to the surface as she remembered how he'd made her promises only to immediately break them and smash her heart to smithereens in the process.

'I beg to differ,' she replied to Martha, knowing that was a little white lie, given that her heart was well and truly closed. She never wanted to feel that dull ache in the pit of her stomach again. It was why she'd kept every romantic prospect ever since at a distance.

'I still can't quite believe she's gone,' said Isla, giving Florrie a look that made it clear she was trying to change the subject. Once again, Florrie was grateful to have Isla as a friend, there to save her from further interrogation from her gran, Martha, by swerving the conversation into a different direction.

Another wave of emotion hit Florrie and her voice faltered when she spoke. 'I can't either. One minute she's here, drinking port, telling tales of the past, the next she's gone. Since the night she passed away, I keep wondering if maybe she knew her life was coming to its end and that's why she got out all the old photographs.'

Dolores pointed to The Vintage Flower Van as they neared it. It had been part of the funeral cortege and was now parked outside the entrance of the church. Looking smart in his dark suit, Drew Allaway, Isla's husband, was standing next to it.

'How you doing?' he asked Florrie gently.

'Holding it together as best I can.'

'It was a beautiful service and Ada will be missed.'

'Thank you.'

'Would you like me to tow The Vintage Flower Van back to the cottage?' asked Drew. 'Or would you prefer it outside the pub for the wake?'

'I think back to the cottage; let's put it back where it belongs. I'm going to place buckets full of flowers outside the van and anyone who is passing can help themselves to a free bunch in memory of Aunt Ada.'

'That's a lovely idea,' said Isla supportively.

'Thank you for taking time out this morning to help me with the van,' Florrie said to Drew. 'I know you have your work cut out up at the farm.'

'Don't be daft, you don't need to thank me.'

Florrie looked towards Drew's truck. 'Do you mind if I come with you? I just want a breather before I go and join everyone else in the pub.'

'Of course,' he replied.

Dolores touched her arm. 'We'll see you over at the pub when you're ready.'

'Do you want me to come?' asked Isla tentatively. 'Or would you rather be on your own?'

'The company would be good, even though I'm not sure the conversation will be up to much.'

Florrie, Isla and Drew watched Dolores and Martha cross the road, then the three of them climbed into the front of the truck. Drew began to drive back towards the village green and past The Old Bakehouse, the road before them covered in flowers. All of Ada's friends had lined the streets for her final journey and as the sombre cortege had made its way through Heartcross the mourners had paid tribute by throwing flowers in front of and onto the hearse.

'Look at all the flowers...' Florrie's voice faltered. 'I've never seen so many people line the streets of the village. It felt like Aunt Ada was a celebrity.'

'I have to admit,' said Drew, 'I've never seen so many people either, but we shouldn't be so surprised. Ada touched the hearts of many. She was well loved, always had a smile on her face, and went the extra mile for everyone.'

As Drew drove up the lane, and Rose Cottage appeared in front of them, Florrie reflected, 'It's strange to think that Aunt Ada won't be standing at that front gate passing the time of day with the locals. This place was her home for all of her married life and you can see why she would never want to leave. It's something special and it feels like an end of an era now that she's gone, never to return.' Florrie flapped her hand in front of her face, doing her best to hold in her tears as another wave of sadness engulfed her.

'You'll be okay,' Isla said gently. 'You have us, the cottage, your business and The Vintage Flower Van. In fact, have you thought about what you're going to do about this place? Are you going to move back in?'

Rose Cottage had been Florrie's home for many years but soon after she set up her own florist shop, she wanted to stand on her own two feet and rented a house on Love Heart Lane. She'd still spent plenty of time at Rose Cottage, of course, especially in the last twelve months as she'd looked after The Vintage Flower Van while Ada started to enjoy her retirement. Florrie also sourced the majority of the flowers for Buttercup Barn from the gardens at Rose Cottage.

'Yes, that's the plan. It'll be daft to pay rent when this place will be standing empty. The cottage and the garden are a huge part of the business and our life. I could have carried on living here with Aunt Ada when I came back from university, but I wanted to make my own way in life so I struck out on my own. Now I'll most definitely take over the reins. In fact, after all the legal stuff has been sorted, I'll let Rona know I'm moving out. I'm sure the house won't be empty for long. And I've been thinking, I'd like The Vintage Flower Van to stay here, rather than moving it to Buttercup Barn, so I may need to advertise for another member of staff to oversee it. I certainly have a few big decisions to make in the coming days and weeks.'

Drew positioned The Vintage Flower Van in its familiar spot on the grass verge. 'Do you both want a lift back to the pub?'

'I think I'll walk back,' said Florrie. 'As I said, I want to open up the van and place some flowers in the buckets for passers-by to take, but thank you.'

'I'll walk back with Florrie, and see you back at the pub. We won't be long.' Isla kissed her husband lightly on the cheek and the two women waved him off.

As soon as the truck disappeared at the top of the lane, Florrie and Isla began to fill aluminium buckets with water then placed them in a line outside The Vintage Flower Van along with a makeshift sign reading:

In Loving Memory of Aunt Ada. Please help yourself to a free bunch.

'I've already made up the bunches of flowers. I was up early as I couldn't sleep,' shared Florrie.

She opened the doors of the van and once again was swamped by emotion as she stepped inside. 'This was her life. For sixty years she was in here every day, selling her beautiful blooms.' Glancing above the door she took in the photograph of her great-grandfather in his full military uniform and gave a tiny gasp. Putting her hands on her heart, she moaned, 'I nearly forgot! And I've only just been talking about the promises I made to Aunt Ada.'

Isla smiled. 'I think she'd forgive your mistake. There's been a lot going on today.'

'But it's Friday and I nearly failed at the first hurdle.'

'But you haven't. There's still time to go back to the cemetery and put flowers on your great-grandmother's grave. I have to say, when Ada first told me that story, it melted my heart. Very romantic.'

'It is, isn't it? It's one of the reasons I wanted to follow in Aunt Ada's footsteps as a florist. I share the story all the time, especially with regular customers who come into the shop week after week buying flowers for their partners.'

Florrie thought back to one of the first times she had shared her great-grandfather's story to an audience. It was the last day of the summer term at university, the same day she'd met Tom Houston.

After he rescued her bottle of water, she watched him walk towards the lecture room. For the past two years they'd sat in the same lectures but on opposite sides of the room. Just like every other girl on their course, Florrie knew the second he walked into any room without even taking a glance in his direction. There was a presence about him; he turned heads. Florrie often daydreamed what it would be like to be on the arm of Tom Houston, but even though they were both studying business she knew that they were worlds apart. She'd often scrolled through his social media channels: as well as boasting a long list of sporting achievements, he came from a family of property developers whose business was worth millions. The most she'd ever won was a handwriting competition in primary school, and her bank account was always in the red, except when her student loan arrived.

He glanced back over his shoulder just then and gave Florrie a flirtatious, heart-warming smile. She smiled back, loving the fact he'd created his own nickname for her. Clutching her water bottle, she followed him in and sat down in her usual seat, on the opposite side of the room to him. She didn't dare glance in his direction.

Within minutes the lecturer appeared and stood next to the podium at the front of the room. He clicked a remote control and the screen behind him switched on. The students hushed as he clipped his microphone onto his shirt.

'One more year to go and you'll walk out of here qualified in your field. Business is the future and today you' – he pointed to the students sitting in front of him – 'are going to pitch your business

ideas. What makes a good business idea? The idea doesn't need to be unique but it must have a USP to capture the attention of its target market. Put it another way, it must offer something different from companies already working in that marketplace, otherwise their credentials and head start will make it practically impossible for you to catch up, let alone compete.'

Florrie knew she wanted to be a florist and follow in Aunt Ada's footsteps. Ada had built a stellar reputation on word of mouth alone, growing The Vintage Flower Van into a success at a time before social media was available as a means of marketing and promotion. She sold to locals and tourists alike, and she rarely had any blooms left over at the end of the day. Her business was a profitable success and Florrie couldn't wait to step into her shoes and keep her legacy alive. Daring to take a quick glance over in Tom's direction, she saw that he was listening carefully to the professor's every word, his pen poised over his notepad on the fixed writing ledge in front of him.

The lecturer continued.' Good business ideas fill a gap in the market, offer a new product, service or invention, provide an innovative solution to an everyday problem or monetise an interest or hobby,' he told them. 'Remember: products must solve a problem or serve a purpose – the value must be clear and immediately evident to your customers. Now, is there anyone brave enough to share their business idea with us all?'

Florrie sat back and listened carefully for the next thirty minutes as different students shared their visions for the future. The lecturer encouraged other students to challenge different business ventures, giving their own opinions and suggestions about how best to help the business succeed. Florrie suddenly found her arm in the air and the lecturer looking straight at her. He nodded in encouragement as he pointed to her. This will be the last one of the day' – he checked his watch – 'and then you'll be pleased to know you can take the summer off.'

All eyes were suddenly on Florrie. She swallowed. This was the first time she'd ever spoken out during a lecture. Usually, she sat back, observed and made notes.

'My name is Florrie, which means blooming.' She looked over in Tom's direction and saw he was smiling at her. 'So it's probably no surprise to hear that I love flowers.' She took a breath, Tom's encouraging gaze helping her to get into her stride.

'What is there not to love? Their fragrance and association with beauty and love make them the ideal gift if you ever need to show your affection for someone or communicate unspoken messages of the heart. Many people have stories about flowers, but my favourite is one I first heard from my great-aunt Ada when I was just a little girl. According to my great-aunt, my great-grandfather brought home a bouquet of flowers for my great-grandmother every Friday without fail. But then the war began and he enlisted. Knowing his military service would keep him away from home, he walked into a florist in the Scottish Highlands at seven o'clock one morning in full military dress. He was leaving town and determined to get his affairs in order before he did, which to him meant ensuring he didn't let my great-grandmother down while he was away. So, he placed an order for fifty-two Fridays' worth of bouquets so that he would never miss a week, no matter how long he was kept away from home.'

'How utterly romantic,' murmured the student sitting next to Florrie.

'And that's the reason I want to be a florist. Flowers are part of the lifeblood of my family and I want to continue our tradition of honouring them. My great-aunt Ada still runs her vintage flower van at the age of seventy-six and grows beautiful flowers in her award-winning garden. I look forward to working with her and I can't wait to take over *The Vintage Flower Van* when she finally decides she's retiring, and expand our family floristry business to new heights.'

'As much as you're pulling at my heart strings, I'm afraid a wonderful sentimental story isn't enough to convince me that a florist shop in a small town would make a good business idea,' challenged the lecturer. 'Flowers can't scale quickly and profits are limited by product availability. A bad season in the garden could put you in the red.'

'Does every business have to be purely about making money though? Isn't being fulfilled and happy with your work, and making enough profit to get by, enough?' disputed Florrie. 'My great-aunt is happy and her life is full of things that she loves.'

'But flowers are seasonal and wouldn't last long with no real refrigeration,' a nearby student piped up. 'Does your flower van have refrigeration capabilities?'

Florrie was just about to put her side of the argument forward when a voice spoke out from the other side of the room.

'I think Florrie has a point. Is it about making millions or about being happy and ticking by?' Tom asked, defending her. She smiled and he held her gaze for a moment longer than necessary. 'When you think about it, businesses themselves are like flowers in that their success or failure hinges on whether or not they bloom at the right time.'

'And what is your USP?' asked the lecturer, returning his attention to Florrie.

There was only one answer. 'My unique selling point is me, Florrie Appleton. There is only one of me, I've been working in the industry since a very young age and I have a unique understanding of what does and doesn't work for the market I serve.'

The lecturer looked impressed with her answer and the whole

room began to clap. Florrie was proud of herself. She had stated her case and presented it well, unwilling to be put off by anyone else's opinion. She wasn't out to run a million-pound empire, she was simply out to do what she loved, and what she knew about best.

Just at that moment the lecturer called time on the discussion. 'That's it, folks. Remember your last essay needs to be emailed by close of play today. Other than that, great discussions today and I'll see you all back in here in the autumn. Stay safe, and enjoy your summer.' He looked at Florrie and nodded for her to meet him at the front of the class. She picked up her bag and walked down the stairs towards him.

'You made a good point today. Business is about different mindsets and knowing what's best for you and your customer. You've even inspired me to drop by a florist's on the way home to purchase a bunch of flowers for my wife.'

'I think she'll love that.' Florrie smiled.

'Plans for the summer?'

'I'm working in my great-aunt's flower van. In my opinion it's the best job in the world. I'll see you in the autumn term.'

'You will.'

As Florrie turned around, she saw that the lecture room was nearly empty, but Tom was still in his seat, looking at her. 'That's quite a story, Red,' he said as she drew closer to him. 'Your great-grandfather sounds like a remarkable man.'

'He was a true romantic at heart and very much in love. What are your plans for the summer?' she asked, not wanting the conversation to end.

'Six weeks living in the south of France on my father's yacht – in St Tropez, to be precise.'

'Oh, the hardship,' she teased.

Tom placed his hand in the small of her back as they exited the classroom. *'But before then I have the use of a private beach house for a couple of weeks. Why don't you join me?'*

Florrie stopped in her tracks and coughed. Her eyes locked on his. 'Sorry, I thought for a moment there that you'd invited me to spend two weeks with you.'

'I did.'

'We don't know each other.'

There was a glint in his eye. 'But after two weeks, we will. Come on, Red, be impulsive.'

Florrie thought about it for a moment. Could she really throw her plans out the window and take off with Tom? It was crazy, it was unlike her ... but it was oh so appealing.

'Okay, Yes!' she said.

He smiled as he took her hand...

———————

'Penny for them? You're daydreaming.' Isla nudged Florrie's arm.

'Sorry, I was just thinking...'

'About...?'

Florrie thought about sharing that she might have seen someone from her past at the funeral, but decided against it. She didn't want to give Tom any more thought time, even though it was very difficult to push him from her mind. 'About how much Dolores and Martha will have had to drink by the time we arrive at the pub,' she said, hoping to throw Isla off the scent of a juicy story.

Isla chuckled. 'They'll undoubtedly be in full swing by now.'

'I think that's exactly what's needed this afternoon.'

After quickly arranging her great-grandmother's favourite bouquet, Florrie led Isla into Rose Cottage. 'I'll lay the flowers on her grave before I go to the wake,' she said, pausing to pick up the pile of post from the mat. She shuffled through the envelopes. 'It's mainly condolence cards; everyone has been so kind. Would you like a drink? I feel like I need one to steady my nerves … and to catch up with everyone else before we walk into the pub.'

Isla pointed to the half-full bottle of port with two glasses at the side of the sink. 'Should we use those?'

Florrie shook her head. 'They're from the night before Aunt Ada passed away,' she admitted, a bit embarrassed. 'I couldn't bear to wash them up and tidy them away. I know that sounds daft.'

'It doesn't. It must be difficult now, but with time it'll get easier. Let's have a glass of Ada's favourite port and we can open the cards together before we head back to the wake.'

Florrie nodded, reaching for clean glasses from the kitchen cupboard.

After the port was poured, they raised a toast to Aunt Ada. 'She always swore by her port, having a glass before she went to bed every night. It was a tradition she carried on from her marriage to Uncle Ewart, something special they'd shared. Shall we sit in the garden?'

Isla nodded and Florrie led the way to the small courtyard. 'Can you smell that lavender? It won't be long until it needs pruning and then hopefully we'll get a second burst.'

'It's such a gorgeous aroma,' replied Isla. 'What a suntrap Ada created out here … and look at that view!'

The view from the courtyard over Rose Cottage's gardens was truly stunning, and there was an inviting calmness about the place. Over the years, Ada had been very self-sufficient, growing her own vegetables and herbs alongside her one true love – flowers. There were numerous gardens and each was a blooming masterpiece. It was a beautiful sanctuary, every flower bed erupting with colour.

After toasting Great-Aunt Ada, Florrie began to open the condolence cards and read the lovely messages inside. 'She had so many friends. Some of these are from her regular customers. Their messages are so kind and full of their memories of Ada.' The last envelope was a letter addressed to her great-aunt from the local solicitors in Heartcross, the bold logo standing out. It was marked 'confidential', prompting Florrie to confess, 'I feel like I'm prying by opening her post.'

'You're next of kin though, and no doubt there's legal stuff to sort out. You're best to open it and see what it's about.'

Florrie slowly opened the envelope and looked inside. 'It's a bill from the solicitors – the invoice for drafting Great-Aunt Ada's will.' Florrie looked up at Isla. 'I still wonder whether she had an inkling about what was to come.'

Isla shook her head. 'I don't think so. I think she was just getting her affairs in order so she could enjoy her retirement. Having a will lined up just made sense – and it will make things straightforward for you.'

'That's true. I'll follow up with them this week to see what the will says. For now, we need to get back to the wake; everyone will likely be wondering where we are.'

They finished their drinks and with the bouquet of flowers in Florrie's hand, they parted ways at the bottom of the lane. 'I won't be long,' said Florrie. 'I'll lay the flowers and be right with you.'

She walked briskly back towards the church and as soon as

she passed through the wrought-iron gates she made her way towards the grave and stood the bouquet up against her great-grandmother's headstone. 'I'll see you all next Friday, if not before.' She edged backwards, still looking at the graves, and as she turned away she bumped straight into someone standing behind her.

'I'm so sorry,' she said hurriedly, brushing back the hair that had fallen into her eyes as she collided with the stranger. 'That was my fault, I wasn't looking where I was going.'

'There's no need to apologise.'

Immediately, Florrie recognised the voice. She slowly raised her head and locked eyes with his. Her jaw fell open and her heart began beating nineteen to the dozen. She couldn't believe it.

Tom.

Here.

Close enough to touch…

Flustered at the thought, Florrie felt herself blush.

'It's been a long time, Red, too long.' The look in his eyes was warm, the sexy, captivating smile that she had once been obsessed with still wide. 'But you're no longer red, I see. The brown suits you, you look…'

Florrie narrowed her eyes and tilted her head to the side, waiting to see what compliment he could possibly come up with after everything that happened between them in the past. After his betrayal.

'More beautiful than the last time I saw you.'

Florrie was still staring at him. She didn't trust herself to speak. She'd thought of this moment many times and rehearsed in her mind exactly what she would say if their paths ever crossed again, but faced with him now, those thoughts had evaporated.

'It's me, Tom. Surely you recognise me? These rugged good looks haven't changed that much. In fact, I think I'm maturing like a fine wine,' he said jokingly. He still had that twinkle in his eye.

Florrie didn't understand what was happening. He was showing no shame whatsoever even though eight years ago he'd left her feeling hurt and betrayed. Tom went to touch her arm but Florrie moved it away.

Of course she recognised him. She'd dreamed of his face for many years after they'd parted and there was no denying he could still take her breath away just by the way he looked at her. Trying to suffocate all the old feelings that were attempting to rush to the surface, she told herself, *Remind yourself how he treated you.* The words turned over in her head as she gave herself a little shake.

'I'm sensing something isn't quite right here,' Tom said, clearly confused by her continued silence.

Her stare turned cold and icy. 'Not quite right' was an understatement.

Tom raised an eyebrow and looked a little uncomfortable but persevered in attempting to thaw her freezing cold welcome. 'I couldn't quite believe when I saw you inside the church earlier. I honestly thought I was seeing things.'

Florrie remained silent.

'Do you have anything to say to me after all this time?' he asked, looking perplexed and sounding confused. 'I'm really pleased to see you and I thought ... I thought you would be too...' He trailed off.

'Why are you here?' Her tone was unfriendly, her gaze unrelenting.

'I came to pay my respects.'

'After eight years you turn up out of the blue after treating me like you did, and today of all days?'

He narrowed his eyes at her. 'What exactly are you insinuating I did? And what do you mean, "today of all days"?'

Florrie blew out a breath. 'Unbelievable.'

'I'm not quite sure what's going on here but I'm sensing there's something that I don't know about.'

'You know exactly what you did, and then to turn up at my great-aunt's funeral like nothing has happened and to claim you're pleased to see me?'

Now it was Tom's turn to stare, open-mouthed. 'Today's funeral ... Ada was your great- aunt?' He looked like a rabbit caught in headlights. How had he not realised Florrie was related to Ada?

'So what were you doing here?' She didn't let him answer. Now that she was speaking she couldn't stop. 'Have you turned up to apologise? What, you assumed I'd be at my most vulnerable and more willing to forgive you? Fat chance of that!'

Florrie averted her eyes for a moment and glanced down at his left hand. There was no sign of a wedding ring. She wasn't quite sure what to make of that ... or of the fact that she'd checked.

'Apologise? What do I need to apologise for? If anything, it's you that needs to apologise to me. But as soon as I saw you, I knew I was prepared to let that go.'

Florrie released a strangled sound from the back of her

throat before she said, 'Me? What would I need to apologise for? You infuriate me.' Did he think he could just slip back into her life unexpectedly without any sort of explanation? Behind her sunglasses she closed her eyes for a second. Even though she wanted to dislike him with every bone in her body, he was right – he had matured like a fine wine, and was now even more utterly gorgeous than she remembered.

The two weeks she'd spent with Tom in that private beach house had been the best two weeks of her life. She'd fallen wholly in love with him, and he with her, or so she'd thought. But soon after she'd discovered that she was nothing more than a bit of fun to pass the time away. He'd had a girlfriend waiting for him in St Tropez. Florrie had seen the photographs of them together on his father's yacht.

'That feeling is becoming very mutual,' Tom said, his bewilderment giving way to frustration and annoyance.

Florrie turned and walked away without giving him a second look.

Chapter Three

F lorrie hurried towards the village pub.

Damn. That just had not gone to plan. Why hadn't she let him answer why the hell he was at the funeral? She thought about going back but the last thing she wanted was a full-blown argument while standing in front of the graves of her loved ones.

Reaching the pub, she took a breath and tried to calm her racing heartbeat before pushing open the door. Instantly she was hit with music and the happy sound of chit chat, and she relaxed. The scene in front of her made her smile. A large number of villagers had gathered around the piano in the far corner where Drew was playing, and Dolores had taken to the microphone and was belting out one of Great-Aunt Ada's favourite songs. Huddled together were all of Ada's friends, including Grace and Andrew from Heartcross Castle, Felicity and Fergus, Flynn and Julia from Starcross Manor, Jinny and Gabe from Bumblebee Cottage, Molly and Cam from The Old Bakehouse, along with the local doctors Ben and Katie. Florrie could see dozens of glasses of port held aloft and watched as Dolores reached the chorus and everyone joined in. She leaned against the bar and the owner, Meredith, slid a drink towards her.

'This is exactly the send-off Ada would have hoped for. A true celebration of life,' Florrie observed.

Meredith pointed to the memory box that was placed on the bar. 'Everyone has been writing down their favourite memories and after the buffet we're going to read them out. I think Dolores and Martha have a couple of other things up their sleeves too.'

Next to the bar was an oversized cork board where friends of Ada had pinned their favourite photos of her, creating a wonderful collage of memories. 'Look at Great-Aunt Ada's hair in that one!' Florrie laughed. 'She looks like a mad professor!' Back in the eighties, when home perms were all the rage, Dolores, Martha and Ada had decided to perm each other's hair one Sunday afternoon … with disastrous results. 'I can remember Ada telling me that even though it was the height of summer they all ended up wearing bobble hats for weeks until their hair had begun to tame.'

Meredith laughed. 'I wish I'd have seen that.'

With the singing still in full flow Florrie caught Isla's eye and headed over to join her beside the piano. Isla slipped her arm around Florrie's shoulder and chinked her glass against Florrie's as they joined in the song, tears in their eyes and smiles on their faces. Soon after, the buffet was declared open, the trestle table was full of Great-Aunt Ada's favourite foods and cakes, all made by Rona from Bonnie's Teashop.

Once the food had been devoured, Florrie stood at the bar next to the memory box with a microphone in her hand.

'I can read the memories out from the cards if you'd prefer?' offered Isla, knowing how difficult this would be for Florrie.

Florrie shook her head. 'I've got this, but thank you.'

As she spoke into the microphone, the pub fell silent and all eyes were on her. 'Thank you all for coming today to celebrate Great-Aunt Ada's life. I do know she'll be having complete FOMO about all this – especially those chocolate flapjacks, they were her absolute favourite.' She smiled towards Rona and Felicity, Rona's daughter, who had been up early preparing the buffet.

The room laughed.

'Now I'm going to share with you all your own happy memories of Ada, followed by a short video, and then I believe Martha and Dolores are going to show us how to play one of Great-Aunt Ada's favourite games from the past. Also, the drinks are free, so please do drink the bar dry. Aunt Ada would be disappointed if we didn't.'

The memories from the box were entertaining and there were a lot of stories that Florrie had never heard before. When the last memory had been shared, a video flashed up on the screen on the wall of the pub and everyone watched the images of Ada from the past, including footage filmed by Ewart on her first day of business, Ada standing proudly in front of The Vintage Flower Van. There were the younger versions of Dolores and Martha, dressed up on Ada's wedding day, and a short clip of Ewart carrying Ada over the threshold of Rose Cottage.

The next ten minutes whizzed by, everyone captivated by the memories.

Taking a sip of her drink, Florrie smiled and briefly looked out of the window. The timing couldn't have been worse, as Tom walked past at that very moment and for an instant Florrie held his gaze before breaking eye contact. As soon as he was out of sight she walked towards the bay window, curious to see where he was heading. At the end of the street, he turned and took the track at the bottom of Love Heart Lane. Unexpectedly, he looked back over his shoulder. Immediately, Florrie took a step back. Damn. He likely knew she'd been watching him.

'You okay?' asked Isla, joining her at the window.

'I am. I'm just taking a moment. All those memories … and the video footage was just fantastic. Great-Aunt Ada would have loved this. The friendships she had were really something special.'

'Just like ours.' Isla nudged her arm and smiled warmly. 'Now look at that pair. Just like we said, they're in their element.'

Dolores and Martha had everyone gathered around. Martha waved over to Isla and Florrie to join them as they introduced the game 'Most Likely', saying they had played it when they were younger, usually when too much alcohol had been consumed.

Twenty minutes later, both Florrie and Isla were giggly, the port was flowing freely and the game Dolores and Martha had introduced them to was in full swing.

Florrie leaned into Isla. 'I'm feeling a little woozy. In fact, I think I'm bordering on very tipsy.'

'I'm with you there, I'm not used to drinking in the afternoon. But this "Most Likely" game is fun.'

Martha was shushing the peals of laughter whilst everyone

waited for the next question. 'Most likely to get a terrible tattoo?'

There were frantic whispers before each person pointed at someone else. Florrie put her hands in the air. 'Definitely not me, I'm scared of pain and needles.' Florrie turned towards Isla. 'Who do you think?'

'I'm saying nothing.' Isla's voice was low.

'Oh my gosh, you have a terrible tattoo, don't you? How terrible?'

'Terrible! Picture the scene: in our youth, myself, Felicity and Allie go on a girls' holiday in Ibiza. We get very very drunk.'

'I'm not liking the sound of this.' Florrie was hanging on to her every word.

'I got a tattoo of what I thought was a lovely dedication to Drew. The farm still belonged to his parents back then but I knew it would be passed down to him in time and that we were going to be together forever. So, in my drunken stupor, I decided to have a tattoo of a cute cow's head. However, after twenty years and stretch marks from childbirth, it now looks like a cross between Kung Fu Panda and Tinky Winky.' Isla raised her eyebrows whilst Florrie let out a peal of laughter.

'I vowed right there and then I was never drinking again.'

'And here we are,' Florrie said, clinking her glass to Isla's.

They both looked over towards Dolores and Martha who'd thrown out a couple more questions. The tears were streaming down their faces, but thankfully they were due to laughter now. The day had certainly had a number of ups and downs!

'I could picture them sitting around the royal yacht, eating caviar and sipping champagne whilst playing this game. How the rich and famous live,' said Isla. 'Oh, to have a life like Dolores...'

'She's really had an amazing life and career, hasn't she? Always dragging Martha and Ada off to those glitzy parties.' Florrie took a sip of her drink then tilted her glass towards Dolores. 'Not only an interesting life but a nice long one. And even at the age of ninety-nine she's never forgotten her roots or her true friends.'

'I'm still laughing about earlier when Gran shared that she and Ada used to cart Dolores around in a wheely holdall when they used to leave parties, so the paparazzi didn't snap a photo of her.'

'It's a good job Dolores is petite! The things that they got up to...'

'One last question,' announced Martha. 'Most likely to go on holiday with someone they've just met?'

Jokingly, Isla turned towards Florrie. 'I'm saying you.'

'Me?'

'Yes, you! I think you probably got up to more things in your university days than you've let on about.'

Florrie put her hands on her chest, pretending to look hurt. 'I'm saying nothing,' she declared. Even though she knew that Isla was teasing, her words had resonated. The last time she'd thrown caution to the wind she'd done exactly that and gone on a two-week holiday with someone she'd admired from afar but had only spoken to once.

It may have only been two weeks in the arms of Tom Houston but he'd swept her off her feet and made her feel like she'd never felt before – or since. Her heart had swelled with happiness and plans had been made but then it all came tumbling down, and she was left – alone – to pick up the pieces of her broken heart.

'I think I'm ready to go home now,' she announced. A lot of the villagers were beginning to head off and the crowd was dwindling.

'Let's go then,' said Isla supportively.

Florrie stood up and began to thank everyone. Then she and Isla strolled back towards Rose Cottage arm in arm. 'Thank you for today,' Florrie said, putting the key in the door and giving Isla a heart-warming smile. 'I couldn't have got through it without you.'

'You don't need to thank me, that's exactly what friends are for.'

'And Drew doesn't mind you staying with me tonight?' Florrie was grateful that Isla had offered to stay; she didn't want to be on her own, not after today. And though she could have gone back to her home on Love Heart Lane, Florrie wanted to stay at Rose Cottage. She felt closer to Great-Aunt Ada there, and it would make it a little easier to prepare the flowers for the van first thing tomorrow morning.

'Of course he doesn't mind. And if you want some help opening up in the morning, I'll be here. What's the plan for The Vintage Flower Van? How are you going to work two businesses?'

They walked into the kitchen and Florrie made them each a cup of tea. 'I've had a chat with Martha about that this evening. I think at the moment I want to keep it where it belongs, outside Rose Cottage, but there's a couple of options to consider. For instance, I could park the van outside Buttercup Barn and have it become an extension of my business, or I could leave it here and hire a florist to man it. In the meantime, Martha has agreed to help me cover both businesses until I make a decision.'

'That decision doesn't need to be rushed. You take your time.'

'I will. For now, I'm going to stay here and open up the van each morning. I can prepare existing orders from Buttercup Barn too. Martha and I can work it between ourselves.'

'That sounds like a plan, and of course I'll help as much as I can.'

They stood on the lavender courtyard outside the back door and looked over the gardens.

'I think it would be good to take part in Flowers in Bloom one last time. For Ada,' Isla said gently.

'I think you might be right. Keeping me busy during this sad time will do me good...' Florrie hesitated. 'I need to be occupied.'

'You say that like there's more going on with you. Is everything okay?'

Florrie thought about sharing what had happened today at the cemetery, but her emotions were already running high, and really, what was there to tell? Hopefully, Tom had got the message loud and clear and he was already headed out of town. He'd made his choices eight years ago and there was no point raking over the past now.

'No, not at all.' Little white lies seemed to be becoming a habit. 'In a funny sort of way, I quite enjoyed this afternoon. Dolores and Martha were fantastic in making it a celebration of life. They certainly did keep everyone's spirits high.'

'Including ours.' Isla hiccupped before taking a sip of her tea.

'I do feel exhausted though.'

'Why don't you have an early night?'

'You don't mind?'

'Not at all. I can use one myself.'

After they finished their tea, Isla made her way up the stairs to bed while Florrie locked the back door and took one last glance at Ada's final glass of port, still sitting on the sideboard. With a tear in her eye, she washed up the teacups then moved Ada's reading glasses to the dresser, along with a newspaper and the box of photographs she'd been looking through the night before she passed away. She hesitated in the doorway and glanced out of the window. 'Good night, Great-Aunt Ada, sleep well.'

Florrie shut the kitchen door and climbed the stairs to bed.

Chapter Four

They sat at the table opposite each other. 'And how did you

F lorrie had been up at the crack of dawn and had spent the past hour preparing The Vintage Flower Van for the day ahead to the sound of birdsong. Martha was due to arrive just before nine a.m. to take over The Vintage Flower Van for the day. As Florrie walked back towards the kitchen she was greeted by the aroma of sizzling sausages and bacon.

'Wow! Look at this!'

Isla was standing in front of the racing green Aga, cooking up a full Scottish breakfast along with huge slices of buttery toast.

'And I thought I'd been the busy one this morning. I could get used to this.' Florrie smiled at Isla as she set the table and switched the kettle on. 'You can come and stay anytime.'

'Don't tempt me. I know I shouldn't say it but I quite enjoyed getting up and only having to worry about myself. That happens once in a blue moon. Felicity is taking the boys to school for me.'

'You deserve the break! This looks amazing, but there's

enough here to feed a small army. Are you expecting guests?' Florrie joked.

'Please don't think I'm nagging, but I did notice you didn't eat much yesterday, which is understandable, so I thought you may be hungry. You do have to look after yourself.'

'I know. For the last week my appetite has been wiped out,' admitted Florrie. 'But I won't be passing on this feast. Thank you. This is just what I need.'

They sat at the table opposite each other. 'And how did you sleep?' asked Isla.

'Out like a light, but I think that was thanks to the drink more than anything else. I'm quite surprised I'm not suffering with a hangover this morning.'

'I'd put out some paracetamol just in case, but quite surprisingly I feel bright this morning too.' Isla plated up the breakfast whilst Florrie made them both a coffee.

With two steaming hot mugs on the table Florrie was just about to sit down when the letterbox clanged. 'Probably more condolence cards.' After retrieving them from the mat she shuffled through them and stopped when she saw another letter from the solicitors.

'I wonder what this can be now.' She held the letter up to show Isla the bold type.

'There's only one way to find out,' Isla replied, placing their breakfasts on the table.

Florrie tore open the envelope and unfolded the letter. 'It's Great-Aunt Ada's last will and testament. She signed this the week before she passed away so there shouldn't be too many surprises.'

Florrie glanced over the legal document as Isla watched and drank her coffee.

'Great-Aunt Ada's left me her engagement and wedding rings, which thankfully I already knew as she'd told me recently, all her belongings in the cottage and, of course, The Vintage Flower Van.' Florrie smiled.

'She's left some jewellery to Martha and a bracelet to you, too,' Florrie continued, turning over the next page. Coming to the end she narrowed her eyes and skimmed over the document again. 'That's strange.'

'What is it?' asked Isla.

'There's mention of savings, small investments, The Vintage Flower Van and her personal possessions, even down to her favourite watering can, but there is no mention of the cottage, whatsoever. Why wouldn't the cottage be in the will?' Florrie passed the paperwork to Isla who glanced over it.

'You're right, I can't see anything about Rose Cottage at all. That *is* strange. Maybe ring the solicitor's office or pop in on the way to Buttercup Barn?'

'It's Saturday today, so I'll have to wait until Monday. I was thinking maybe there's a page missing or something, but this looks all in order.' Florrie took the will back from Isla and placed it on the table.

'Eat up, and try not to worry. There will be a simple explanation.'

Florrie picked up her knife and fork but her appetite had dwindled again. She was worried and the more she thought about it, Great-Aunt Ada had never mentioned the cottage to her in conversation. Even though Florrie had rented a house on Love Heart Lane, she always thought Rose Cottage would become her home again, one day. 'Hopefully, it's just an oversight.'

'It will be,' reassured Isla.

Hearing a knock on the door, Florrie put down her knife and fork. Opening the door she found Ash, the postman, standing on the doorstep. 'Florrie, it was a lovely service yesterday.'

'It was.'

'Sorry to bother you but I missed this letter a second ago when I pushed the others through the letterbox. It's recorded delivery and I need a signature.'

Florrie signed the handheld machine that Ash held in front of her before she took the letter then returned to the kitchen.

'It was Ash. He had a letter that needed signing for and look how it's addressed. "To whom it may concern", yet the address is Rose Cottage.'

'It looks very official. Who are W. Houston Property Developers? That's the logo on the envelope.'

Florrie stared at the envelope. Her heart began to race.

Houston.

As in Tom Houston.

From online searches she'd done all those years ago she knew that the company was owned by his father, and given his course of study at uni, it had seemed inevitable that afterwards Tom would join the family business.

Was it possible that Tom had written her a letter after she brushed him off in the cemetery? Curious to see what he'd written, she ripped open the envelope, aware that Isla was watching her intently.

The first thing that Florrie noticed as she took out the letter from the envelope was the bold red writing stamped across the top of the letter: EVICTION NOTICE.

Her hands began to tremble and, as she read the letter, she experienced the feeling of blood draining away from her face.

She was thankful she was sitting down as she suddenly felt light-headed, as though she could collapse at any moment. 'I don't believe this is happening.'

'What is it?' asked Isla, concerned.

'An eviction notice.'

'What do you mean, an eviction notice? Eviction from where?'

'Here. Rose Cottage.' Florrie's eyes were fixed on the signature. The letter was signed by Thomas Houston, Managing Director of W. Houston Property Developers. Florrie could feel her pulse racing. The absolute cheek of the man. Not only had he turned up after all these years, he was also now evicting her! She shook her head in disbelief. She wished she'd had this information when she'd come face to face with Tom yesterday.

'This has got to be a mistake. I don't understand.' Florrie passed the letter to Isla. 'This letter is insinuating that Aunt Ada didn't own Rose Cottage and she's been renting it since she moved in with Uncle Ewart over sixty years ago.'

Isla looked as confused as Florrie felt. 'Rented? Surely not?' Once Isla had read the letter, she glanced back towards Florrie. 'You're right, that's exactly what the letter is saying.'

Florrie exhaled. 'I wasn't expecting that.'

'Definitely a shock to the system.'

'All Great-Aunt Ada's possessions have to be removed and the cottage left empty by the last day of the month.' Florrie looked around the kitchen, which, just like every other room, was packed to the rafters with Ada's possessions from the last sixty years. 'I can't do this. I don't *want* to do this. Not only is it a mammoth task, but I'm also just not ready to sort through her life. I'm only just coming to terms with losing her!' The tears in her eyes welled up and Florrie reached for a tissue from the box on the table. 'If what's in this letter is true, I've not only lost Great-Aunt Ada, I've also lost our home and the gardens, too.'

'I'm so sorry, Florrie. I didn't even know the house was rented. Who are W. Houston Property Developers? Have you never had any dealings with them before?'

Florrie tapped on the printed signature on the letter.

'Yes, I have,' she said tersely.

'You look like you want to tell me something but you're not quite sure.' Isla held her gaze.

'I know him. In fact, I had a run-in with him in the cemetery yesterday.'

Isla raised an eyebrow. 'You never said.'

'I wasn't quite sure at first whether I was seeing things.'

'How do you know him?'

'Tom Houston is my … was my…' Briefly, Florrie closed her eyes. 'I spent two weeks at a private beach house with Tom the summer before my final year of university.'

'You're a dark horse! And why don't I know anything about this?' Isla teased.

'Because he broke my heart and I was completely humiliated. I was hoping I'd never have to cross his path again.'

Florrie took a sip of her drink and thought back to that afternoon she'd thrown caution to the wind, stuffed her clothes into a small suitcase and climbed into his silver soft-top BMW. With her hair blowing in the wind as they drove along the coast road, Florrie had had hundreds of fireflies fluttering at high speed in her stomach. They'd laughed and sung at the top of their voices and before they'd even arrived at the picturesque, oak-beamed seventeenth-century cottage that looked like it was straight out of a fairy tale, Florrie had decided that one day she would marry Tom.

The rural cottage stood amongst lush green grass with cattle and sheep next door. As soon as Tom pulled up outside, Florrie was greeted by a wooden gate that led to an oak-beamed porch that tumbled with pink clematis. She gasped as her eyes flitted along the open veranda with its two wicker rocking chairs and small table.

'It's beautiful, isn't it?'

Florrie turned to answer but was struck mute by the wicked glint in his eye and lopsided grin. Was it possible he meant her, rather than the cottage?

'Isn't it just,' she said coyly, casting an appreciative glance of her own over Tom before turning back to the view. At the end of the porch was a vista of glistening sea.

'You haven't seen anything yet.'

After taking the luggage from the car, Tom opened up the mizzle green front door. The inside of the cottage was just as breathtaking as the outside. Facing the furnishings was a grand rustic fireplace with an old bread oven. Up the wooden stairs were a couple of bedrooms, the first light and airy with floral patchwork quilts on the rustic double bed, along with a small chest of drawers and a table lamp. The window overlooked the beautiful enclosed garden. The landing housed an inviting snug space with a bookcase and a sofa to settle into with plush blush-pink velvet cushions. In the primary bedroom was a stunning iron-framed bed covered in simple white linen, as well as exposed redbrick walls and its own log burner.

'Take a look out of the window.' Tom gestured towards it.

The view was simply stunning. Her eyes followed the gravel path at the side of the cottage, which led down to its own private cove.

'It's called the hidden bay,' said Tom. 'Let's go and take a look.' He gave her a sideward glance that caused Florrie's heart to race. Spontaneously grabbing each other's hands, they ran outside and through the garden to the cove. It seemed the most natural thing in the world to touch him, to be close to him.

The sun was beating down on the horseshoe-shaped beach, and the glassy sea was simply stunning, worthy of a picture postcard. Taking her by surprise, Tom pulled Florrie towards the water's edge. She had a wide smile on her face but as soon as the cold water hit her feet, she gasped out loud and started to hop from one foot to the other.

'It's not that cold.' He grinned. 'The sun is shining and it's at least twenty-six degrees.'

'That doesn't stop the sea from being freezing.'

'Such an exaggeration. And anyway, cold water is good for your soul and boosts your mental health.'

'I'll take your word for it,' she murmured, taking in the magnificent view. She'd never seen anything so beautiful. 'And this cove belongs to the cottage?'

'It does, and as you can see it's private. No one can see us, Red.'

The tiny, secluded beach of sparkling beige sand had low white cliffs on either side, with a cascading waterfall.

'Who exactly owns such a wonderful property as this?'

'A friend of my grandfather's.'

Before he finished his sentence, Tom had stripped his T-shirt from his body. A tiny thrill ran through Florrie as she flashed her eyes up and down his toned torso. With her eyes locked on his he kicked off his shoes and with a quick tug on his belt his trousers fell to his ankles. As he stepped from his clothes the intensity of his gaze made her tingle, and her heart beat wildly. She tried to avert her gaze but was unsuccessful as he confidently turned and she watched him walk naked into the sea before he dived under. As he came up for air, he threw his head back and ran a hand through his tousled hair, slicking it back from his face. He took her breath away.

He looked back over his shoulder and gave her a sexy grin. 'Come on, Red.'

Feeling slightly nervous, she slipped off her shoes, followed by her shorts and T-shirt. It was glorious to feel the sun upon her skin as she walked into the water wearing her underwear.

With a racing pulse she swam towards him. As soon as she was within arm's reach, he took both her hands and placed them around his neck. He pulled her body against his.

'You, Red, are beautiful,' he murmured.

Florrie could feel her whole body trembling in anticipation of his touch. Their faces were now centimetres apart, their bodies bobbing in the rhythm of the waves. He bent his head slowly, his lips brushing against hers.

They let the waves sweep them backwards and forwards as they kissed, time standing still in this perfect moment. Finally pulling apart, they laughed as the waves picked them up and eventually swept them back to the shore. Tom's arm was draped around her waist, and Florrie let herself lean into him, dropping her head to his wet chest as they fell into a heap on the sand, their wet bodies joined at shoulders and hips. Trying to catch her breath, Florrie watched the rise and fall of her chest before she briefly closed her eyes.

'I can feel you watching me,' she said after a moment. Opening her eyes and taking a sideward glimpse towards Tom, she saw he was leaning on his elbow looking at her. He gently pushed her hair off her face like it was the most natural thing in the world.

'You intrigue me, Red.'

'Why?' she asked. The intensity of his gaze caused goosebumps to spring up all over body, making her shudder.

'Because you're not like other girls.'

'Is that a good thing?' she asked, her eyes not leaving his.

'Definitely a good thing. It's nice to let go and have fun, don't you think?'

'Absolutely,' she murmured, thinking that if anyone had even suggested when she woke up in the morning that before the day was out she would be frolicking in the sea with the most handsome man on campus, she would have sworn they were deluded. She leaned up on both elbows, staring up at his face. The intoxicating warmth of the coastal air was the perfect setting for whatever was unfolding between them. She willed him to kiss her again.

He did.

Softly at first, but then their hands and mouth began exploring each other with an urgency neither of them could control.

Florrie gripped his strong arms, feeling his skin next to hers. Living in the moment, and not thinking of the consequences, had brought her here – and this was only the start.

'What exactly did this man do to you?' Isla asked, breaking Florrie's reverie. 'And I have to say according to Google, he's pretty damn hot and a successful businessman.' Isla's eyes widened. 'He's also on numerous rich lists.'

'He runs a business that was passed down from generations before. It doesn't mean he's the reason for its success.' Florrie might have sounded a little bitter but she wasn't going to let him take the credit. That business was of his grandfather's making. She knew all about his family. After all, she'd spent hours researching who was who after their short-lived love affair had ended, because she couldn't quite let go.

'Are you avoiding the first part of my question?'

'Maybe.'

'You can't leave it there.'

'What he did to me was take advantage. We shared two weeks of pure raw sex and emotional connection. We explored the coastline in a private boat, took naked midnight swims under the starlit sky. We drank copious amounts of champagne and slept naked in front of fires we'd made on the beach. It was two weeks of excess and boisterous fun and I thought it was just the beginning. We'd talked about the future… Anyway, after our two weeks came to an end, he went to St Tropez to spend the summer holiday with his family on his father's yacht. He promised to keep in touch and told me he would see me at the beginning of term for our last year in university.'

'And?'

'Almost immediately, I learned he'd deceived me. Photos of him and a woman named Sophia Henley frolicking on his father's yacht in the south of France were posted online and the headline claimed that it was on the cards that the childhood sweethearts would soon announce their engagement. He wasn't single, Isla, and yet he still spent that time with me. Still gave me false hope for a future he knew would never happen. I blocked him from every form of communication after I saw the photos, and when he didn't return to university that autumn for our final year, I assumed he'd begun working for his father's business, which now I know he did.'

'Blimey, you blocked him and didn't give him the chance to

explain? Maybe there was a rational explanation,' suggested Isla, always the voice of reason.

It had been a knee-jerk reaction, but Florrie hadn't been able to help it. 'I had that very thought numerous times, but I felt humiliated and the only saving grace was no one knew I had been with him so there was no public humiliation. It hurt so much, Isla. How could he just forget to tell me he would be spending the summer with his childhood sweetheart on his father's yacht?'

'When you put it like that...' Isla was tapping away on her phone. 'Sophia Henley ... an entrepreneur since the age of sixteen and heavily involved in charities—'

'Tom Houston is a pig who grabbed a bit of fun whilst he could,' cut in Florrie, still thinking about the pain that twisted in her heart when she first saw that photo of him and Sophia together.

Isla was still looking at her phone. 'She may have been his childhood sweetheart but according to Google she's now married to a very famous lawyer who represents celebrity clients. And from what I can see Tom doesn't post much about his private life on social media.' Isla was still scrolling. 'Ooh! Actually, here's a bit of interesting information. Tom Houston is single and in fact one of the world's most eligible bachelors.'

Even though Florrie had seen for herself that there was no ring on his finger, she was surprised to have it confirmed that he was single. After blocking all forms of communication from him eight years ago, she'd vowed never to look him up again – even though at times she'd had to fight her curiosity hard – but she'd assumed he'd be married with kids by now.

'He may be an eligible bachelor but he's also evicting me

with only a few weeks to remove all of Great-Aunt Ada's belongings.'

'That won't be him personally. You'll just be on a database. He'll have numerous teams and bosses and they will have been informed Ada has passed away. I bet it's somehow linked to the will,' offered Isla.

Florrie knew Isla was talking sense, but she still couldn't piece it all together. 'What is he doing turning up in Heartcross though?'

'I'm not sure. Maybe it is something to do with Rose Cottage? Perhaps he's here to look over the property, the land and gardens, with a view to putting it on the market now that Ada's no longer renting it? You should have asked him why he was here.'

The welcome Florrie had given him was far from friendly and she knew it was unlikely she was going to talk to Tom anytime soon. 'And what's does this part of the letter mean? It says there will be a follow-on letter with a list of all the things that belong to the cottage, and there will be an inspection to ensure the property is left in a habitable state. Do you think the cottage was furnished when they moved in?' Florrie felt worried. 'Surely Ada has changed the furniture over the decades.'

'Let's not panic just yet,' said Isla calmly, trying to smooth the way. 'I bet this is a standard letter that they send out. Surely they could just transfer the tenancy to you, as this has been your home for many years? I bet it's a simple transaction. You could maybe talk to them about valuing the property and buying it from them.'

'If this cottage doesn't stay in the family, it's going to have a huge effect on business.' Florrie stood up and looked out of the window. 'We grow the majority of our own flowers in these gardens. What am I going to do without them?'

'I know this is a little unexpected, but try not to panic until we know the full facts. Surely the cottage will be rented out again – and why not to you? Better the devil you know, and all that.'

Isla was talking sense, but Florrie had a tiny niggle in the back of her mind. 'Isla, The Vintage Flower Van. I promised Aunt Ada it would live on. It's been in that spot for decades.'

'I was just thinking the same, but it won't be the end of the van. Like you've already considered, we can tow it to Buttercup Barn and have it as an extension to your florist shop. It won't be quite the same but it would allow the van to live on and keep trading.'

'How did I not know this place was rented?'

'One phone call to W. Houston Property Developers will sort everything, I'm sure.'

Despite Isla's attempts to reassure her, Florrie felt her chest squeezing tight as she looked over the letter again, worry still etched on her mind. This had been her childhood home for many years and Aunt Ada's sanctuary for many more. It was going to break her heart leaving it all behind.

Chapter Five

'It's ten to nine. I really should be getting over to Buttercup Barn. Would you be able to wait until Martha arrives? The Vintage Flower Van is all set up and ready to go and I'll pop back during my deliveries this morning to see how's she going,' asked Florrie.

'Of course, and take this letter with you.' Isla handed Florrie the letter. 'Ring them from the shop and I'll pop in on the way back to the farm.'

Quickly clearing away the dishes and starting the dishwasher, Florrie picked up her bag and the letter and walked out to her van. As she sat behind the wheel, Tom Houston was very much on her mind. There was a part of her that was torn. If the conversation didn't go the way she wanted when she telephoned W. Houston Property Developers, should she track down Tom and try and speak with him? 'Absolutely not,' she said, thinking out loud.

She turned the key. The van didn't start but the radio sang out. She smiled to herself, used to going through this same rigmarole every morning. She knew that on the third turn, Rose, her reliable van, would start … and it did.

The song on the radio took her by surprise and she froze. It was the same song she and Tom had declared their two-week holiday anthem all those years ago. Her eyes flitted from the radio to the glove compartment. She hesitated for a second then opened it and reached right to the back. She lay her hands on what she was looking for and brought out an iPod that had once belonged to Tom. When their holiday had come to an end, Tom had dropped her back at the university and helped her pack up her belongings for summer. Wheeling her suitcase into the car park he'd asked which was her car. She'd pointed and a wide grin had spread across his face.

'I always wondered who that van belonged to; I should have guessed.'

'Meet Rose, named after…'

'The flower,' he guessed. 'I've not seen anything quite like it.'

Her turquoise van covered in hand-painted roses was unique and full of character. 'No other flower is as famous or popular. The Rose outshines everything else.'

'Just like its owner,' Tom added, locking eyes with Florrie, making her stomach flip with multiple somersaults.

'I love her. She's part of the family. She takes a while to start, the heater is broken and the left-hand window doesn't close properly, but it's a great way to store flowers, especially in the winter as the van has its own refrigeration going on.'

Tom laughed. 'And what is your favourite flower? The rose?'

Without hesitation she said, 'The red tulip, the perfect love. The dark centre of the flower represents a lover's heart, darkened by the heat of passion.'

Tom pulled her in towards him, kissed her passionately then

whispered, 'I've left you a present. It's in your bag.' There was a twinkle in his eye. After she watched him drive away, she immediately opened her bag to discover his iPod with a small note tied around it. The note had a hand-drawn heart with her and Tom's initials written on either side. Turning the iPod on she found that Tom had created a playlist of all their favourite songs from the two weeks they'd spent together. Florrie hadn't listened to that playlist in eight years.

Taking the plunge now, she connected the iPod to the van, and as the first song sounded through the speaker, Florrie was instantly transported straight back into Tom Houston's arms.

Five minutes later, Florrie parked outside her florist shop and took in the delicious aroma that wafted past her from the creperie. Crossing the path, she walked towards Buttercup Barn, which always looked delightful with its olde worlde charm. The beautiful shopfront was full of colour and happiness, with artificial flowers tumbling around the oak-beamed porch. The display highlighted the natural beauty of the season with two wooden cartwheels adorning each side of the oak door with its wooden heart hanging in the centre. After unlocking the door Florrie picked up the post from the mat before walking over to the counter and taking the letter from W. Houston Property Developers out of her bag. Then, with a pounding heart, she picked up the phone and dialled the number printed on the letter. Within three rings the phone was answered. 'W. Houston Property Developers, how may I help you this morning?'

Florrie took a deep breath and crossed her fingers. 'Hi, my name is Florrie Appleton and I currently live at Rose Cottage, Heartcross Village. The property was rented from you for many years by my great-aunt Ada who's recently passed away.

I've now received an eviction notice and I'd like to discuss transferring the lease to myself, with maybe a view to purchasing the property from you in the future. I'm hoping you can help me.'

'Let me put you through to the right department. Please hold the line.'

The call was transferred and it seemed like the longest two minutes of her life. Florrie listened to the classical music playing from the other end of the line whilst she waited for the next member of staff to become available. Willing them to hurry, she was finally connected.

'Miss Appleton, how may I help you?'

Once again and still with her fingers crossed, Florrie explained the situation and waited whilst she heard the woman on the other end of the phone tap away on her keyboard. After going through a few security checks, and confirming she was indeed Ada's next of kin the woman said, 'I'm so sorry to tell you, Miss Appleton, but the lease on Rose Cottage will not be renewed. The cottage is no longer available for rent. The eviction date will stand and the property needs to be vacated by the last day of the month.'

Not quite believing what she was hearing, Florrie asked, 'Please can you tell me why?' She heard her voice crack. 'This is my home, and my family business is run from here. Is there a right of appeal? Surely someone can help me?' she begged, feeling desperate.

'I'm sorry, Miss Appleton. According to the records, Rose Cottage was under very old lease terms and though W. Houston Property Developers honoured that lease during your great-aunt's lifetime, it was terminated with her passing. All I can tell you is that the file says the property will no longer be available for rent.'

'Is that because it's going to be sold? Because if there's any chance I can have right of first refusal...' Ada had left Florrie a few investments and though she still wasn't sure exactly how much she had, and whether she could afford to buy a property, she was determined to make it work somehow.

'I'm sorry. The property is not for sale,' the assistant repeated. 'I can also confirm another letter has been sent to the property notifying you that there will be an inspection visit to make sure everything is left in good order. Once that has been completed the original deposit will be refunded to you in the amount of...' There was more tapping on the keyboard. 'Thirty-five pounds. Is there anything else I can do for you today?'

Florrie was aghast and lost for words. She could feel herself beginning to tremble. After hanging up the phone she promptly burst into tears. Hearing the bell tinkle above the door she looked up to see Isla walking through the door.

'Thank God it's you and not a customer.' Florrie held up the letter.

'Oh Florrie, I was just coming to see how you were getting on but I'm assuming it's not good news?'

Florrie managed a shake of her head, the tears still rolling down her cheeks. 'They said the lease cannot be transferred, and the property is not for rent or for sale. I just don't understand.'

'Did you speak to a supervisor? Maybe they could look at this case in more detail? I don't know what else to say.' Isla walked over to the door and locked it before displaying the closed sign. 'Let's have a breather for a minute.'

Florrie stood in front of the window and took a second to compose her thoughts. 'They did say there was another letter coming in the post with further details.'

'That could be this one. The post came just as I was leaving.'

Florrie took the letter from Isla. Seeing the name 'W. Houston Property Developers' now brought instant dread. 'What I don't understand is, if the cottage is not for sale or rent, then what's going to happen to it? I feel so sad – all of Great-Aunt Ada's hard work in maintaining the place over the years will have been for nothing. She's added so much value to the property. It is so unfair. They don't seem to want to take any of that into consideration.'

'I agree with you there.'

'It's an absolute blow. I feel sick to my stomach.' Florrie tore open the letter.

'Let's try and stay positive. Maybe we could take some legal advice,' suggested Isla. 'We'll do our best to find a way through this.'

Feeling like her whole world was collapsing around her, Florrie read the letter. 'It's things that need to be left in the cottage, or equivalents. This is a little silly. As if Aunt Ada is going to have kept things from sixty years ago. But it's quite general. There shouldn't be too much of an issue.' Florrie turned to the second page and her eyes widened as she read the words. 'Oh no, just when I didn't think things could get any worse!'

'What is it?' asked Isla.

'This letter states that The Vintage Flower Van belongs to Rose Cottage.'

'That's ridiculous,' said Isla, aghast.

'It cannot be removed from the premises,' Florrie continued. 'Which means Great-Aunt Ada's business of sixty years will have to fold. It can't! I promised her I'd look after the van.' Florrie exhaled. 'Just ... why are they doing this?' She handed the letter over to Isla. 'The Vintage Flower Van is iconic, and has been a part of this community for decades. Everyone will be up in arms.'

'It looks like it came with the cottage. Aunt Ada must have rented it, too.'

Florrie briefly closed her eyes. 'It's just one thing after another. It seems never-ending. My guess is if they weren't accommodating about the lease then they aren't going to allow me to have the van.'

'But surely it can't be any use to them.'

'Great-Aunt Ada's business meant the world to her. Her legacy needs to live on.'

Hearing the locked door rattle they both looked up to see Flynn trying to open it. He cupped his hands against the glass and peered inside, spotting them straightaway and tapping his watch. 'Open up,' he shouted, jokingly, with a smile on his face.

Florrie unlocked the door and Flynn stepped inside. 'I know it's short notice, Florrie, but I'm organising a huge charity conference up at Starcross Manor. It's going to be a big deal, with the national press attending and major coverage on social media platforms, and I was wondering – well, hoping – you'll take care of all the floral displays in the reception area along with the room, and dress the tables for the lunch.' Flynn looked between the pair of them and immediately realised there was something wrong. 'Have I caught you at a bad time?

Sorry, I've not even asked you how you are. Here's me barging straight in.'

'Don't be daft, you know you're my favourite hotel owner and of course I'll help. I'll get my diary.'

'Thank you. Are you doing okay?' he asked tentatively. 'Especially despite the latest news. I'm not sure how I'd be feeling.'

Florrie was perplexed. 'Latest news? Feeling about what?' she asked, glancing from Flynn to Isla. 'What have I missed?' She knew Flynn couldn't know about Rose Cottage or The Vintage Flower Van as she'd only just found out herself.

By the look on Flynn's face, he'd realised he must have said something he shouldn't have.

'Flynn?' queried Isla.

He took a breath. 'I may have put my size nines in it. You don't know, do you?'

'Not until you tell me,' encouraged Florrie, knowing by his expression that whatever he was going to tell her wasn't something she wanted to hear.

Looking nervous, he said. 'W. Houston Property Developers are intending to sell off the land and gardens attached to Rose Cottage and have applied to build a number of new houses on the plot. I never knew that cottage was rented, I always thought Ada owned it.'

Florrie stared at Flynn in disbelief. 'Say that again.'

'Surely you must be mistaken?' chipped in Isla. 'Where have you got that information from?'

'I'm afraid I'm part of a property developer's group and we keep each other updated with what's happening in the area. A member of the group posted an article they'd spotted online.'

'We've only just buried Ada. This is unbelievable!' Florrie

couldn't keep the astonishment out of her voice. 'What is wrong with these people?' Frustrated, she pointed out of the window in the general direction of the cottage. 'Ada nurtured that land for *decades*. She grew flower after flower. That garden is idyllic. The perfect cottage garden, it's beautiful and shouldn't be demolished just to make money.'

The actions of W. Houston Property Developers felt so personal, so painful. 'I'm not going to let this happen even if I have to get out there with placards and throw myself in front of the digger. Great-Aunt Ada would be crushed by this.'

'Sometimes property businesses have no scruples. It's all about making money and it doesn't matter who they trample over. Have they not said anything to you at all?' Flynn asked.

Florrie shook her head. She was still trying to get her head around what he'd just told them. 'No wonder they wouldn't divulge any information over the phone to me. Do you by any chance have the article? I'd like to see it.'

Flynn pulled out his phone from his pocket. He tapped the screen then passed it to Florrie. Isla looked over her shoulder. There was a photo of Rose Cottage and the article described how W. Houston Property Developers was hoping to convert the acres of land belonging to it into a number of new-build semi-detached houses.

'This is heartbreaking. I actually want to cry,' admitted Florrie, fanning her hand in front of her face. 'Firstly, the eviction, then The Vintage Flower Van and now the land. Surely, we can object?'

'You can appeal against the plans,' reassured Flynn. 'We all can. Sometimes direct action is the way to go and all the community would be behind you. We need to make everyone aware of this.'

'They don't waste time, do they? This article says that plans have already been submitted, which sounds to me as if this was ready to go and they were just waiting for Great-Aunt Ada to…' Florrie swallowed and laid her hands on her chest.

Isla touched her arm. 'Try not to get even more upset.'

'"Rose Cottage has belonged to the Houston Family since the 1940s,"' Florrie quoted from the article. 'This makes it sound like they've always lived there. It's just because tourism is thriving and people want to move to Heartcross – they see a chance to cash in by "offering a solution so new families can enjoy the Heartcross way of life".'

'They've put a good spin on it, I have to say,' remarked Flynn.

'And you're right, we need to make everyone aware of this. The community will be up in arms when this gets around.' The acrimony in Florrie's voice was clear and she could feel the anger rising up inside her. 'I'm not standing for it or allowing anyone to bulldoze Great-Aunt Ada's hard work. She's spent hundreds, if not thousands – maybe even tens of thousands! – of pounds over the years on flowers for that land, not to mention countless hours and days working the land with her bare hands. I want to speak to Houston's. Those gardens should be opened up in memory of Great-Aunt Ada and everything she has achieved in this community. She was one in a million. Do you know since she started her business in The Vintage Flower Van, she's provided flower arrangements for every funeral in this village free of charge? She always went out of her way to make everyone's lives a little easier.'

'I didn't know that,' said Flynn admiringly. 'She truly was such a remarkable woman.'

'Aunt Ada was the type of person you could aspire to be

like, not like W. Houston Property Developers. To me that article highlights the fact that they're driven by money, when it's people, happiness and memories that count for a lot more. Call themselves an honourable family business? "We make all the difference." Their tag line is a *joke*.'

'It is wrong,' agreed Isla.

'I know they're entitled to do what they can with their own cottage but it feels like a stab in the heart so soon after we've buried Ada.' Florrie took a breath. 'I feel like I'm riding the fastest roller-coaster in the world. I don't know which twist or turn is coming next.'

'It's yet another unexpected shock,' added Isla as Florrie gave Flynn his phone back.

'I wonder if Great-Aunt Ada ever tried to buy the cottage from them over the years? We'll probably never know. Heartcross has become more and more popular, but to flatten the gardens, and destroy all the wildlife and all the birds nesting in the hedgerow... Decades of growing nature will be destroyed in an instant.'

'I agree, it's one of the most beautiful gardens I have ever seen. So much love went into it on a daily basis, and winning Flowers in Bloom for so many years shows just how outstanding the gardens are,' said Isla supportively.

'And now I need to ring them again. They're taking The Vintage Flower Van.' Florrie looked towards Flynn.

'Surely not. That van is an iconic part of our community.'

'Apparently, it came with the cottage.'

'I'd have a chat with Jaydon at the solicitors, I'm sure he could draft a letter if needs be. In fact, he's with me tomorrow. Why don't you come over, take a look at the room that needs the flower displays and have a chat with him?'

Florrie nodded. 'Thank you, I'll do that. But I can't afford any type of costly battle.'

'If there's one thing I've learned about Heartcross in the time I've been here, it's that this community will not stand for any wrongdoing or unfairness. W. Houston Property Developers will have a fight on their hands if they say no to you keeping The Vintage Flower Van.'

'Flynn is right. Depending how far you want to fight…'

'But that's a cost.'

'Social media costs nothing to make people aware of wrongdoing, and we're all behind you. Look at when the bridge collapsed in the storm all those years ago. The story spread like wildfire due to social media and that was the reason this village became so popular overnight. Anything that's happening in Heartcross is news and this is definitely news.'

'Let's hope it doesn't get to that. Surely, they'll have no use for The Vintage Flower Van and they'll be kind enough to give it to me, or at least let me buy it. If the worst comes to the worst and they do bulldoze the gardens at Rose Cottage I'll be taking my spade and digging out all the flowers myself before that happens – though I may need to rent some land off you to replant them all.' Florrie forced a smile as she looked at Isla.

'We'll all be pitching in and helping.'

'We sure will,' confirmed Flynn. 'I'll see you tomorrow morning. I know it's easier said than done but try not to worry.'

'Thanks, Flynn.'

As Flynn walked to his car Florrie spotted a familiar figure coming out of the creperie. 'And there he is, the destroyer of all things good.' She nodded and Isla followed her gaze.

'Tom Houston? And what brings him to Heartcross today?'

He was sitting on a bench enjoying a crepe only a few hundred yards from where they were standing.

'How do you feel about seeing him sitting there?' asked Isa, still looking over in his direction.

'I want to go across and slap this letter right against his chest and demand he explain what the hell is he playing at, but I'm not going to. I'm going to keep my dignity and get advice from Jaydon first even though it's extremely tempting to confront him right now.'

Isla was quiet for a moment. 'Given the information we've just discovered from Flynn, I think we need to be playing our cards very close to our chest. I know exactly what I would be doing.'

'Which is what?'

Isla pointed to the poster on the lamppost right next to where Tom was sitting.

'We need to be ingenious and I think the answer is simple. Now you have even more reason to make sure you and Rose Cottage win Flowers in Bloom this year. Think of the publicity that would create! "W. Houston Property Developers to destroy winning gardens of Flower in Bloom and bring a well established business to an end,"' Isla projected in a theatrical voice. 'I can see the news headlines right now.'

Florrie didn't need to contemplate Isla's words for long. 'You're absolutely right! The gardens are still in tip-top condition and I could create enormous publicity and news articles dedicated to the memory of Great-Aunt Ada and ensure The Vintage Flower Van is a huge part of the day. And that's exactly what I'm going to do.' With a smile on her face, she looked across at Tom, who had just stood up. He tossed the wrapper from his crepe into a nearby bin and turned towards Buttercup Barn, he must have sensed someone was watching him. Their eyes met through the window and he held her gaze for a moment before he turned and walked along the path to Love Heart Lane. He didn't look back.

Florrie felt her mood slump further. Seeing Tom again had ignited all of the feelings that she'd tried so hard to squash over the years, and as much as she wanted to fling open the shop door to confront him about the letter she was holding, she was also disappointed he hadn't attempted to come over and speak to her.

Isla smiled. 'If W. Houston Property Developers don't play fairly, let's make things as uncomfortable as possible for Tom Houston. He'll soon wish he'd never heard of Heartcross or crossed Florrie Appleton!'

Chapter Six

The next morning Florrie's eyes began to tear up as she left Rose Cottage and walked past The Vintage Flower Van, which was arrayed with beautiful blooms that she'd cut from the garden first thing. Yesterday, she'd had a second conversation with W. Houston Property Developers, which was short and not so sweet. When she asked if they would consider allowing her to keep or buy The Vintage Flower Van, their answer was non-negotiable, their clear, concise 'no' still ringing in her ears.

When her head had hit the pillow last night, Tom had been in the front of her mind. This all seemed to be a little personal to her. She'd always thought she was a good judge of character, and after going over and over it again in her mind she couldn't believe how Tom had treated her in the past, or how he was treating her now. The more she thought about it, the more she felt confused about him. Why had he seemed genuinely pleased to see her? Had he completely forgotten betraying her?

Now, behind the wheel of her van, Florrie headed towards

Bonnie's Teashop, planning to grab a quick bite before heading up to Starcross Manor to meet Flynn and Jaydon. She beeped and waved at the Union Jack-roofed Mini coming towards her and Martha waved back.

After a conversation on the phone last night Martha had agreed to swap roles from tomorrow, manning Buttercup Barn whilst Florrie threw her heart and soul into doing whatever it takes to save The Vintage Flower Van and the gardens at Rose Cottage.

Florrie parked the car outside the terraced house she was currently renting from Rona on Love Heart Lane. For a moment she stayed behind the wheel of the van and gazed at the line of whitewashed terraced houses, which looked utterly gorgeous, their potted plants with tumbling flowers full of colour guarding the duck-egg blue front doors. The view in front of her was as stunning as usual. Across from the houses were the comical-looking alpacas grazing in the field, and, to cap it all, the majestic Heartcross Mountain stood tall at the top of the lane against a beautiful cobalt sky. She fully understood why Heartcross was flooded with tourists all year round. After leaving university, she'd lived with her great-aunt at Rose Cottage but had soon craved her independence. With Ada's help, her dream of opening up her own florist shop had become a reality, and she'd moved into her own house. She'd lived on Love Heart Lane for five years now and knew she'd had the best of both worlds – her own space and Great-Aunt Ada only a short walk away.

As she walked through the door of Bonnie's Teashop the bell tinkled above her head, causing Rona and Felicity to look up from behind the counter. She was met with huge, beaming smiles and Rona rushed towards Florrie, swiping her hands on a tea-towel before enveloping her in a hug.

'It's good to see you out and about. I know when my mother passed away all I wanted to do was hide from the world. Ada's service was beautiful and I'm glad to see The Vintage Flower Van is open for business and blooming in all its glory. Heartcross wouldn't be the same without it.'

Florrie pulled slowly away from the hug. She was going to have to tell them about the possible demise of The Vintage Flower Van. 'Thank you both for taking care of the buffet. You did an excellent job. Please don't forget to send me your invoice.'

'You're very welcome and we'll do no such thing. Ada was our friend and you're our friend and we wouldn't think of charging you.'

Florrie was truly touched by Rona's gesture. 'Thank you, that's so kind.'

'And I know you've probably come to talk to me about giving up your lease on the house but don't worry, you aren't leaving me in the lurch. Vacant houses are hard to come by in Heartcross, so I have no doubt that it'll soon get snapped up.' Hearing the oven timer beeping from the kitchen, Rona picked up the oven gloves that were lying on the counter and turned to go and grab whatever was ready. Before she could, Felicity took the gloves from her.

'I'll get the sausage rolls out,' she said before disappearing through the kitchen door.

'About the house...' said Florrie.

'Honestly, I don't want you worrying about anything.'

'I won't be moving out.'

Rona looked perplexed as Felicity walked back towards

them and placed the freshly baked sausage rolls into the savoury display counter.

'I just assumed you'd be moving back into Rose Cottage.'

'Why aren't you moving back into Rose Cottage?' asked Felicity, leaning on the counter.

'Because it's not my cottage to move into.'

Felicity raised an eyebrow. 'I wasn't expecting that.'

'I'm in a little bit of shock, if I'm truly honest with you.'

Rona pointed to the empty table just in front of the window. 'We have a quiet moment so why don't you sit and I'll rustle up a pot of tea. Tea is always good in a crisis … and it sounds like a crisis might be brewing.'

Sitting at the table a few minutes later, Florrie hugged her mug of tea. 'Everyone is going to find out soon enough, so I'll just come out with it. The cottage wasn't owned by Great-Aunt Ada. I've only just found out myself. It turns out it was rented.'

'Who from?' asked Felicity.

'A company called W. Houston Property Developers,' replied Florrie.

Rona looked deep in thought. 'That's right. I'd forgotten all about that, probably because Ada had lived there so long. The company is a family business created many years ago by William Houston, who was well known and respected in these parts. He was the kind of man you called a pillar of society, a genuine man with a very good reputation. Everyone loved him, unlike his son, Edward Houston.'

This little bit of information was a surprise to Florrie. 'Hang on a moment, are you saying that William and Edward were … locals?'

'I believe so.'

'And what gives you the impression that Edward wasn't liked?' asked Florrie, intrigued.

'I was unashamedly nosy. I eavesdropped on private conversations between my mum, Martha and Dolores when they got together for drinks in the front room. That's how I used to find out all the gossip in the village.' Rona chuckled.

'Mum!' Felicity said, looking stunned.

'I'm not proud of it now but their conversations were better than any of the celebrity gossip columns in the magazines. And I remember one thing they said about Edward was that he rubbed people up the wrong way. At one time he was included in all the social events – likely living off the good reputation of his father – but then something turned sour and Edward became an outcast within Heartcross social circles. Dolores and Martha would be the ones to ask if you want more specific details. I believe Edward's son has taken over the business now, even though Edward is still involved in some capacity. I read an article about them in a Sunday newspaper, but it must have been some time ago though.'

'That would be Tom Houston and from what I know, he's more like his father than his grandfather.'

Felicity pointed at Florrie. 'Tom Houston! That was the guy who introduced himself to me this morning. I noticed him the second he walked through the door because he stood out from the usual crowd of hikers. I have to admit, I couldn't help but admire his rugged good looks. He was dressed in a fine Italian navy suit. Very smart.'

'And did he say what he was doing here?' asked Florrie.

'If I remember correctly, he's attending a charity event of some sort,' replied Felicity. 'But why did you say he's like his father? How do you know?'

'Because he's already rubbed me up the wrong way.' Florrie decided not to share that she'd known him from university or that for a short time she'd known him *very* intimately. 'W. Houston Property Developers have applied to build new houses on the land where Rose Cottage currently stands and, to add insult to injury, The Vintage Flower Van apparently also belongs to them and they're refusing to sell it to me. So after all my promises to Great-Aunt Ada to keep the van going,' Florrie swallowed, 'it seems I've fallen at the first hurdle and it will likely have to close its doors on the last day of the month, which is the same day all of Ada's possessions need to be removed from the cottage. I'm losing her home and business in one fell swoop.'

Rona gasped. 'That's preposterous! They can't take the van from you. It's iconic. People travel far and wide to buy flowers from the van. It's its very own tourist attraction.'

'They won't transfer the rental lease of the cottage to me either. It's all such a major blow.'

'Florrie, this is heartbreaking. I'm so sorry,' Felicity said kindly.

'It is. Flynn is the one who shared with me that the company has plans to build houses on the land.'

'Why would you want to demolish such outstanding natural beauty?' Rona was dumbfounded.

'Because these people have no morals and are all about the money,' cut in Felicity. 'New houses are popping up everywhere. Most of them no bigger than a postage stamp and spoiling the natural beauty of the countryside.'

'What can we do to stop them? The community won't be happy with this,' Rona said heatedly.

Those were exactly the words that Florrie was hoping to

hear. 'We can pull together in the community spirit Heartcross is known for and show Tom Houston exactly who he is messing with. Firstly, I will be entering Flowers in Bloom, creating as much publicity as possible for Rose Cottage and its award-winning gardens. A community meeting also needs to be arranged to make everyone aware what's going on so we can come up with a plan of action.'

'I can't see any resident of Heartcross being in favour of destroying the most beautiful gardens in the area for new houses, or handing The Vintage Flower Van over to them. Let's see what we can all do to stop this,' said Felicity.

'W. Houston Property Developers has clearly underestimated the power of Heartcross. You let us know when the meeting is and we'll arrange the refreshments,' said Rona.

Florrie smiled at their immediate and unequivocal support. This is what she'd always loved about the community in Heartcross – in times of need, they all stuck together. 'Thanks, Rona. I'm headed up to Starcross Manor as I have a meeting with Flynn and a lawyer so would it be possible for you to put one of your delicious cinnamon swirls in a bag for me?'

'Of course.'

Five minutes later, Florrie was following the winding lane through the woodlands to Starcross Manor and manoeuvring her way past the gatehouse and up the tree-lined driveway. The historic Georgian manor house had been transformed into a magnificent five-star hotel set in a hundred acres of lush green woodland, which incorporated formal gardens, a deer park and a wildflower meadow. It was truly stunning. Even the driveway leading up to the entrance was grand, sweeping into a wide circle around an ornate fountain. The hotel was extremely popular with tourists and was now also the number one wedding venue in the Scottish Highlands.

There wasn't a cloud in the sky and today the temperature was going to be a whopping twenty-six degrees. The weather buoyed Florrie's spirits and she thought the ducks had the right idea, lapping up the sunshine while swimming in the lake and then nestling under the cascades of branches at the water edge to cool off. With the impressive stone steps leading up to the oak doors of Starcross Manor in view, Florrie slowed down the van and headed towards a vacant parking spot opposite a very posh car that was surrounded by traffic cones. As she climbed out of her van, she decided to satisfy her curiosity and take a closer look.

She quickly realised it wasn't an average posh car, it was in fact a Mansory Vivere Bugatti Veyron, usually only owned by high-profile millionaires. With its modified wings, shortened bonnet and striking monochrome design the car had serious attitude. Florrie couldn't help but wonder who'd be driving a car like this. She wasn't all that surprised to see it though. Starcross Manor was well known for its celebrity appeal and, with a number of famous people living in the village of Heartcross, it was becoming the prime holiday destination in Scotland for everyone, including the rich and famous. A swift glance towards the main door of the hotel confirmed that there was no one in sight, so she walked up to the car. The interior was seriously impressive – it reminded her of a lavish hotel suite – and close up she could see how the exterior paint job caught the light, like ice on the ground on a frosty morning.

'Someone must have worked hard for this car,' she murmured to herself, knowing it was probably worth more than she would ever earn in her lifetime. As she walked back past Rose, Florrie locked the van door, threw the keys into her bag and patted her on her bonnet. 'But I love you more.'

As Florrie made her way up the stone steps, she heard the quacking of ducks, which made her look back over her shoulder. There was a proud, plump, dappled mallard leading her family across the car park in a long line towards the lake, where a weeping willow arched out over the water.

Smiling, she shielded the sun from her eyes and watched them for a moment before a movement caught her eye. The smile slipped from her face rapidly as she let out a trilling gasp. She'd forgotten the handbrake and Rose was on the move!

'NO, NO, NO...' Feeling a squeezing sensation in her chest as well as what felt like a rush of blood pounding in her head, Florrie bounded down the stone steps two at a time whilst simultaneously attempting to frantically fish out the van keys from the bottom of her bag. But she was too late. Freezing on the bottom step, Florrie watched in horror as Rose smashed straight into the bonnet of the Bugatti.

'Shit! Double shit!' She exhaled, briefly closed her eyes and wished she was anywhere else but here.

'What the hell do you think you're doing?' bellowed a voice she instantly recognised.

'Oh God, could this get any worse? Why me?' she uttered under her breath.

'You've nearly smashed my car to smithereens.'

Taking a sharp intake of breath, she turned and locked eyes with an angry-looking Tom, who was striding down the steps towards the car.

It was *his* car, apparently.

'Well, don't just stand there.' Tom threw his arms up in the air before he loosened the top button of his shirt, shaking his head in disbelief.

Florrie slowly walked towards him. 'I'm so sorry, it's all my fault. I must have forgotten to engage the handbrake.'

Lifting an eyebrow, he composed himself. 'Please can you get Rose moved so I can see the damage?'

Florrie stopped in surprise. 'You remembered her name?'

'It's not that easy to forget.' Tom stared at her and for a second Florrie wondered if he meant her or the car.

'Please pull her forward,' he repeated.

'Yes, sorry!' she said, fishing the keys out of her bag and opening the door. After turning the key in the ignition and nothing happening, she rushed out, 'Don't worry—'

'I know, she starts on the third turn...' Tom interrupted, before trailing off. Looking up at him Florrie followed his gaze towards the iPod, which was lying on the dashboard. Of course the song they'd heard together before they fell asleep in each other's arms under the starry sky on their final night started playing out of the speakers just then, right on cue, and Florrie didn't know where to look, her cheeks instantly flushing red.

'Is that my iPod?' Tom asked, his tone hard to read.

Her eyes darting back towards him, Florrie knew there was no point trying to deny it, but thankfully Rose started just then, buying her time before she had to answer. Florrie hit the accelerator hard by mistake causing the van to kangaroo forward, then in a second blunder pressed the brake with enough force to catapult herself forward. Feeling a fool, she squeezed her eyes shut as she heard the loud clang of Rose's bumper falling onto the ground behind her. Tom Houston was making her *very* nervous.

She took a deep breath. 'I'm so sorry.' Her voice was shaky. 'I could have hit you.' Her white knuckles were still gripping the steering wheel.

Tom's expression softened. 'You're shaking. I ... I didn't mean to shout at you. It's just that I only got the car a few days ago. Here, let me move Rose.' He held out his hand and Florrie hesitated for a moment before letting Tom help her down from the van. The touch of his hand made her tingle and she could feel herself turning slightly crimson as she noticed the familiar aroma emanating from him. He was wearing the same aftershave as he had eight years ago. Standing to the side, she watched as he gently drove Rose back into the space she'd rolled from and parked her.

'The handbrake is on, this time,' he said with a smile as he stepped out of the van. 'And are you okay?'

Florrie knew Tom had every right to raise his voice but he didn't. He seemed genuinely concerned and more like the caring Tom she remembered. 'I'm okay, but I think Rose needs some TLC.' Florrie's eyes were fixed on the bumper, which was still lying on the ground. 'You need to assess the damage to your car,' she reminded him.

Tom walked up to his car. 'From what I can see there's just a couple of dents and a smashed front light. Let me take your details.'

'Yes, of course.' She grabbed a business card from her bag and passed it to Tom. 'All my details are on there.'

He turned the card over in his hand. 'I assumed you changed your phone number. After...' He paused. 'I tried this number many times but ... it never...' Tom looked hurt.

Florrie hesitated. 'It never connected because I blocked your number after what you did.'

Tom raised an eyebrow. 'Unbelievable.'

She wasn't quite sure what he meant by that, but it wasn't a conversation she wanted to get into right at this second. There was no point dragging up the past. Even though there was a part of her that wished it had never happened, to forget about those two weeks they'd spent together, their bodies entwined, would mean she also lost out on some very special memories they'd shared. 'I'll unblock you now.' Florrie took her phone out from her bag.

'You still have my number stored in your phone eight years after blocking it?' he asked.

'It appears so,' she replied, tapping on her phone.

Tom's phone began to ring. Florrie leaned over his shoulder to take a look at the screen. 'That's me, but I see you've no longer got my number stored.' She wasn't sure how she felt about that; maybe there was a twinge of disappointment?

'I haven't, no, after what *you* did,' he said, a bit pointedly.

It was now Florrie's turn to raise an eyebrow but she brushed past his implication. 'You can contact me about the damage and the costs.'

'Rest assured, I will.'

Florrie was beginning to feel a little agitated. She dropped her phone back into her bag before opening the back doors of Rose. Hauling the bumper up into her arms, she placed it down into the back of the van. As she shut the doors, she glanced down at her white T-shirt and saw that it was now sporting a black stripe right across it. Damn.

Tom smiled in amusement, which irritated her that little bit more. 'It's not funny.'

He held his hands up in protest and at that moment his

phone rang again. He looked at the screen. 'It's the office. I need to take this.'

Florrie watched him walk off towards the lake and remembered that she was here for a meeting with Flynn and Jaydon, which she'd now have to take covered in grime. Hearing an engine, she spotted Isla driving towards her in the farm van. She parked near to Florrie then jumped out of the driver's seat. 'I'm just dropping the fresh meat to the kitchen.' She clocked Florrie's T-shirt. 'What have you been doing and what's happened to Rose?'

'I've had a little bump.' Florrie nodded her head towards the Bugatti.

'Woah! Out of all the cars in the car park, you've bumped into the most expensive one. Surely it must belong to a film star or someone equally rich and famous.'

'It's worse than that. Would you believe me if I told you the car belongs to Tom Houston?'

Isla followed Florrie's eyes in the direction of Tom, who was leaning against the gate leading to the lake, still talking on his phone. 'No way. How did he react to that?'

'To be fair, he's been quite good about it, especially considering he's only had the car a few days.'

Isla let out a low whistle. 'His business must be doing very well.'

'And that's the reason I'm here. To try and put a stop to some of that business.'

'You can't deny he's drop-dead gorgeous.'

Florrie stared in his direction before turning back to her friend and scolding her. 'Isla, you're meant to be on my side.'

'Oh, I am, believe me. I and the whole community will be behind you, but he does have the perkiest of bums and that shirt is clinging to every muscle. Bad boys are always more appealing.'

'Isla!' Florrie rolled her eyes ... even though she couldn't help secretly agreeing. Florrie acknowledged the fizzing inside her that Tom's presence stirred up, but what she needed to focus on right now was keeping her promise to Great-Aunt Ada and making sure she did everything in her power to stop Tom and his company destroying the gardens at Rose Cottage.

Chapter Seven

S tepping inside the grand foyer was still as impressive as it had been the very first time she'd done so. At either side of the reception desk stood an olive tree with twinkling lights, which had been provided by Buttercup Barn along with the week's stunning collection of vibrant stargazer lilies paired with classic and timeless memory roses. Pistacia added a finishing touch of lush greenery, making the flowers in the glass vase on the reception desk a stunning focal point.

Florrie's shoes tapped on the slate floor, and the receptionist looked up and greeted her with a warm smile.

'Florrie, how lovely to see you! Flynn is expecting you. He's waiting for you in the Grand Hall along with Jaydon. They're just through there.' The receptionist gestured towards the double oak doors to the right of her.

'Thank you.' Florrie sailed into the Grand Hall, which she admired every time she saw it. She'd dressed this room on many occasions for weddings and functions, but even stripped back and void of decoration, it was still a room of beauty. The open fire, though not lit, was at the heart of the room. Regal arched oak beams ran the length of the ceiling. The elegant panache and charm of the room made it an instant hit no matter who was using it or how.

Flynn spotted Florrie the moment she walked in and was up on his feet to greet her.

'Please excuse my T-shirt,' she shared immediately, embarrassed by the state of her clothes. 'I've had a little van trouble on the way.'

'Oh no, is there anything I can help with?'

'Honestly, it's fine, just a tiny mishap, but thank you,' replied Florrie, not wanting to go into the misfortune of the last thirty minutes.

'Do you know Mr Fairbrother?' said Flynn. 'I'm sure your paths must have crossed at some point.'

A tall, slim man stood up. 'Please, call me Jaydon. It's lovely to finally meet you as I've heard so much about you. I've been your great-aunt's solicitor for many years.'

Florrie shook his hand. 'Pleased to meet you, too.'

Flynn gestured to one of the leather-bound chairs with a blush-coloured cushion, positioned in front of the floor-to-ceiling window that overlooked the vast maintained gardens. They were edged with flowerbeds and featured a fountain in the middle of the lawn. 'Take a seat and help yourself to tea and biscuits.'

All three of them sat down.

'The Grand Hall is the room I need dressing with flowers for the important charity event I'm hosting. It's going to be a huge deal and featured in national magazines along with TV adverts. Ten Scottish charities that go above and beyond have now been selected and this event will give them an expanded platform to help bring national awareness to the causes they're supporting. They'll also each receive a donation from myself. Each charity has its own logo and colours so I was thinking about having arrangements in their company colours on their individual tables. What do you think?'

Florrie nodded. 'Absolutely.'

'The stage is going to be in front of those windows there,' he said, pointing towards them, 'with the backdrop of the gardens and the mountain behind. We'll want some arrangements on it that work cohesively with the individual table decorations, if that's possible. If I email you the list of charities, will you be able to take a look at each one and see what you think might work best?'

'Yes, of course. I can get that back to you early next week.'

'I'll email you the list when I get back to my office.' Changing course, Flynn glanced in Jaydon's direction then back towards Florrie. 'I've brought Jaydon up to speed with what we've learned about Rose Cottage and The Vintage Flower Van.'

'We have got to do something to stop W. Houston Property Developers in their tracks,' urged Florrie.

'I agree,' replied Flynn, looking to Jaydon for guidance.

'First, please let me offer you my personal condolences for your loss. I was very fond of your great-aunt, and I've been a regular customer of The Vintage Flower Van for over fifteen years. Every Wednesday I've bought my wife some of Ada's gorgeous flowers, which are always displayed proudly on our farmhouse table.'

'And I hope you continue to do so...' Florrie paused. 'Well, at least for another few weeks. You won't be able to after that if I'm not successful in negotiating a deal to keep the van.'

'As far as The Vintage Flower Van is concerned, I think we need to apply pressure to W. Houston Property Developers and let's see how they respond. A legal letter will be passed to their management to deal with. In all fairness, they may not even be aware of what is going on here. Then we can take it from there. But with Rose Cottage, I'm afraid it's a different story. W. Houston Property Developers can apply to do whatever they wish regarding the land, but there is still the right to object.'

'And that's what we all will be doing. I'm going to organise a community meeting and let everyone know what's happening and what we're facing. I wouldn't like to be the administrative assistant at the council offices on the day all the objections flood in! Did you know that Ada didn't own the cottage?'

'Ada came to see me around six months ago, saying she wanted to get everything legally tied up, especially the bonds and investments, to give you financial support in the future. It's not unusual for people of a certain age to start getting their affairs in order. When I asked her about the cottage, all she said was that there was an agreement about it between herself and William Houston.'

'The founder of W. Houston Property Developers,' said Florrie.

'Yes. She said that she was going to have a conversation with you about it, but I'm assuming that didn't happen?'

Florrie shook her head. 'And despite trying multiple times, they won't transfer the lease to me. They're adamant that all of Great-Aunt Ada's possessions need to be removed by the last day of the month. Thankfully, Isla and Drew have storage space at the farm that they've said I can use. Still, it's going to be a mammoth task, and I'm not ready to say goodbye to the cottage.'

'And they've sent you a couple of letters outlining this, I believe?'

Florrie took the letters out of her bag and relayed all the information from the telephone calls.

Jaydon looked over the letters. 'Okay, according to these documents, the property and its contents, including The Vintage Flower Van, belong to W. Houston Property Developers. Even though it is theirs to keep, anyone with any ounce of decency would let you keep the van so that the business could continue operating, especially considering the fact that it's been the heart of the community for sixty years and is an iconic and historic family-run business.'

'We've got to try and keep The Vintage Flower Van up and running. I promised Aunt Ada. It's about the sentimental value it holds, not the monetary value.'

'All we can do is appeal to their better nature. Flynn also mentioned the Flowers in Bloom competition is fast approaching. I know Ada won the competition many years in a row.'

'Ada's garden is one of the primary reasons people travel from all over to come and see Flowers in Bloom. Ada's garden looks like it should belong to a stately home,' commented Flynn.

'The competition started out many years ago,' Florrie explained, 'when all the keen gardeners in the village came together and invited the community to come and view their gardens. Then the next year they began selling tickets and donated the money to charity. Tickets are sold from Hamish's shop and the morning they go on sale people queue for them because there are only a limited number. Flowers in Bloom has grown over the years and has become a nationally recognised event amongst garden enthusiasts. It's been covered in gardening magazines, and one year the TV show *Gardener's World* presented the show from Rose Cottage. It's become quite famous in its own right,' she said proudly.

'And this is the same garden that they're proposing to bulldoze in order to build new properties?' Jaydon raised an eyebrow. 'Surely W. Houston Property Developers would know the history of the cottage?'

'You'd think so, but even if they do, would they care? Probably not as long as they're making money,' replied Florrie.

'Do you know what's specifically happening to the cottage?' asked Jaydon.

Florrie shrugged. 'Your guess is as good as mine. They won't rent it to me and they claimed it's not up for sale.'

'My educated guess is they possibly have a two-tier plan. If they're successful and planning permission is granted, they may let the cottage go to rack and ruin, claiming it's unfit to live in and easier to knock down so they can build more new houses on the land.'

'That's criminal.' Florrie was horrified.

'I've seen it before. They make a hefty profit that way.'

'I'm not going to let that happen,' Florrie's tone was defiant. 'But I do fear the likes of me standing up to them will have no effect whatsoever.'

'Don't underestimate the power of this community and social media,' reassured Flynn.

'That's exactly what Isla said.'

'And she'd be right,' said Jaydon. 'This afternoon I'll draft a letter regarding The Vintage Flower Van and I'll send it over to you by email. Once you've okayed it, I'll send it to W. Houston Property Developers.'

Flynn passed Florrie a pen and a piece of paper. She scribbled down her email address and handed it to Jaydon.

After Jaydon took photos of the letters with his phone, he looked over at Florrie. 'The key here is to get all this noticed. You need to snowball publicity about The Vintage Flower Van. Does it have its own social media account?'

Florrie shook her head. 'Aunt Ada couldn't get to grips with doing her accounts online, never mind posting on social media. I tried to show her all the reels I'd created about Buttercup Barn but she liked using the old-fashioned way of word of mouth and reputation.'

'I'd set up an account for The Vintage Flower Van. Create content and post online including all about its history. Show it off with all of the wonderful flowers. Tell everyone you've taken over the business after the passing of your great-aunt – making it clear that it's a family business that's spanned decades and generations. If you can increase the followers by appealing to the masses, W. Houston Property Developers will be forced to sit up and take notice. And if they still refuse to play ball, then you post all about how the business is being forced to cease trading after sixty years because of—'

'Idiots with no common sense,' interrupted Florrie.

'I'll leave you to decide on exactly what to say in the posts.' Jaydin smiled. 'And entering Flowers in Bloom is a must. To be blunt, you need to win. But no pressure!' he said, trying to lighten the growing tension in the room. 'Believe me, people are going to get behind you. They'll feel very passionately about saving the gardens from being demolished.'

Florrie knew Jaydon was talking sense and she was

determined to make sure that everyone in Scotland knew about The Vintage Flower Van and the proposal to flatten the land. 'I'm going to make it my mission to not only win that competition but also to make The Vintage Flower Van as famous as possible.'

'So, just to recap,' said Jaydon, 'I'll get the letter drafted this afternoon and emailed across to you. If you're happy with it, I can then get it sent to them straightaway.'

'Can I just ask how much it's going to cost me for your services and advice?' asked Florrie, a bit worried that she hadn't asked sooner.

'Absolutely nothing. I'm happy to help you out in memory of Ada. Like I said, I was very fond of her.'

'That's very kind, thank you. Next Wednesday's bunch of flowers is on the house. I insist.'

'Deal,' replied Jaydon. 'Here's my card.' He looked at his phone. 'There's three weeks until the eviction, so make sure you're maximising publicity while you still have access to The Vintage Flower Van and the grounds of the cottage.'

Florrie nodded. 'I understand and I'm on it. Thanks, to both of you.'

After walking back through the foyer, Florrie headed out towards the car park and immediately noticed Tom's car wasn't there. As soon as she got home, she knew she needed to notify her car insurance provider and book Rose into the garage to get her bumper fixed. As she got behind the wheel, something caught her eye. She narrowed her eyes at the folded piece of paper flapping under the windscreen wiper. Knowing that Starcross Manor was not the type of establishment to bombard you with marketing leaflets, she climbed from her seat and grabbed the piece of paper, curious about what it might be. She was surprised to see her name neatly written on the front.

Unfolding the paper, she read:

Just for the record, my favourite song on the playlist was track 4.

She instantly knew the note was from Tom, and her heart gave a tiny leap. Track four was her favourite, too. It had been playing the first night they'd spent together. It might have been the oysters they'd shared, or the champagne, or the intoxicating warmth of the sea air, but whatever it was, that night, no matter how hard she tried, would be etched on her mind for ever. It had been truly beautiful and for a moment she was lost in the romance of it all, but as she looked back towards Starcross Manor she remembered the reason she was here. Tom Houston was the owner of the company that was demolishing everything Aunt Ada had worked for. But why would he want her to know his favourite track? Perhaps to make her remember what they had had together for those two weeks? Or did he know what was happening at Rose Cottage and was this a feeble attempt to distract her and make her fall under his spell again whilst he surged ahead with his plan to make as much money as he could?

'You don't know me at all,' Florrie said angrily, screwing up the note into a ball and tossing it into a nearby bin on the edge of the car park. She wasn't going to let herself fall for his charms again. Her head was well and truly in the game of fighting for what was right.

Driving back to Buttercup Barn, Florrie was thankful it was half-day closing, her mind busy with everything that had gone on that morning. After parking the van outside the shop, she waved at Isla, who was serving inside the farm shop. As soon as there was a lull in customers, Isla walked towards her.

'How did the meeting go?'

'Jaydon is going to draft a letter regarding The Vintage Flower Van and it's on my list to arrange a day and time for the community meeting. I'm thankful its half-day closing today. What are you doing this afternoon?'

'Just general chores that I need saving from. What are you thinking?'

'I'm thinking of setting up social media for the flower van and posting its first reel. I may need a cameraperson.'

'I'm in! I'll see you up at Rose Cottage just after two p.m.'

For the next couple of hours Florrie was run off her feet and by midday there were only a few bunches of flowers left to sell. It was her first breather of the day and as she stood in the doorway of the shop, hugging a mug of tea, she heard the computer ping.

Checking her inbox she saw that there were two new emails.

The first, as promised, was from Jaydon. Reading through the letter he'd prepared, Florrie was impressed. He'd laid out a concrete moral case for The Vintage Flower Van staying in the family and as a gesture of goodwill being handed over to Florrie. He'd included dates of trading up until Ada had passed away and links to articles The Vintage Flower Van had been featured in. Florrie felt hopeful. Surely anyone receiving this email wouldn't hesitate to give her the van. She quickly typed a reply, agreeing that Jaydon should send it. Her fingers were crossed that the email would make a difference.

The second email was from Flynn, listing the ten charities being celebrated at his event, in alphabetical order. He had included their logos and links to their websites. She quickly glanced down the list and stopped on the eighth entry.

The William Houston Foundation.

Florrie couldn't quite believe it. The Houstons were turning up everywhere! She clicked on the link, which took her through to the charity homepage. There was a photograph of William Houston. Florrie did a double take. There was no mistaking Tom was from the same family! He had the same rugged good looks and charismatic smile as his grandfather. The homepage described when and why the charity was set up; it seemed William had suffered a heart attack and he wanted to give something back to the people who had cared for him during his recovery. That's when he'd set up the William Houston Foundation, with every penny raised going to NHS charities.

According to the website, the charity was now run by Edward Houston, but Tom Houston was in the midst of taking over the reins ... which would explain why Tom was in Heartcross. Maybe he was networking in the area before the charity event to help create more awareness for his grandfather's charity?

Curious to know more about William Houston, Florrie Googled him. There were numerous articles about him online, with one national paper suggesting that he should receive an OBE for services to the property and development industry. Florrie put her hand on her heart when she read how William had housed a number of factory workers when their houses near a local mine had been destroyed by a natural disaster. Out of the goodness of his heart he'd constructed new houses, keeping families together and charging low rent. He was well respected, a pillar of society, genuine, and his extensive charity work was admirable. He was a man who just kept giving. Clicking on the next article, Florrie read the bold headline.

Respected Property Millionaire William Houston Dies
After Health Complications.

The article outlined how he'd battled with a number of health conditions following his heart attack and yet had never given up campaigning for his charity. His funeral was packed, mourners spilling out into the road as there wasn't enough space in the church – a church she recognised from the photo. William Houston's funeral had been held here in Heartcross, just like Ada's.

She carried on reading. Tributes had poured in, the most notable from Dolores Henderson. *'My good friend, William Houston, taken too soon. I will miss you dearly.'* The article went on to state that in memory of William, Dolores had donated all of the profits of her next concert to the William Houston Foundation. This came as a complete surprise to Florrie. She hadn't realised there was a friendship between Dolores and William, but why would she? They were a couple of generations apart and Dolores had had no reason to mention a friend who'd passed away such a long time ago.

But what Florrie couldn't figure out was why a company that was founded on good principles and strived to help others would want to destroy one of the most established gardens in the oldest cottage standing in Heartcross, and bring to an end a business that had been in operation for over sixty years.

Florrie flicked between photos of William and Tom and even though there were similarities in their facial features, it was obvious to Florrie that Tom wasn't William. Tom wasn't a decent, genuine bloke who would go out on a limb for workers who had lost their houses. No, the business was now about destroying beauty that had taken years to cultivate, in favour of making money.

'I might be a one-woman florist,' said Florrie, staring at Tom's photograph, 'but I'm going to become a constant irritant to you, Tom Houston.' And she was in no doubt that the whole of Heartcross would be behind her.

Chapter Eight

'You look like a proper florist,' exclaimed Isla, wandering into the courtyard at the back of Rose Cottage.

'That's because I am a proper florist! But I'm curious, how does a proper florist look?' Florrie asked, amused.

'You know, exactly like you. A bit quirky, out there. You have your own style going on.' Isla looked her up and down. Florrie's mousy hair was tied up in a messy bun with a fresh rose speared through the middle of it, giving it an extra touch of charm. Her jeans, rolled up at the ankles, had coloured flowers embroidered down each leg. Her T-shirt was orange, and a lightweight crimson scarf was wrapped around her neck and matched her fingerless gloves.

'I've had this style for as long as I can remember.'

'I know and your followers will be able to tell you're the real deal and authentic.' Isla pointed. 'I have to ask though: fingerless gloves and a scarf in the height of summer?'

'When you're working with flowers all day these things are

a lifesaver. The number of times I've got a thorn stuck in my hand from the roses... And it's only a lightweight scarf.'

Catching her reflection in the garden mirror that hung on the brick wall Florrie repositioned the rose in her hair before they walked around the cottage towards The Vintage Flower Van. Florrie smiled. She was a lover of bright clothes that reflected her personality and she intended to allow her character and passion to stand out. That's what would make people stop and view her reels on social media.

'So, what's the plan?' asked Isla. 'You've already got a successful following from Buttercup Barn. Isn't it possible to direction the traffic from that account to the new one?'

'I could but I don't want this to be about me. I want followers to fall in love with The Vintage Flower Van so they'll want to come to buy flowers here. This' – she flung her arms open in front of the van – 'is a thing of beauty and I want it to become a national treasure. I know I have my work cut out but soon the whole of Scotland will be fighting to keep this van and those gardens alive.' Florrie could hear the passion in her own voice. 'What we need is short reels. I need to make it entertaining, pick trending music, use hashtags and emojis, and I need to vary the posts. Telling everyone exactly what The Vintage Flower Van is all about will create awareness, build the number of followers, and hopefully even grow the business.'

'Are you sure you aren't a marketing executive on the side? You sound very professional and knowledgeable,' teased Isla.

'It's exactly like yourselves when you opened up the farm shop. You had me hooked and logging in every day to see what you'd posted. You started off by introducing the farm and showing pretty reels of the mountain terrain, the river that runs through the field, and the lush grass, then followed that up with milking the cows, introducing the followers to a baby cow, lambing season, etc. – and not forgetting the alpacas! They were an instant hit. Every child in Scotland wanted a pet alpaca, thanks to you.'

Isla laughed. 'That's very true. The profits of the shop were phenomenal from day one and I've lost count of the number of times that customers have told me they'd visited the farm shop or booked "walk an alpaca" days because they'd seen me on TikTok. It's all about getting the word out there and it really does work if you get it right.'

'Exactly. And if we can do the same with The Vintage Flower Van... The only thing we haven't got in our favour is time.' But Florrie was not going to let that stop her. 'Even if, and it's a big if, W. Houston Property Developers let me keep the van, we still need to publicise where the majority of the flowers are sourced and the history behind the stunning gardens at Rose Cottage, along with Flowers in Bloom.'

'So, let's get started! Shall we pretend it's first thing in the morning and you're opening up for the day? You can show your morning routine,' suggested Isla, looking up at the sky. 'The sun is shining. You have the perfect backdrop of Heartcross Mountain, and I did bring this...' She reached inside her bag and pulled out a long string of triangular floral bunting. 'Everyone loves bunting! And there's more.' She opened the boot of the car. 'Give me a hand. I thought these would look amazing too.'

Florrie poked her head into the boot and agreed. 'Those painted milk churns are gorgeous.'

'Aren't they just? It's all about the aesthetics and creating a look that makes everyone want to visit. There are cushions too, in a mix of colours, patterns and textures to complement the van, creating a cosy, inviting look that makes people want to visit and buy your flowers.'

Impressed, Florrie asked, 'Are you sure it's not you that's a marketing executive?' She laughed.

Together they set out decorating The Vintage Flower Van, hanging the bunting across the front. 'How about grabbing the bistro tables and the wrought-iron chairs from around the back of the cottage? It'll add character and charm,' Isla suggested.

'Perfect.' Florrie disappeared back into the courtyard then positioned the table and chairs in front of the van. After placing the cushions on the chairs, Florrie positioned the milk churns before cutting flowers from the garden and placing them in the buckets in front of the van. They both took a step back to admire their handywork. The Vintage Flower Van radiated romance; it was elegant and full of charm. 'I'm going to have all the girls sending their men to buy them flowers from The Vintage Flower Van.'

'And maybe meeting a man for yourself? After all, according to Gran, The Vintage Flower Van is your road to destiny. Your happy ever after is tied to the van somehow.'

Hearing those words, Florrie immediately thought of Tom. As much as she'd tried to dismiss all thoughts of him since his surprise arrival, he was still very much on her mind.

'If that's the case, the clock is ticking and the love of my life needs to hurry up. They may only have three weeks to reveal themselves.'

They both laughed.

'You daft thing, now let's take some footage whilst the sun is shining.'

Isla was in full film-maker mode now. She opened the door

of her car, pulled out a wheeled tripod and rested Florrie's phone in the cradle.

'Look at you with all the gear.'

'This is a brilliant bit of kit. I just push it on the wheels and it follows you, and with this handle I can move the phone in any direction. It keeps the image steady.'

'I'll start off by introducing myself, something like... Hi, I'm Florrie, come with me and take a look at The Vintage Flower Van. Then I'll collect some flowers from the buckets and make a beautiful bouquet, which we can set to some music.' Florrie spotted a gardening trug just inside the cottage gate. 'Oh, this is perfect, let's fill it with freshly cut roses. It's all about creating those visuals.'

'And I'll put a soft filter on the reel to give it that dreamy kind of look.'

Florrie took a handful of roses from the buckets and, swinging the wooden trug full of pale blush roses, slowly walked towards The Vintage Flower Van. Isla captured the beauty of the moment along with the stunning background of Rose Cottage and Heartcross Mountain towering in the distance.

'Hi, I'm Florrie, this is my vintage flower van, come with me and take a look around.' She hovered on the steps of the van for a moment before Isla shouted, 'Cut!' like a proper director.

'That was perfect and so natural.'

Florrie smiled. 'And fun! I'll collect the flowers from the bucket and make up a bouquet whilst sitting at the bistro table.'

Thirty minutes later they finished filming and sat on the bistro chairs with a glass of lemonade each. Florrie set up the social media accounts on her iPad, whilst Isla edited the reel with a soft filter and twinkly music. 'Just adding the captions. We need to let everyone know where they can find this vintage van of happiness. And how about the first fifty followers receive a discount code for money off their first purchase? Everyone loves a discount.'

'Perfect.' Florrie sat back and as soon as Isla finished editing the reel, she passed her the phone. 'Team effort, what do you think?'

The reel played out and Florrie gave a tiny gasp. It was captivating, romantic and enchanting,

'I want to go and buy flowers immediately from here,' Florrie said, smiling. 'It's a job well done.'

Isla had caught the ambience perfectly, the captions and the background music adding to the magic of the reel. 'Everything looks so dreamy! The Vintage Flower Van will undoubtedly capture hearts and Rose Cottage looks like something straight out of a fairy tale.' Florrie was impressed and smiled at Isla. 'Dream team indeed.'

Florrie typed in a punchy bio on the new Vintage Flower Van social media accounts then uploaded the reel. The social media campaign to save The Vintage Flower Van had officially been launched!

'All I need to do now is arrange the community meeting and then it's Heartcross against the world.'

Taking a sip of her drink, Florrie tilted her face up to the sun and closed her eyes for a moment. 'The sunshine makes the day more pleasant and helps the flowers grow, but I'll have a mammoth job of watering the garden tonight,' she mused, hearing her phone beep. Glancing at her screen, she sat up abruptly. It had been eight years since that name had flashed on the front of her phone.

Her pulse began to race as she hovered over the message icon for only a second before pressing on it to see what Tom had written.

Hi, it's Tom. Please could you send me your insurance details x

The message was brief and the first thing that Florrie noticed was the kiss. She'd only ever received one text message from Tom before, and there it was on the screen as she scrolled up. She'd never deleted it.

What an amazing two weeks, I never wanted it to end! I'll be listening to songs from our playlist every day and remembering our special time. There's something about you Florrie Appleton. I don't want to wish the summer away but I can't wait to see you again xxx

Florrie had never replied. The text had landed just after she saw the photos of Tom and Sophia.

'Everything okay?' asked Isla, noticing Florrie had gone quiet.

'It's Tom Houston asking for my insurance details. Do you know what I discovered today?' Florrie looked up. 'That Dolores led the tributes to Tom Houston's grandfather when he passed away. She was friends with William Houston and donated money from her concert to a charity that he'd set up. I found articles about it online; his funeral was held at Heartcross Church.'

'Wow, small world. Have you had a chat with her about what's happening at Rose Cottage?'

'Not yet, but I'm intrigued about their friendship and can't help wondering if that has any connection with Tom Houston being at Ada's funeral.'

'If William's funeral was held at Heartcross Church, he must be buried there.'

'That never even crossed my mind.' Thinking back to the time she'd spent at the private beach house with Tom, she was sure she had told him she lived in Heartcross … so why hadn't he mentioned his own family connections to the village?

'Gran would know,' added Isla.

'I just think it's a strange coincidence that everywhere I turn the name Houston is popping up.'

'Dolores would have crossed paths with many celebrities and high-flying businessmen. She has always been discreet about her private life so it's entirely possible she knew William much better than we think. We don't have a clue who she was friends with when she was our age, other than Ada and Martha.'

'So true.'

'And what's going on now? Is he sending more messages? Your phone is beeping off the scale.'

Florrie's eyes widened. 'The account has new followers! Our mission to save The Vintage Flower Van and Rose Cottage and gardens has begun!'

'Keep up the momentum. If anyone posts comments make sure you interact.'

'I will.'

'Judging by that pinging, you're going to be in for a very busy night.'

'Let's hope so… There are already one hundred followers in less than ten minutes!'

It was exactly what Florrie had hoped would happen.

Chapter Nine

'Isla, the comments... I've woken up to hundreds of comments on my first ever post and the followers ... I just can't believe it. How does this happen?'

It was early morning and Florrie was sitting in bed with a cup of tea in one hand and her phone in the other whilst staring at her iPad, balanced on her bent knees. She knew Isla was an early bird and couldn't wait to talk to her so had called her right away. 'Do I reply to all these comments?'

'Hang on, I'm just logging on to take a look.'

For a moment, there was silence at the other end of the phone. 'Florrie! You've nailed it! This is brilliant. Yes interact, make these people feel part of your journey. You have to keep on top of this and post again today.'

'I will. I just need to think of something.'

'It's a beautiful morning out there, why not introduce your followers to the grounds of Rose Cottage and let them see where the beautiful blooms are grown? Or you could take your followers on your deliveries. Just keep posting! I'll see you tonight. I have a full day at the farm but let's catch up later. Maybe we could grab food in the pub? Drew is taking the children to Primrose Park; he's discovered his old fishing rod in one of the barns and has promised to take them to the fishing lake after work for a picnic.'

'Yes, that sounds perfect,' replied Florrie, knowing that she hadn't been eating much. Her appetite had dwindled since the death of Great-Aunt Ada. 'And I'm on it, I'll post the next reel this morning.'

After hanging up the call, Florrie turned back to her iPad with a wide smile on her face. The social media campaign was off to a flying start. Everyone loved The Vintage Flower Van. She was amazed how much momentum the account had gained overnight. She began to scroll through all the lovely comments.

What a beautiful vintage flower van. I've booked my trip to Heartcross!

I'm on my way to Heartcross to visit this utterly gorgeous flower van.

Just look at that flower van, you have the best business in the world! Its stuff dreams are made of!

These were the types of comments that Florrie had hoped would be posted. If she could make random strangers fall in love with The Vintage Flower Van and the gardens at Rose Cottage as much as the community, she would be able to use them in her fight against W. Houston Property Developers.

'Oh my gosh,' she said, thinking out loud. 'Maybe I could

organise an online petition. "Save The Flower Van and Rose Cottage Gardens.'" Of course, she would have to wait for Jaydon to get a response from W. Houston Property Developers first, but Florrie was at least starting to feel hopeful in her quest to save Ada's beloved business.

There was comment after comment, and lots of questions about growing flowers. Florrie was stunned by the number of people who had taken an interest in such a short time. Isla was right, she needed to build on that immediately. For the next ten minutes she answered questions about the different varieties of flowers in the bouquet she'd made up yesterday. She was in her element; this was exactly what she loved doing – talking about the thing she loved the most.

What's your favourite flower? asked one follower.

That was an easy question to answer.

The red tulip as it represents elegance and grace. Not only that, red tulips mean the perfect love. The dark centre of the flower represents a lover's heart darkened by the heat of passion.

As soon as she'd typed the words, she was transported back eight years when she had told Tom the same thing and he'd kissed her. Right at that moment she'd been on top of the world. She'd believed she was in love in Tom Houston. Even now, as Florrie stared at the screen, she couldn't get him off her mind.

Over the years she'd fought with herself about whether to unblock him and have a peek at what he'd been up to. She'd resisted temptation until now, and before she could stop herself, she clicked on her privacy settings and unblocked Tom.

With her heart racing she typed in his username and briefly closed her eyes. When she opened them Tom's profile picture was staring back at her. It felt like he was looking at her the same way as he did on that first afternoon they'd spent together. His stare intense, his wolfish grin sparking tiny explosions of joy throughout her body.

His face was tanned in the profile picture, and he had the unshaven thing going on, which she found deeply attractive. There was something about Tom Houston that she just couldn't shake off.

Navigating her way to his photos, Florrie couldn't quite believe there had been no posts in the past eight years. She couldn't help thinking that was strange. Maybe he'd set up a new account since then? Florrie typed his name into the search bar but the only account that came up was the one she was already looking at. Being careful not to double-click the screen and draw attention to the fact she was looking at his social media, she looked at the photos. They were exactly how she remembered them.

The first showed Tom and Sophia frolicking on his father's yacht in swimwear, Tom's arm around her waist, Sophia gazing up towards him with a look in her eyes that Florrie recognised because she'd looked at Tom in that way too. The second photo was of Tom and Sophia sitting by the water's edge, outside a bistro in St Tropez, enjoying a glass of wine. Florrie recognised the bottle as Chablis, a wine that Tom had first introduced her to. Sophia looked stunning with her bronze tan, designer sunglasses and straw fedora. Even though Florrie had seen these photographs eight years ago, she still felt a twinge of jealousy. Sophia had been tagged in the photograph and Florrie couldn't resist the temptation to click through to her profile.

Sophia Henley had brains and beauty. Every photograph was the very definition of 'Instagram worthy'. In one photo she was dressed in luxury outdoor gear with a black Labrador at her side. In the next she was on stage talking into a microphone with a room full of people seated in front of her. Florrie immediately recognised the logo on the screen behind Sophia from Flynn's email – it was for the William Houston Foundation. The caption had a link to a website and Florrie clicked it and found herself back on the foundation's site. Three faces looked back at her from the top of the screen: the CEO Edward Houston, the Foundation Director Tom Houston, and the Fundraising Manager Sophia Henley. Did that mean Sophia would be arriving in Heartcross for the charity event? Florrie felt a little put out even though she knew she shouldn't be. What was it to her if they were still in touch and working together?

Throwing back the duvet she swung her legs to the floor and jumped straight into the shower. Last night, she had nipped back to Buttercup Barn to set up the shop to make things a little easier for Martha in the morning. Before she headed back to Rose Cottage, she'd stopped at her home on Love Heart Lane and grabbed her insurance policy. After hopping out of the shower she took a screenshot of the policy details and pinged it over to Tom in a text. Almost instantly he replied.

Thank you x

She stared at the text. No, she stared at *the kiss*. Was he being so nice because he wanted her onside to make his life easier? Did he think it would help him to profit from the houses he planned to build on the Rose Cottage land without her putting up much fuss? If he was, he had another thing coming. She and the community of Heartcross were going to create more publicity than a royal wedding, which meant she would definitely be butting heads with Tom in the very near future, which would bring a swift end to any future kisses in texts.

As soon as she was dressed Florrie headed to the kitchen and with her phone in her hand opened the back door. She was greeted by an effect of harmony that pinned her to the spot. The sky declared that it was going to be another glorious day ahead. Just outside the back door was a short walk through the courtyard to the walled garden, an original feature of the cottage. It was a sheltered square on the south side of the cottage, with high walls of greyish-pink stone. Ada had gardened this part productively, with vegetables, fruit and flowers for her table.

Ada had also erected a row of glasshouses on the west side of the walled garden, which were crammed with cucumbers, tomatoes and fruit vines clambering up the pink, lime-washed walls. At the furthest corner the garden led into a wilder grassy orchard and then a buttercup meadow, the River Heart rushing along the perimeter. All in all, the garden covered two acres – land that had seen a huge transformation since Ada had moved in.

Morning was Florrie's favourite part of the day, and she wanted to capture the beauty of the place in the next reel. As she began recording, she used the same opening as yesterday's reel. 'Hi, I'm Florrie Appleton. Come and explore the beautiful gardens of Rose Cottage, where I grow the flowers that are sold from The Vintage Flower Van. This garden was first brought to life over sixty years ago by my great-aunt Ada. You could perhaps think you're in France, but you'll discover this utterly gorgeous garden in the beautiful village of Heartcross in the Scottish Highlands – and on August twenty-third it will be open to the public for one day only during the annual Flowers in Bloom competition. Why don't you come and visit, take a look around? I'd love to see you.'

Florrie carried on walking and recording multiple reels, capturing all of her surroundings and plenty of content to use over the coming days. She took the path, along stepping stones laced with lavender, to the archway of grey-pink stone that led to a collection of white-painted furniture, placed to look down over gracious sloping lawns studded with perfectly spaced topiary. The lawns were edged with generous borders full of beautiful flowers. Everything looked spectacular in the early morning sun. Florrie filmed close-ups of the wonderful flowers, giving a quick description of each, whilst chatting about Ada's vision and her transformation of the gardens, and her attention to detail. Florrie referred to Ada as a distinguished portrait painter, explaining how her endless passion for growing flowers had led to the creation of a picturesque garden that was still flourishing today.

As Florrie reviewed the footage, she couldn't quite believe how magical the whole place looked. Taking a moment to enjoy the beauty of the garden, she sat in Aunt Ada's bistro chair. Remembering how Isla had added soft focus to yesterday's reel, she did the same, wanting to create a consistent visual style for The Vintage Flower Van's account. If the followers kept growing, she knew they too, as well as the community, would be up in arms at learning all this was going to be destroyed for new-build houses. It was criminal.

Five minutes later, the reel had been uploaded to her social media channels and whilst she waited for responses to start coming in, she checked her diary, which was lying open on the kitchen table. She smiled. No matter how many times she'd tried to encourage Aunt Ada to use technology and switch from the old method of accounting to a computer, Florrie herself still loved an old-fashioned diary and preferred it to logging her appointments on her phone.

The community meeting needed to be held as quickly as possible, with objection letters splattering the council office desks soon after. Wednesday seemed as good a day as any so Florrie drafted a text to the community WhatsApp group, titling it 'SAVE THE FLOWER VAN AND THE GARDEN OF ROSE COTTAGE'. Within minutes her friends in Heartcross began reaching out to her. First Flynn and Julia, then Molly and Cam, quickly followed by Grace and Andrew. This is what Florrie loved about the village of Heartcross: no matter how busy people were running their own businesses, everyone always pulled together in times of crisis. Those who didn't know already were now on board, and the rest of the villagers were already beginning to confirm their attendance at Wednesday's meeting.

There were two issues at stake: The Vintage Flower Van ceasing trading if Jaydon's letter was unsuccessful, and the gardens being potentially flattened to build houses. With a day and time set for the meeting, and support already flooding in, Florrie was hopeful the village of Heartcross would have some impact on both.

For the next thirty minutes, Florrie prepared The Vintage Flower Van for the day. Checking her phone, she saw that this morning's reel was already gaining traction and had over one hundred comments. Followers were also enquiring where they could buy tickets for Flowers in Bloom. Florrie couldn't have hoped for a better response.

She quickly punched a text to Isla.

Next reel uploaded and WhatsApp message sent to the community group.

In addition to Rona offering to provide tea and coffee and homemade treats, Flynn had promised to supply a pile of picnic blankets, which had been used for a summer wedding, for everyone to sit on.

Watching the reel again, Florrie smiled. 'We're going to cause a riot, Aunt Ada,' she murmured. 'We aren't leaving here without a fight. Everyone is on board.' Looking at the clock on the wall of the kitchen, she saw it was time to open up. After grabbing a bottle of water from the fridge, and her diary, she made her way outside. The bunting and the colourful milk churns had added something special, complementing the van and today's flowers beautifully. Going back into the van and turning the pages of the order book to today's date, she glanced up at her great-grandfather's photograph. 'I know it's Friday. Don't worry, I've not forgotten.'

Suddenly, she had an idea. After slipping her phone into the tripod that Isla had kindly left behind, she set it up to record in the corner of the van. 'Hi, I'm Florrie Appleton, welcome to The Vintage Flower Van. Today I'm going to tell you a very special story that spans decades.'

Florrie held the camera over the historic entry in the order book, followed by the photograph of her great-grandfather, before she began to tell the romantic story of her great-grandparents, hoping it would capture the hearts of her followers. After that, she filmed another reel of herself choosing the best flowers for today's bouquet from the garden. After she removed any leaves and thorns, Florrie used shears to strip the remaining foliage from the plant stems before choosing her favourite flower as the focal point of the bouquet and then adding the supporting flowers around it, with the flower heads at different angles. The next step was to add filler flowers – smaller flowers and greenery – giving the bouquet a more natural aesthetic. Then she added volume with myrtle and eucalyptus before firmly tying the stems together using floral wire. For a stunning finishing touch she added a decorative wrap and tied it with colourful ribbon that complemented the flowers.

With twenty minutes to go before opening time, Florrie prepared today's flowers for the van and made up another bouquet for Aunt Ada then carried on filming as she placed the bouquets on Rose's passenger seat and drove towards the church. After parking on the road outside, Florrie filmed up to the wrought-iron gates and along the path of the cemetery. She rested the flowers on her great-grandmother's grave before ending the recording. After laying the second bunch of flowers on Aunt Ada's grave and whispering, 'Love you, miss you,' she took a moment to remove the wilting flowers from the previous week that were resting against the headstone. As she was leaving, she walked over to the compost bin and laid them on top.

'Florrie.'

She nearly jumped out of her skin. A second ago, there hadn't been another soul in sight. With her hands on her heart, she turned around and came face to face with Tom. She was surprised to see him again and especially at this time in the morning.

'Sorry, I didn't mean to make you jump.'

'You're here again. Are you looking for another funeral to gatecrash?' Seeing those old photographs yesterday had opened up some old wounds and sparked her barbed comment, but looking at Tom now, Florrie couldn't help but notice he looked tired. In fact, he looked exhausted, as if he had the weight of the world on his shoulders. 'I need to ask. What exactly were you doing at my great-aunt's funeral?'

'I was there on my grandfather's instruction.'

Florrie was confused. 'But your grandfather has passed away.'

'Yes.' Tom pointed to a grave a couple of rows back. 'He's buried here in Heartcross.'

'What exactly do you mean, you were there on your grandfather's instruction?' Florrie pressed.

'My grandfather and Ada were friends. In fact, from what I can gather, they were the best of friends.'

Florrie was amazed. She didn't remember Aunt Ada ever mentioning William Houston, though if he had been friends with Dolores it would make sense that he had also known Ada. 'Best of friends?' Feeling her hackles rise, Florrie couldn't hold back. 'And that obviously means nothing to you as you're destroying everything she ever worked for.'

A look of pure puzzlement crossed Tom's face. 'I have no clue what you're going on about. I think we need a conversation to clear the air.'

'Starting with an apology would have helped to clear the air.'

'I don't know what you mean. I've been nothing but polite

and genuine towards you since arriving in Heartcross.' He stared at her, waiting for an explanation.

'You turn up here, after eight years, being disingenuous and pretending to be honourable—'

'I'm not pretending to be anything but myself and I have to say I think I'm a decent person.'

Florrie scoffed. She hoped her voice sounded steadier than she felt. 'We're a decent and close-knit community in Heartcross, and you walk in with your agenda to make money...'

'That's what charities do, they raise money and give it to worthy causes.'

'That's not what I'm talking about. You can stand there all you like being holier-than-thou but it won't wash with the people in Heartcross; they'll all see through you.'

Tom looked a little stunned, his tired face paling further.

'I suppose you're going to tell us it will be good for the community, without giving a second thought to what you're destroying as long as it puts money in your pocket.' Her eyes were firmly fixed on him. 'You know exactly what I'm saying here.'

Tom looked exasperated. 'I really don't.' He shook his head then ran his hand through his hair. 'I've no idea what you're going on about. But it seems to me you're dying to pick a fight with me for whatever reason and this isn't the time or the place. I've got more important things going on.' He stared at her with such intensity she suddenly wished she could read his mind.

'Haven't we all.'

Tom threw his hands up in the air. 'Fine! I'll leave you to it.

I'm not really sure what's going on here but whatever it is I think you have it all wrong.'

As Tom walked off, Florrie took a deep breath. With the emotion pouring through her body, she blinked back frustrated tears. She didn't like confrontations of any sort but how could he stand there and blatantly deny things, saying he didn't know what was going on?

Watching him disappear through the wrought-iron gates, she looked over at the gravestones and walked along the next two rows until she found what she was looking for.

She stared at the gravestone.

In Loving Memory of William Houston.

From the dates engraved on the stone, she could see that, William Houston was taken too soon.

Chapter Ten

'Florrie! I didn't expect you to be working the van this morning,' Ash said, walking towards her with a bright smile on his face.

She looked up over the hatch. 'Martha and I have done a swap. She's going to be working at Buttercup Barn whilst I try and save the van and the cottage.'

'I saw the WhatsApp message. I can't believe it.' He snuck a glance towards Rose Cottage. 'No one in their right minds would destroy any part of this place. It's full of character and history. I'm actually lost for words.'

'I know, heartbreaking is the only word I can muster up, but hopefully at the meeting I can encourage everyone to write objection letters. Surely the council would have to listen to us if we bombarded them?'

'We'll all happily do whatever it takes. I'll spread the word on my rounds.'

'Thanks, Ash, I really appreciate it. Before the meeting I'm upping my presence on social media, and I've invited the world to Flowers in Bloom so hopefully I can get the story of this place into the press.'

'Good plan. Here's today's post.' Ash looked down at the envelope then at Florrie. 'Actually, I'm not sure you'll be wanting this.'

Florrie took the envelope and her eyes fixed on the dreaded logo of W. Houston Property Developers. 'Here we go again.'

'I'll leave you to it, but anything you need just shout.'

'I will.'

As Ash headed down the lane, Florrie turned the envelope over in her hand. 'Think positive,' she told herself. 'This may be good news.'

Tearing open the envelope, she quickly read the letter then rang Isla.

'Isla, you're not going to believe this. I've had another letter from W. Houston Property Developers.'

'Please tell me it's good news.'

'The letter is informing me of the date they're coming to inspect the property to make sure everything is in order before they kick me out of the cottage.'

'Which is?'

'The same day as Flowers in Bloom. You know what this means? I need to make this a visit for them to remember. The timing is brilliant. Not only will they be greeted by the whole community, but hopefully the publicity will also have gained huge momentum by then and I can organise the press being here.'

'They couldn't have planned it better if they'd tried. Wait until you tell everyone at the meeting. We can have some serious fun with this.'

'Can't we just.'

'I've got to go as the farm shop is busy, but I'll see you later at the pub, around six-thirty.'

Florrie hung up the call, her mind in overdrive. Flowers in Bloom couldn't come soon enough.

Sitting outside The Vintage Flower Van, Florrie edited the second reel of the day. As she watched herself share her great-grandfather's story, it captured her heart just as much as it had the first time she'd heard it. She knew that her new followers were going to fall in love with their story. Five minutes later, the reel was edited, and Florrie felt she'd chosen the perfect background music. She uploaded it to all of her social media accounts and wondered how long it would take for people to interact with it. She looked up to see a steady queue of people heading towards The Vintage Flower Van. Florrie wasn't sure what was going on but there was a certain buzz in the air.

'It's Florrie! Look, it's Florrie Appleton!'

A group of tourists were heading her way, each waving madly with one hand, their phones held aloft in the other. Was it possible that these were some of her online followers, here to capture pictures of her and The Vintage Flower Van? What a result!

Bunch after bunch of flowers were sold and Florrie wondered if this was what it was like to be famous. Everyone in the queue was talking about the van and Florrie couldn't wait to see their reactions to her great-grandfather's story. All the flowers were sold out by three p.m.; Florrie had never seen anything like it, and she'd lost count of the number of times she'd had her photograph taken with a customer in front of The Vintage Flower Van.

With nothing left to sell, she began to close up for the day, wondering if today was a one-off and whether the excitement would quickly dwindle. She hoped not. There had even been customers asking for her autograph! She felt silly about it, but it had started her thinking. Maybe The Vintage Flower Van needed more of a personal touch, a little extra keepsake for all those buying flowers from the van. Maybe some sort of label – 'Flowers by Florrie'? – which she could sign and attach to the wrapping of the blooms.

Her phone rang, and she was pleased to see it was a call from Martha. 'Buttercup Barn is all clean and tidy, the books are balanced and I'll be back in the morning.'

Florrie knew that she couldn't have gotten through this difficult time without Martha and Isla but she also knew she couldn't keep putting Martha to work, as she should be relaxing and enjoying her retirement. As soon as Flowers in Bloom was over, she'd advertise for help, when she had more time to shift through application forms and could arrange interviews.

After she hung up the call, she checked her social media accounts.

She gasped.

The story of her great-grandfather had gone viral! Her notifications were off the scale with hundreds of comments, likes and shares. This was exactly what Florrie had hoped would happen!

With the community and this kind of backing behind her, she could already imagine how people were going to react when they heard exactly what was going on behind the scenes. W. Houston Property Developers would be splashed all over the news for all the wrong reasons.

'This is fate,' she murmured, locking up The Vintage

Flower Van. As she walked back towards the cottage, email notifications began to ping, and top of the list was one from Jaydon. She opened it immediately but her joy was short-lived. W. Houston Property Developers had replied and said The Vintage Flower Van belonged to the cottage and was non-negotiable. Disappointed, she stood at the gate of Rose Cottage and looked back towards the van.

She rang Isla. Thankfully, Isla picked up on the first ring.

'Isla, W. Houston Property Developers won't let me keep the van.'

Isla was quiet for a moment, 'I'm actually thinking this is an advantage for us at this stage.'

Florrie was flummoxed. 'How do you make that out?'

'Everyone in the shop today has been talking about your great-grandfather's story. People are really connecting to your social media – they're emotionally invested in The Vintage Flower Van. Your passion and warmth radiate in every reel and everyone can see how much you love being a florist and how much that van means to you. When people realise that they can't buy their flowers from The Vintage Flower Van that has been standing for years, and then they discover the gardens along with all the wildlife and flowers are going to be destroyed, there will be a lot of passionately angry people out there. Believe me. One cause will help to highlight the other. A fight worth fighting is worth fighting hard for.'

Blitzed by myriad emotions, Florrie could see exactly what Isla was saying. Her thoughts were running wild. 'With the community meeting scheduled for Wednesday, can you imagine how many objections the planning permission people will receive by the weekend? I'm actually beginning to believe that we might have enough clout to put a real spanner in the works.'

'I believe we do.'

Florrie had fire in her belly. She wasn't sure why, but the idea of fighting W. Houston Property Developers suddenly excited her rather than scared her.

Chapter Eleven

J ust after four p.m. Florrie was sitting in the courtyard cashing up the day's takings. She was amazed to see they'd nearly tripled those of the day before. Even after The Vintage Flower Van had closed for the day, people had been walking up the lane and taking photos of the outside of the van. Closing the accounts book, Florrie turned to face the garden. The scene in front of her was enchanting; the view of Heartcross Mountain alive with purple heather always took her breath away. Turning her gaze towards her great aunt Ada's favourite spot, the rose garden, Florrie hoped The Vintage Flower Van would see a lot more days like today.

Lifting the lid on her laptop, which was in front of her on the table, she viewed the regular orders from the wholesalers. The orders always increased during the winter months, but now, with the possibility of losing the garden, the orders for spring and summer would also need to be boosted. The next year in the business was certainly going to be a learning curve and very different from anything Florrie had experienced in the past.

She had also pulled out Ada's old flower bible. The book was handwritten by Ada herself and was over sixty years old. Ada had updated it on a regular basis. It outlined the distinct areas of the land attached to Rose Cottage and the volume of flowers grown in each different section. She had also kept a log of which varieties sold best over the years – pink peonies and violet roses were clear frontrunners. Florrie turned the pages carefully, thinking that the amount of meticulous, intricate detail that had gone into this book was commendable. Looking back at the laptop, she decided to increase the volume of flowers from the wholesalers for tomorrow's delivery, especially if today was anything to go by.

As soon as that was done, she took a quick look over the comments that had been posted since she'd uploaded her great-grandfather's story. They were utterly heart-warming, her followers having instantly fallen in love with the story, just like she did. The Vintage Flower Van was becoming an overnight triumph on social media and that was exactly what Florrie had hoped for. Feeling loved by all the new virtual friends she was making, she began to scroll through the likes and comments, replying to as many as she could.

Finishing off her drink, she began to feel peckish and was grateful she would be meeting Isla at the pub in half an hour. Taking all her stuff back inside, she placed her laptop and the accounts book on the kitchen table and placed the flower bible on the dresser where it belonged. Taking a look around the kitchen, Florrie knew in the next week she was going to have to make a start on packing up Ada's belongings, a job she wasn't mentally prepared for. She exhaled and grabbed her bag. She didn't want to think about that just yet.

With the sun still providing warmth, Florrie set off towards the Grouse and Haggis pub, taking the path through Primrose Park, a route she'd often walked with Ada, who loved long summer evenings like this one. Every Monday evening, she would wander down to the Grouse and Haggis for a game of cards and a glass of port with her friends. The permanent ache in the bottom of Florrie's stomach hadn't subsided since Ada passed away, but she was learning to manage it a little more each day.

Having climbed over the stile into the wooded area, she carried on walking along the tree-shaded path. She passed through the deer park and by the side of the lake, and then stepped out alongside the gravel car park in front of Starcross Manor. Taking a sideward glance Florrie slowed. Parked to the left of the stone steps that led to the Manor's front door was Tom's car. She was amazed to see it had already been fixed. No doubt, with the circles he moved in, he could afford to pull in favours. She'd never made a claim on her insurance in her life, but knew that her premiums would go up because of this stupid mistake and she couldn't afford to offer to pay Tom for the damage direct.

Feeling a little discouraged, she carried on down the long driveway and was soon heading up the high street. Hamish Henderson, Dolores's son, was busy outside his village shop straightening up the fishing nets. Just as he was about to go back inside, he noticed Florrie and shouted over to her, 'Flowers in Bloom, how many tickets do you think the village can manage this year?'

Florrie knew it pulled in an average of 1,500 villagers and

tourists each year, with entry times staggered throughout the day. With each ticket costing twenty-five pounds, which included a cream tea at Bonnie's Teashop, Rona recouped some costs, whilst the rest of the money – thousands a year – went to charity and was much appreciated.

'Do you think we can handle more than usual? It is the height of the tourist season, after all,' Florrie ventured.

'I had exactly the same conversation with Ada last year and she thought we could try for another two hundred and fifty tickets. It's okay with Rona, they can manage the numbers, but I appreciate this may be a little overwhelming for you, having such a huge crowd traipsing through the cottage gardens.'

Florrie thought for a second. 'There will be people to help me. What's another two hundred and fifty? If we can sell them then why not.' Her way of thinking was that it meant another two hundred and fifty people would be talking about the possible closure of the gardens.

'And I'm sorry to hear about Rose Cottage. I couldn't believe your WhatsApp message when I read it. People have started to talk in the village and they aren't happy about the proposal. No doubt the meeting on Wednesday will be a lively one.'

'I'm all for lively, especially if we can make any sort of difference,' replied Florrie. 'And I've been thinking – but do say no, as I appreciate this has been your domain for many years – but would it be possible this year to sell the tickets from The Vintage Flower Van? Only because it would make more people aware that The Vintage Flower Van and the gardens are going to be no more if W. Houston Property Developers get their way.'

'That's absolutely fine by me. The ticket details go on to the website on Thursday, so I can bring you over the first printed batch at the community meeting.'

Florrie noticed that Hamish was looking over her shoulder as he spoke, as though he'd been distracted by something behind her. Just as Florrie turned to see what had caught his eye, the Bugatti drove past them.

'This village gets more like Hollywood every day.'

'Hamish! Your mum is one of the most famous women in the world and lives here!' Florrie said, laughing.

Hamish gave a chuckle. 'I've never seen her as famous, she's just my mum.' He gave Florrie a wave before heading back inside the shop to serve some customers.

Crossing the road to the Grouse and Haggis, Florrie realised she was a little ahead of time. Just as she was about to enter the pub, she heard her name being shouted from the other side of the road. Turning around she was greeted by Dolores smiling widely as she navigated crossing the road with the aid of her stick.

'Aunt Dolores!' Florrie beamed. 'You look amazing, and we were just talking about you!'

'Hamish told me I'd find you out here.'

Dolores really did look phenomenal. The tall, slim woman was never without her cherry-red lipstick, and today she had a matching bright red beret on top of her curly blonde hair. She was dressed to impress, as always, this time in her favourite vivid peacock-blue blouse, which was draped with orange beads, along with her favourite black skirt and green tights. She looked bright as a button.

'And you have to stop calling me Aunt Dolores, it makes me sound so old.'

Florrie laughed. 'Age is just a number, and you have a youthful spirit, just like Peter Pan.'

'You're right. Not bad for ninety-nine years old! I can't believe I'll hit a century at the end of this month.' She blinked her black spidery eyelashes at Florrie.

'No way! One hundred? I can't believe it! What have you got planned for your special day?'

Dolores had had a colourful past with a very successful singing career. Back in the day, fans used to queue for hours in the hope of getting tickets to one of her gigs. She was a sex symbol who'd constantly sold out concert halls and appeared regularly on the covers of magazines and in newspapers all around the world. Every chat-show host wanted her to be sitting on their couch because they knew the viewing figures would rocket. An idol and an institution in her own right, she'd hung out with the rich and famous. In fact many decades ago she'd been linked with royalty, and Scottish newspapers had published dramatic headlines suggesting she had spent time on the arm of Prince George before he married. Little did they know that at the time it was all a cover and Dolores was loved up with her partner Charlotte.

Dolores had a mischievous glint in her eye. 'I've been thinking about exactly what I'd like to do on my special day.' She waved her walking stick towards the bench outside the pub. 'Have you got time to take a seat?'

Florrie nodded. She was intrigued and sensed that Dolores had something very special she wanted to plan.

The two women sat.

'I hear you've been having a tricky time since Ada passed away.'

'I have. It's all a bit of an unexpected mess and now they're determined to take The Vintage Flower Van from me.'

Dolores nodded. 'I can imagine … but we'll see about that.'

'What do you know about W. Houston Property Developers?' Florrie wanted to know everything.

Dolores stared in front of her. 'W. Houston Property Developers was founded by my dear friend William Houston. He was a man of morals and everyone adored him. When he walked into a room, heads would turn.'

Florrie realised Dolores had tears in her eyes and placed a hand on her knee.

'William was taken too soon. He'd missed out on so much life but he certainly made an impression when he was alive. He bought numerous properties across Scotland and when he passed away, the company was taken over by his son, Edward.'

Dolores paused and Florrie could see that she was battling with whether she should share something with her. She evidently chose not to; perhaps she was being loyal to William's memory?

'Let's just say that Edward wasn't – and isn't – of his father's calibre or the family man he liked to portray. He's crossed my path many times in the past. We moved in the same circles and frequented the same parties. He flirted with the rich and famous and exaggerated his contacts to influence new friendships that would benefit him in some way.'

'Are you saying he used people?'

'In my humble opinion.'

'In my humble opinion, I don't like W. Houston Property Developers at all,' added Florrie. 'My heart is breaking. To demolish the gardens and take The Vintage Flower Van makes no sense to me whatsoever, but I'm going to create so much publicity that hopefully someone will take notice. Did you know that Aunt Ada didn't own Rose Cottage?'

Dolores nodded. 'Yes, I know there was an agreement between William and Ada.'

'And what do you know of Tom Houston?' probed Florrie. 'I saw him at the funeral.'

Dolores arched an eyebrow. 'He was at the funeral? Are you sure?'

'I'm sure.'

'Was Edward with him?'

'I didn't see his father.'

'That's good because that man isn't welcome around these parts. He's still a major part of W. Houston Property Developers and there's only one thing that drives him – greed. If William had had his way, he...' Dolores stopped herself in her tracks and didn't finish the sentence. 'As for Tom, by all accounts he is more like his grandfather than his father, thankfully.'

Florrie was a little surprised by this. She had never known Dolores to badmouth anyone, except maybe the press on a few well-deserved occasions.

With a glint in her eye, Dolores took hold of Florrie's hand. 'I have a proposition for you. I think I may be able to help you to create a little publicity.'

'Tell me more.'

'You know that I create commotion everywhere I go, and even at my age it still hasn't calmed down?'

Florrie knew only too well. Only last week, Dolores had flown to a restaurant in Edinburgh. As soon as she'd arrived, there was a paparazzi frenzy followed by a huge commotion outside, once her fans realised she was inside. The restaurant had had to close its doors as a tsunami of people surged inside hoping to get a table. The whole incident had made it onto the ten o'clock news.

'I certainly do.'

'And that's why I've come up with a plan.'

'Which is?'

'The press has not been off my back for the last two months, trying to get the exclusive of how and with whom I'll be celebrating my one hundredth birthday. The offers from TV and radio have been pouring in, everyone wanting me to appear on their programme that day. Talk shows on prime-time TV have offered ludicrous amounts of money – and, would you believe, that programme that takes place in the Australian jungle has even approached me to see if I'd make a guest appearance! Do I look like I want to eat bugs and kangaroo penis at my age?' Dolores rolled her eyes.

Florrie chuckled. 'Those were not words that I ever expected to hear today.'

'I'm all about the finer things in life and they don't include long-haul flights and they've never included penises.' Dolores smiled.

'Aunt Dolores!'

'That's one of the joys of being my age, I can get away with saying anything,' she replied with a chuckle. 'But the point is that whatever I do on my birthday it will be splashed all across all media channels. So I think we can help each other.' She hesitated. 'And between you and me, this would rile Edward Houston a little, which I am all for.'

The way she said those words, Florrie knew that something had gone on between them in the past.

Dolores continued. 'Ada was a loyal, discreet person and had my back for many years, and now I'd like to do something for you and her. There will be no houses built on those gardens as long as I'm alive ... though I'm not exactly sure how long that will be.'

'Don't say that, Aunt Dolores!'

Dolores smiled and pointed her finely manicured nail towards the poster stuck on the lamppost. 'I want to help you with Flowers in Bloom.'

'Oh, Dolores, that's very kind but you don't need to help out on the day. We'll have everything covered, but do come along for a cup of tea.'

'A cup of tea? I'll be drinking champagne because it will be a day to celebrate!' She leaned into Florrie. 'It's happening on my birthday and I would love nothing more than to hold a special gig in the gardens of Rose Cottage in memory of my dear friend. All my lifelong friends and neighbours will be there, and when the press discovers where it's being held, can you imagine the publicity? Those beautiful gardens will be splashed across every TV screen in the world. Rose Cottage will be a name on everyone's lips. The public will get to enjoy the gardens and see me perform my last ever gig.'

'It's always your last ever gig,' joked Florrie. Dolores had tried to retire many times but it just never happened.

'We need to keep this secret for the time being, until the Flowers in Bloom tickets have been sold, but I'll be dropping hints I will be performing a gig on my birthday, and the press will go wild. During my birthday speech, I will tell everyone about my friend Ada and what Flowers in Bloom means to the village, how many times the Rose Cottage Gardens have won the competition, and the fact that those gardens were transformed by Ada and now there's a planning proposal to demolish the lot.'

Florrie's eyes were wide. 'You'd do that for me?'

'I'd do anything for you and Ada ... and for William. He would never be demolishing those gardens.' Dolores looked up towards the sky. 'I'm hoping there is life after death because we will have one hell of a party when we're all back together.' She nudged Florrie's arm. 'But in the meantime, let's create havoc.'

'There's something else I need to tell you,' Florrie confided. 'W. Houston Property Developers are coming out to do an inspection on the cottage to make sure everything is in order. The date on the letter is the same day as Flowers in Bloom and your birthday.'

Dolores's smile widened. 'Then they're going to be in for a big shock. This publicity is going to be on a different scale.'

'I really don't know what to say.'

'Say yes, dear. But I must warn you. There will be a frenzy in the media. Can you handle it? The paparazzi will be swarming around Rose Cottage when they discover where the gig is being held.'

'Most definitely,' replied Florrie, without hesitation. 'Her pulse was racing and she held out her hand. 'Look, I'm actually trembling. I'm not sure whether that's nerves or excitement.' Feeling her eyes well up with tears, Florrie held out her arms and hugged Dolores. 'I can't thank you enough.'

'You don't need to thank me; your great-aunt was a wonderful woman and I know she would do the same for me. That's what we do in Heartcross, we always have each other's backs.'

'I still can't quite believe this. Dolores Henderson

performing in the garden of Rose Cottage on her one hundredth birthday.'

'As long as you're sure?'

'It's a definitive yes from me. The tickets go on sale on Thursday, and everyone who purchases a ticket will be in for the biggest surprise of their lives.'

'Just like W. Houston Property Developers.'

Florrie did have one slight reservation, and couldn't help but voice it. 'As much as all this will be amazing, this is your one hundredth birthday. Shouldn't you be taking it easy and just relaxing? This is going to be a full-on day with all the media spotlight on you.'

'Should I be taking it easy? Never,' Dolores said, with a twinkle in her eye. 'Absolutely not. I'm a lucky girl and whilst I have all my faculties, and my looks are hanging on in there –' she chuckled '– and my voice is still going strong, I'm going to use what I've got. You have to live every day as though it's your last, especially at my time of life.'

Florrie knew that only too well after the passing of Aunt Ada. 'And what's your secret for a long, happy and healthy life?'

'Always remember your own self-care, learn to say no, and look after yourself because the only person you can ever rely on is yourself. Well ... there is one exception to that ... you'll always have someone you can rely on while you live in Heartcross. What else? Friends are the most important people in your life and you should treat them as you want to be treated; if you do, those friends will be there for you no matter what. Looking after each other is a must. And my final bit of advice is something your great-aunt Ada swore by – have a glass of port every night before you go to bed. I've also found that a glass of champagne every day has done me no harm.'

Dolores was a true superstar, a national treasure, and here she was, at the age of ninety-nine, still at the top of her game and still grounded and helping out the people she loved the most, the community of Heartcross. Florrie had always admired Dolores's zest for life.

She gave Dolores's hand another little squeeze. 'Growing up at Rose Cottage was so magical. My friends and I running wild in the garden, climbing the apple trees and paddling in the shallow parts of the river…'

'I agree, it is a magical place. Ada held some good times in that courtyard. We did get up to some mischief over the years.'

'Tell me the story about her and Martha carting you around in a holdall to escape the paparazzi.'

'That was Ada's idea. The press followed me every single minute of the day. It was like a military operation trying to give them the slip. There were no social media back in those days. The only way anyone found out about anything was through newspapers and magazines so they would hunt you relentlessly. One summer evening we'd all been at a party on a house boat that was moored outside The Little Blue Boathouse when Ada and Martha invited me back for drinks. We could see the paparazzi waiting on the edge of the jetty and there was no way we were ever going to get past them without them taking a photo. There were two options: we could wait until late and swim for it – but I wasn't going to do that, I was wearing Mary Quant and it would never be the same again after that river water – or we could try Ada's marvellous idea to outsmart them.' Dolores gave a chuckle. 'She'd noticed a holdall in the boat and because of my tiny frame she suggested they squeeze me into it and wheel me off the boat and along the river path until the paparazzi were out of sight. It was the bumpiest ride I've ever experienced!'

Florrie threw her head back and laughed. 'You three are hilarious.'

'Of course, we were all also very intoxicated. We laughed the type of laughter that made your sides ache as I tried to squeeze into the thing, and then they wheeled me along the stones, staggering on their heels and trying to hold their laughter in until they were clear of the press hounds. I can't quite believe we got away with it. We found out later that the photographers had camped out at the houseboat for a couple of days, convinced I was still onboard, and then weren't sure how I'd managed to escape.

'Later that same night Martha decided to contact the spirits … and I don't mean just the alcoholic kind. We were sitting in the courtyard and out came the Tarot cards. Martha was on top form and had us all reeled in. It came to my turn…' Martha put her hand on her chest and smiled widely. 'She told me that someone new would be walking into my life and just at that moment we heard footsteps, heels echoing on the wooden floor. They were getting louder and we all froze. Petrified, I was. I can remember thinking my heart was going to pound out of my chest at any moment. We all held each other's hands, our eyes fixed on the back door. There was a shadow approaching . . . and all of a sudden Bonnie walked through the door. She'd spotted me being wheeled in the holdall and thought we might like some late-night snacks so she brought a pile of pastries from the teashop that had been left over. Those were good days. I've met my fair share of people over the years, but I've always known that *they* were my true friends, the friends I could rely on if I ever needed anything.'

'Those friendships have been passed down generations,' said Florrie, grateful for her own close relationship with Martha's granddaughter Isla, and Bonnie's granddaughter Felicity.

'We share so many good memories. Most of them go back to the gardens at Rose Cottage. We're not having the likes of W. Houston Property Developers bulldozing them to build houses. If it comes to it and the planning is granted, we will lie in front of those diggers! But hopefully it won't come to that,' she added hastily.

'That would definitely make the news.'

'We will win this fight, those gardens will be saved and The Vintage Flower Van will live on. Believe me, there are times when I don't like fame – it can be intrusive, and reading things about yourself in the newspapers that are simply untrue is never fun – but there are also times when you can use it to your advantage.'

'Thank you, Dolores, this means a lot to me. Would you like to join us for a drink? I'm just waiting for Isla.'

'That would be lovely but...' She reached for her walking stick and nodded towards the timely Isla, who was crossing the road towards them. 'I'll leave you two to it. Anyway, McCartney will be missing me. Typical man, he never likes being on his own.' Florrie laughed at how Dolores spoke about her deaf dog as if he was a human being.

Isla gave Dolores a swift kiss on her cheek as she passed her then narrowed her eyes at Florrie. 'What's been going on between you two? You look like the cat that's got the cream.'

Florrie stood up and linked her arm through Isla's. 'You're not going to believe what I'm about to tell you.'

'Good or bad?'

'Definitely good.'

'Let's get a drink and you can tell me all.'

Chapter Twelve

Isla stood at the bar with amazement written all over her face. Her mouth fell open. 'Are you being serious?'

'Absolutely serious. Dolores Henderson, world-famous superstar, will be singing in the gardens of Rose Cottage on her one hundredth birthday, but for the time being we have to keep this quiet.'

'Scouts' honour,' replied Isla with a huge smile.

'You were never a Scout.' Florrie laughed.

Isla pretended to look hurt. 'I'll have you know that I went once but got kicked out. It wasn't entirely my fault. In fact, I blame Allie and Felicity, I was just an innocent bystander.'

Florrie laughed. 'The publicity Dolores's performance brings in will be off the scale and W. Houston Property Developers will find themselves splashed all over the news.'

'They won't like that, will they?'

'Dolores told me William Houston was a good friend of hers, but his son Edward was a different kettle of fish – disingenuous, driven by greed and far from a people person.'

'And did she mention Tom?'

'I asked the question and she suggested he was just like his grandfather.'

'And he happens to be over there.' Isla nodded discreetly towards the far side of the pub. Florrie glanced over and saw Tom was sitting on his own, his laptop open in front of him, talking in hushed whispers on the phone. 'How do you feel seeing him sitting over there?'

'He's a two-timing rat…'

'But Goddamn sexy.'

'Isla!' Florrie watched him for a moment. The conversation looked heated.

'He actually looks stressed. Should we start feeling sorry for him?' Isla ventured.

'Tom will be even more stressed when he discovers Flowers in Bloom, Dolores's birthday and the day of W. Houston Property Developers' inspection all coincide. Dolores is going to announce the gig at the last minute because that will take everyone by surprise, especially W. Houston Property Developers.'

'I'm assuming Dolores is doing this in memory of Ada but why would she be standing up against the company that was set up by her own friend?'

'Dolores was adamant that William would never destroy anything to do with Rose Cottage because he and Ada were good friends too.'

'So, she's making a stand against Tom?'

'I think it's mostly against his father Edward, whom she didn't seem to like at all, but as Tom is the midst of taking over the company he may as well start with a bang. We can put a solid plan in place on Wednesday at the meeting.'

Florrie glanced back at Tom, who had stood up. He had his back to them now and was looking out of the window while he continued his conversation. He raked a hand through his hair, a quirk Florrie recognised because it was something she did herself when she was stressed.

'Let's get a couple of menus and a bottle of wine,' suggested Isla.

After ordering, they grabbed a table on the opposite side of the pub to Tom. Florrie opened up one of her social media profile pages and passed the phone to Isla. 'The interactions regarding my great-grandfather's story are off the scale.'

'This is remarkable,' Isla said as she began to scroll. 'So many comments saying they've fallen in love with your great-grandfather's story and The Vintage Flower Van.'

'It is amazing, isn't it?'

'Now it's been confirmed The Vintage Flower Van is non-negotiable, when are you going to shout that from the rooftops?'

'I thought at the meeting we could maybe organise a protest, make placards, get as many villagers to stand in front of the van as possible – and then we can blast it all over social media and invite the local paper so that the story grows.'

'I'm sure it will spread like wildfire. Never underestimate the power of Heartcross.'

The waitress placed their food down on the table and topped up their wine before disappearing back into the kitchen.

'Flynn has asked me to organise flowers for a charity event he's holding at Heartcross.'

'I've heard about it. He's donating a considerable amount

of money to several charities. It'll give them all a huge financial boost.'

'One of those charities is the William Houston Foundation.'

Isla raised an eyebrow. 'Has Flynn linked the Houston name to what's going on at Rose Cottage?'

'If he has, he hasn't said anything, but I don't think so. I looked into the charity and Sophia Henley works for them.'

'The girl who married the lawyer after stealing your man?'

'I wouldn't quite put it like that.'

'But that's what happened. So they're still in touch then?'

'It appears that way. Why hasn't he got someone? He's good-looking, successful...'

'But look how he treated you.'

'I've been playing it over in my head. What if I got it all wrong?' The Instagram photos had cut her deep. They'd been so close over those two weeks, she didn't know why he wouldn't have mentioned Sophia or any kind of pre-existing promise he'd made.

'Then you have to talk to him about it.'

Florrie did want answers and was annoyed that he'd never tried to get in touch after she blocked him. The sensible part of her pointed out that he couldn't have, given that she'd blocked him, but he was a rich and powerful man. Surely if he'd really wanted to reach her, he could have easily tracked her down and come to Heartcross. She looked across at him. No, there were more important things than her getting answers at the moment. 'I'm sure our paths are going to cross many times before the end of the month.'

They finished their food and placed their knives and forks across their empty plates.

'I needed that,' said Florrie, resting her hands on her stomach. 'I'm that full I don't think I can manage a dessert.'

'I know exactly what you mean.'

The waitress took away the empty plates and Isla crossed her arms and leaned on the table.

'What's the plan for the next reel?' she asked. 'I believe we're in for light drizzle tomorrow. Maybe you could use it to your advantage?'

'Can you imagine, me wandering around the gardens in the light rain, wearing a beautiful dress that flows behind me as I walk, carrying the garden trug of freshly picked roses.'

'Sounds very enchanting,' replied Isla.

'Just one problem, I don't actually own a dress of that description.' She laughed, glancing down at her beloved jeans that she'd worn nearly every day since they were purchased.

'I'm sure we can find you a dress,' replied Isla. Hearing Florrie's name being mentioned they both looked up. 'Someone is looking for you,' Isla said as she nodded towards the bar.

Florrie looked over and met the grin of Aidy Redfern, the local journalist, who was hurrying over towards them.

'Florrie! Please tell me I'm the first.' His enthusiastic question caused Florrie to look at Isla in amusement.

'The first for what? What's going on? You seem a little—'

Before Florrie could finish her question Aidy had pulled up a chair and sat between them clutching his notepad in one hand and his pen in the other.

'Has any other journalist got hold of you before me?'

'No, why?' Florrie kept her voice low; she didn't want to draw attention to herself, mainly from Tom, and hoped that Aidy would follow suit.

'Believe me, you're going to be in demand tomorrow. I just have a little advantage as I knew where to find you.'

'In demand? Tell me more.'

'The story about your great-grandfather has hit the headlines. The Vintage Flower Van has become famous, your social media post activity is off the scale, the radio channels are talking about it and the national press have contacted our office as they're wanting to run the story. This is going to be brilliant for your business. My guess is that vintage flower van of yours will be inundated with customers tomorrow and you'll be invited to appear on national TV.'

'Are you serious?' Florrie's excited voice rose an octave and the couple at the next table looked over in her direction. Florrie leaned towards Aidy and lowered her voice. 'Are you actually serious?'

'More than serious. This story has everything – history, romance, feel-good appeal – and the fact that you have taken over a business that has been a part of your family for generations. Did you know Ada and The Vintage Flower Van were featured in the local newspaper on their very first day of trading?'

'No, I didn't know that. Do you have a photo?'

'I do, I'll bring it first thing in the morning.'

'Morning?'

'Yes, morning. I'll be at Rose Cottage first thing. If it's okay with you, I want to interview you before all the press descend on your doorstep. My gut feeling is the way this story is snowballing, everyone is going to know who you are by the morning.'

Florrie's eyes widened. 'In that case, I'll see you at six a.m.'

'And please don't talk to any other journalists tonight.'

Aidy stood up. 'I'll be at your meeting on Wednesday. This attention is really going to increase the profile of The Vintage Flower Van and Rose Cottage. I hope you're ready!'

They watched Aidy leave the pub before Florrie gave a tiny squeal. 'National TV, can you imagine? That'll set the cat amongst the pigeons.' Florrie briefly looked over in Tom's direction but he was no longer at the table on the other side of the pub. He must have slipped out whilst she was talking to Aidy.

'I *can* imagine,' replied Isla. 'And I'm going to be over at yours first thing in the morning as I want to be there the moment you become famous.'

'I think famous is a little over the top, but if Aidy is right, this is huge. I bet W. Houston Property Developers never banked on me being on national morning TV! And if that's the case, I can tell the world what's going on right here in the village of Heartcross.'

Isla picked up her glass and chinked it against Florrie's. 'Here's to tomorrow.'

Chapter Thirteen

The weather the next morning couldn't have been further from the forecast. As Florrie pulled back the curtains, she was met by a clear sky and the sun rising above Heartcross Mountain. Excellent! She took a moment to take in the view, pushed open the window to welcome the light breeze ... and then nearly jumped out of her skin when she was greeted with the sight of Isla staring back at her. Bringing her hand up to calm her beating heart, she choked out, 'Blooming heck, you're up with the larks!'

Isla had a beaming smile as she flung open her arms. 'More like up with the cows. They're milked, all the animals fed and the children are still sleeping. It's a beautiful day and, as Aidy predicted, you're indeed famous. Come on, let me in.'

Florrie smiled. 'On my way.' Hotfooting it down the stairs, she opened the back door.

Isla breezed past her into the kitchen waggling her mobile phone in her hand. 'You're everywhere. I've heard your great-grandfather's story on the radio and your TikTok has been mentioned on national TV. My guess is you haven't been online this morning?'

'I've not had time.'

'Look, here it is on the TV.'

Florrie pulled out the kitchen chair and sat at the table, her eyes fixed on Isla's phone. 'Oh my...'

As the clip started to play the newsreader was sitting at her desk with a photo of The Vintage Flower Van showing behind her.

'How did they get that photo?' Florrie asked.

'No idea, but it's a good one.'

The newsreader began to speak. 'It's the story capturing the heart of the nation and potentially the most romantic story ever to be told. When Willem Hughes went off to war in 1914 he made sure that his wife would continue to receive flowers every Friday whilst he was away. Now, decades later, his great-granddaughter, Florrie Appleton, keeps the tradition alive, supplying weekly bouquets from The Vintage Flower Van, which has been in her family and in business for more than sixty years. Florrie Appleton's TikToks about The Vintage Flower Van have become an overnight sensation with record numbers of views...'

Florrie didn't hear anymore. She frantically swiped her phone open and checked her social channels. 'No way!'

'Yes way!' confirmed Isla.

'This is madness, complete madness!' She checked through all her apps, then the local and national news sites. 'It's being reported everywhere.'

'I know, it's marvellous, isn't it? You wanted to create publicity and you've done it! Sharing your great-grandfather's story was a genius stroke.'

'I need a coffee, something to calm my nerves.' She held out her hand. 'Look. I'm shaking … though I'm not sure if it's shock or excitement.'

Isla made the coffee and pushed a mug across the table towards Florrie. 'This whole thing is going to rocket further as soon as the press discover where Dolores will be performing on her birthday. Florrie Appleton will be known by the world and W. Houston Property Developers will have a riot on their hands.'

'Even though we have to keep Dolores's birthday celebrations a secret for now, I'm thinking that this is the perfect time to share that The Vintage Flower Van is being forced to cease trading after sixty years. With a bit of luck the media will run with the story!'

'I think you're right. We might need to get some advice on how to navigate the media though.'

'Media? I'm your man.' Aidy was standing outside the open back door.

'Whoa! Does no one sleep in this village?' Florrie said jokingly. 'Come on in. The story is spreading by the second. I've even got comments on my social media from people in other countries. It's unbelievable.'

'I know, I've been monitoring it since the early hours.' Aidy smiled as he reached inside his bag and brought out a copy of the original article and photo of Ada on her first day of trading. He handed it to Florrie.

Isla shuffled closer so she could see too. 'Just look at that, Aunt Ada looks so young and so thrilled. That smile … she's radiating happiness.'

Ada was proudly standing in front of The Vintage Flower

Van – which was in exactly the same spot as it still was today – with her arms full of flowers.

Florrie read the headline out loud. *'Heartcross Flower Van Blooms into Business.'*

The article outlined how Ada had qualified as a florist at the local college in Glensheil and then achieved her dream of running her own business.

'The community of Heartcross have welcomed the colourful flower van, claiming it brings happiness to all around, and Ada hopes The Vintage Flower Van will be around for many years to come.'

Overcome with a sudden rush of emotion, Florrie blinked back the tears.

Isla gently bumped her shoulder against Florrie's. 'It's wonderful, isn't it?'

'It is, but I can't help but be saddened by the part where Aunt Ada says she hopes The Vintage Flower Van will be around for years.'

'About that. I understand that W. Houston Property Developers have declined to hand the van over to you after Ada's death?' asked Aidy.

'That's correct.' Florrie was downcast.

'That seems a little harsh. What is it to them?'

Florrie shrugged. 'I don't know. It's starting to feel like it's some kind of personal vendetta. Why else would they be so determined to flatten the land to build new houses? Rose Cottage is my family home and it was home to Aunt Ada and Uncle Ewart for their entire married life. Aunt Ada's business was built here and she turned the gardens from this…' Florrie stood up and walked over to the dresser. She took out a pile of photographs from the drawer and then placed them in front of Aidy and Isla. '…into what they are now.'

Aidy flicked through the photographs of fallen-down sheds, large areas of hardened soil full of stones, overgrown bushes… There wasn't any colour or a flower in sight.

Florrie tapped the next photo, which showed the gardens as they were now. 'My aunt Ada created these gardens. She cared for and loved each plant out there. That was all her hard work. It was a shock to learn she didn't actually own the cottage, and I know I can't do anything to change that, but hopefully we can stop W. Houston Property Developers from destroying everything that Ada created.'

Aidy stood up and walked towards the back door. He looked out over the garden. 'It's stunning. The whole place is like a work of art. They can't bulldoze it. Everyone needs to object to this development.'

'They do and that's the point of the meeting on Wednesday – to get the word out that we need help to stop this from happening, and brainstorm further ideas to do so. I should also mention that W. Houston Property Developers have arranged to inspect the cottage on the same day as Flowers in Bloom.'

Aidy gave a small chuckle. 'I wouldn't like to be in their shoes when they come face to face with the community of Heartcross.'

'Me neither,' agreed Isla.

'Okay,' said Aidy. 'We need to keep the momentum going and keep your plight at the front of the news. Everyone has fallen in love with the story of your great-grandfather. Do you have a photo of him?'

Florrie nodded. 'There's one in The Vintage Flower Van.'

'Would it be okay if I shoot a little footage this morning and then circulate it with the photo of your great-grandfather?'

'Absolutely,' replied Florrie.

'And whilst you're setting up The Vintage Flower Van for today, I'm going to make a call. I've got a contact at the TV studios and I want to try and arrange a slot for you on their morning show tomorrow. Would you be free and be able to get there?'

'Wow! Really?'

Aidy nodded. 'I'll give it my best shot.'

Florrie looked at Isla who nodded. 'We can cover the van if needs must,' Isla offered. 'This is the perfect opportunity; you have to do this.'

'I can be free, I am free! Yes! Thank you, Aidy.'

'I'm sure you'll have numerous journalists flocking to the van today, so time is of the essence. Would you be available to take some photos as soon as you set up?'

Florrie glanced at the clock. 'I need to take a quick shower, and then cut the flowers, and the wholesalers van will be here in a minute. In fact…' Florrie got up and opened the back door wider. The sound of a van's reversing sensor could be heard. 'It's here now.'

'You go and get yourself ready and I'll unload the flowers from the wholesalers and fill up the buckets,' suggested Isla.

'Thank you.' Hurrying up the stairs and switching on the shower, Florrie couldn't quite believe there was a possibility that she would be appearing on national TV tomorrow morning. She'd never done anything like that before, but even though she was already feeling slightly nervous she was also excited to tell The Vintage Flower Van's story to the nation.

Ten minutes later she heard a frantic call from Isla. 'Florrie, are you out of the shower? You need to hurry.'

Pulling on her clothes and dabbing on some lipgloss, Florrie declared herself ready. Isla was waiting at the bottom of the stairs.

'What's up? We've got ages before we open up.'

Isla playfully pushed her towards the living-room window, which overlooked the lane.

'What's going on? What are you doing?'

'You need to take a look at this but don't make yourself too visible.'

Slowly edging towards the curtain, Florrie took a peep out of the window. 'Holy moly! Where have all these people come from?' She watched for a moment as Aidy made his way through the crowd, stopping now and again to speak to people. 'Is he interviewing them?'

'He is. These people must have heard your great-grandfather's story and wanted to see The Vintage Flower Van for themselves. The buckets of flowers will diminish fast.'

Florrie's heart began to race. 'This is incredible. With a crowd this size we'll likely be sold out in the next hour.'

'I'm not sure I would even give it that long. This is going to be good for business. I've got to get back to the farm but do you want Gran to come over here and help out? And what do you want to do about Buttercup Barn?'

Florrie thought for a moment. 'I can put together Buttercup Barn's deliveries from here. Would you be able to put a note on the door telling everyone it's closed today but The Vintage Flower Van is open for business?'

'Yes, and I can send Gran over here.'

Florrie nodded. 'Yes please.'

'Now, come on, let's get you out there and get that pretty face of yours plastered all over the internet, in the national newspapers and on TV screens.'

Heading to the front of the cottage, Florrie was overwhelmed by how fast this campaign was moving. She'd never anticipated this level of interest in her social media channels or The Vintage Flower Van. The number of people already queuing seemed implausible for this time in the morning and as she walked up the path of Rose Cottage, she saw that phones were pointed in her direction and Aidy was busy taking photos. There was excited chatter all around her as Florrie opened up the van and began to sell flowers.

She spent the next thirty minutes chatting to every customer about flowers and romance, The flowers were being sold at record speed and as hordes of people parked their cars at the end of the lane and walked towards The Vintage Flower Van, Florrie began to worry that they wouldn't even make it to mid-morning.

Martha appeared at her side.

'This is unbelievable,' whispered Florrie before turning towards the next customer. 'And what brings you here today?' she asked.

'We just had to visit.' The woman linked arms with her partner. 'We're on holiday, staying at the B&B in town, and when we saw your story on TikTok we couldn't believe the gorgeous flower van in the video was right here in Heartcross. What we would like is' – the woman looked towards her partner then back towards Florrie – 'the same bouquet of flowers that your great-grandfather sent your great-grandmother every week, because we're getting married very soon and I hope we'll make each other happy and share love for a very long time, just like your great-grandparents.'

Florrie put her hand on her heart. 'That's a lovely thing to say. Congratulations!' She walked to the front of the van and picked out thirty tranquil stems of baby pink, dusky lilac and creamy white roses from the buckets, expertly hand-tying them. 'Some of them are still in bud, which will help extend the vase life of the bouquet. For a longer-lasting display, trim an inch off the stems and place in lukewarm water with the florist food in this packet. This arrangement should last between five to seven days.'

With a smile, Florrie handed the bouquet over to the woman. Approving sounds could be heard from the people behind them in the queue. After taking payment Florrie posed for a photo with the happy couple.

After that, it took over an hour before either Florrie or Martha got a breather. They looked at the empty buckets. 'I just can't believe this is happening. How busy was that?' Florrie asked rhetorically.

Aidy was standing in front of the open hatch of the van, snapping a few more photos. 'This is a very lucrative business.'

'I know,' replied Florrie. 'But it was never about the money for Great-Aunt Ada. She did it because, as she said, "Flowers make people happy and it's a short commute to work. Win-win."' Florrie laughed.

'I've taken some fantastic footage. I'm just waiting for a call back from my contact at the TV studios.' As soon as he said those words, his phone rang. 'And this is the call I'm waiting for.'

Aidy walked away from the van to answer the call and Florrie and Martha turned towards one another.

'I bet you didn't think it would be this manic this morning,' said Martha.

Aidy hung up and walked back to them. 'Florrie Appleton, I'm pleased to say that you'll be sitting on the sofa of *Today's Scotland* when they air tomorrow morning. I'll forward you the details of times and where you need to be.'

With feelings of excitement yet trepidation racing through her, Florrie knew this was the perfect opportunity to share Rose Cottage and The Vintage Flower Van's plight, and to put a definitive wrench in the plans of W. Houston Property Developers.

She gave a little shriek as she hugged Martha before turning back to Aidy. 'Thank you.'

Aidy nodded and then headed towards his car, clearly eager to file his story.

Florrie turned to Martha. 'Do you think W. Houston Property Developers has any idea that all this is going on around them?'

'If they don't, they soon will.'

Chapter Fourteen

F lorrie was sitting at the kitchen table recording the day's takings. According to the accounts book, she'd made more money today than the busiest day of last year, Valentine's Day. It wasn't that much of a surprise though, just as predicted the flowers had sold out by early afternoon. After tripling tomorrow's order from the wholesalers, Florrie checked over the email that Aidy had forwarded with all the details from the TV company about tomorrow's schedule. She would be appearing in the first segment of the show, which meant she would need to be up and out early, arriving at the station by six a.m.

Knowing she needed to be prepared, she scribbled down the facts of her great-grandfather's and Great-Aunt Ada's stories on a piece of paper. She memorised the dates of when Aunt Ada was married, the day they moved into Rose Cottage and of course when the business began. Once she'd pulled on the viewers' heartstrings, Florrie planned to announce the sad news that The Vintage Flower Van would have to close its doors. Florrie was not going to leave any stone unturned.

Aidy's article was now online and Florrie quickly copied the link and pinged it over to Isla with the caption 'This is brilliant'. The article included photographs of the long queue outside The Vintage Flower Van and Aidy had woven into the story the couple who had asked for the same bouquet that her great-grandfather had chosen for her great-grandmother. The comments were so lovely, with people even suggesting it had the makings of a great romantic movie.

As Florrie began to scroll through the rest of the day's news, she stopped on an article with the headline *Tom Houston Prepared to Take Over W. Houston Property Developers*. Florrie quickly scanned the accompanying photo and easily picked out Tom and Edward Houston. As she looked at the other faces, she knew who she was looking for … and there she was: Sophia Henley. Tom was quoted as saying, 'This is the next chapter of my life and I'm excited to carry on my grandfather's legacy.'

'And that's exactly what I'm going to do with Great-Aunt Ada's legacy. Just you try and stop me,' she murmured.

Staring at the photograph, Florrie suddenly became worried. These people had money, influence and no doubt a huge legal team at their disposal. Was she was doing the right thing in taking them on? What would happen if she ended up entangled in some legal battle that she couldn't afford to pay for?

Florrie FaceTimed Isla. 'Where are you?'

Isla didn't have time to answer as she was budged out of the way by a beast with long horns and flowing red locks.

'That highland cow has terrific hair,' joked Florrie.

Isla appeared on the screen again and grinned. 'As you might have gathered, it's milking time. You okay? I heard from Gran that it's been an incredibly busy day at the van. What a brilliant article by Aidy, by the way. This sets up your TV appearance tomorrow perfectly.'

'Isla, I'm worried.' The smile dropped from Florrie's face. 'I've got this feeling in the pit of my stomach that I'm going to get myself tied up in knots and it might come back to bite me on my bum.'

'What do you mean?'

All Florrie could think about was the fact that she would have to come face to face with Tom at some point and it was highly likely to become confrontational. How was he going to react when he discovered she'd been on national TV and made sure his company was exposed in not so good a light? What if the whole thing somehow backfired and she ended up looking stupid?

'They're a huge company and I've just got me.'

'Us,' corrected Isla. 'And how will it bite you on your bum? You aren't going out to destroy someone's character, you're giving facts, and the facts are that they're unfairly taking away the business and planning to destroy the land. Just stick to the facts and try and keep your emotions in check and you'll be fine. The key is, don't get personal.'

'The more I think of Tom, the more I want to get personal,' Florrie admitted, feeling the familiar hurt twisting in her stomach, old wounds resurfacing.

'I'm not surprised, but just remember to stay calm, focused and on track. The public will fall in love with the warm, kind Florrie we all know and already love.'

'You're right. It won't do me any good to get personal.'

Isla nodded. 'There's one more important question you'll need to consider before tomorrow, which is: what are you going to wear?'

Florrie had been putting off thinking about that dilemma. She was all about comfort and the majority of her clothes were very unconventional and unsuitable for a TV appearance.

'I honestly have no clue.' Florrie began to panic a little. She thought about all the celebrities that had been interviewed on the same sofa. They wore the latest designer brands but the only smart suit she had in her wardrobe was the one she'd worn for Ada's funeral.

She glanced in the mirror. Her eyebrows had a mind of their own and were sticking up in every direction. 'I also need some grooming.'

Isla laughed. 'You sound like you're one of my alpacas.'

'Look at me though. My clothes are the colour of a rainbow, I wear fingerless gloves every day of the week including summer, my trainers are falling apart, my jeans are embroidered with flowers and my hair…'

'All of that is what makes you Florrie Appleton and we love you being you. Don't go pretending you're someone you're not. Your followers follow you because you're authentic, genuine, kind, warm … the list is endless. They aren't interested in how you dress; they're interested in your story.'

'You make it sound so simple.'

'You'll be a natural. I will see you tomorrow night at the meeting. It's going to be a busy day. Good luck!' Isla hung up the call.

Sitting in the kitchen with the back door wide open Florrie opened up her social media accounts on her phone. Her followers were still increasing in droves and she decided to get them involved in her debut TV appearance. Heading upstairs to her wardrobe, she slid the clothes back and forth on the rail. She definitely had her own style going on. Pulling out two outfits she began to make a set of stories, the first of which she captioned. *'Tomorrow I have my debut TV appearance. I need your help choosing an outfit!'* Florrie filmed herself in two outfits, the first trousers and a shirt, the second her usual style, and of course her signature fingerless gloves. She gave a twirl in each and then posted both clips and finished with a voting poll and a selfie with the caption *'Tune in to Today's Scotland tomorrow at 8am. to see which outfit I've chosen!'*

The votes started coming in almost immediately but deep down Florrie already knew exactly what she was going to wear. Because just like Isla suggested, she needed to be herself.

Chapter Fifteen

Florrie pushed the key into the ignition of the van. After quickly punching the postcode of the TV studio into Google Maps, she placed her phone in the holder on the dashboard. The response to her outfit poll had been outstanding. Thousands of followers had voted and – thankfully – the outfit that had received the most votes was the one she was wearing today – her usual attire. Smiling at her fingerless gloves, she turned the key a second time and on the third attempt Rose's engine started. There were times when Florrie thought of trading Rose in for a newer model but they'd created such a bond over the years and had shared so much; Florrie wasn't ready for the break-up just yet. Putting Rose into first gear Florrie made her way slowly up the lane. As she drove past The Old Bakehouse, she spotted Martha walking across the green. Florrie pulled up at the side of the road and wound down the window.

'Morning, Martha, I'm just off. The nerves are kicking in!' Florrie screwed up her face.

'You'll be brilliant but I must warn you: there won't be any sales while you're on TV.' Martha held up a makeshift sign that read: *The Vintage Flower Van is closed for twenty minutes whilst I watch the owner on Today's Scotland!*

Florrie laughed. 'I think I can live with missing a few sales.'

'Am I okay to watch on the TV inside Rose Cottage?'

'Martha, you don't need to ask. Now wish me luck!'

'Good luck! The whole village is behind you, literally.' Martha winked then touched Florrie's arm through the open window before she walked away.

Florrie was puzzled – what was with the wink? She carried on driving towards the high street and as soon as she turned the corner she got her answer.

'Oh my…' She was lost for words.

The community of Heartcross had lined the pavement and as soon as they spotted Rose, they let out a cheer and began waving flags. Isla was standing next to Felicity and Rona, all holding up good luck signs. Florrie pulled up beside them.

'Let me guess, this is all down to you?' she asked.

'Maybe!' said Isla. 'We couldn't let you go off without you knowing the whole village is behind you. We love you and Ada and we wish you all the luck in the world. We'll all be watching. Meredith and Fraser are putting on brunch in the pub so we can all come together to watch your debut TV performance.'

Overwhelmed, Florrie swallowed the lump in her throat and looked at the line of familiar faces and the bold and colourful signs.

Save Rose Cottage Gardens
Save The Vintage Flower Van
Good luck today, Florrie!

Everyone was supportive and it meant a lot to Florrie to have them all behind her. Fanning a hand in front of her face, she said, 'I've come over all emotional.'

'Don't cry, you'll have puffy eyes and that won't be a good look for TV.' Isla smiled. 'We'll all see you tonight at the meeting.'

'Eek! I'll see you later. Here I go!'

'Break a leg!' cried Rona.

Florrie set off slowly, waving out of the window with one hand whilst beeping the horn with the other. Uplifted, she joined the track at the bottom of Love Heart Lane and drove over the bridge into Glensheil, on a mission to save everything Great-Aunt Ada had worked so hard to achieve.

Thankfully, there were no delays on the roads and Florrie spent the journey rehearsing numerous things in her mind that what she wanted to say, but as she turned left and saw the impressive TV building in front of her, the nerves kicked in and her mind went blank. She slowed as she approached the security barrier and wound down her window. The security guard greeted her with a smile. She gave her name and the passcode that had been emailed to her. He looked at her and for a moment she thought there was a problem, but then he smiled again. 'Florrie Appleton, you're the reason my wife has just booked us a weekend away in Heartcross! She's in love with that vintage flower van of yours, in fact she's obsessed. She's a lover of flowers and all things romantic and for our anniversary all she wanted was a weekend away in Heartcross and a bunch of flowers bought from your famous flower van.'

Florrie's heart swelled with happiness. 'That's so lovely to hear, and so romantic. If you want to send me a message on social media, I'll make sure I have her favourite bouquet made up for you on the day.'

'I will, thank you. She won't believe you're here today.' The security guard looked towards the TV building and then back at Florrie. 'We aren't really allowed to ask but would it be possible to get a selfie with you? My wife wouldn't believe me otherwise.'

Unclipping her seat belt, she stepped out of the van. 'Of course!'

Feeling like a celebrity, Florrie had her photo taken then climbed back behind the wheel.

'I'm sending it to her now.' As soon as the photo was sent the security guard handed over a visitor's badge, which Florrie displayed in the window of the van, and a lanyard, which she placed around her neck.

'That car park space is for you' – he pointed to a space in front of the entrance to the building – 'and just inside the door you'll find the reception.'

'Thank you.'

After she parked the van, she nervously headed up to the double doors and stepped inside. The walls were bright pink. One featured rows and rows of framed pictures of TV presenters who had worked on shows from this very building. In front of her was a tidy reception area, with one desk, one computer and a phone. The receptionist – Rachel, according to her name badge – glanced up as soon as the door opened.

'Florrie! It's you! I've been waiting to meet you all morning! I follow you on social media and I voted for that very outfit. I thought the other one looked way too official. And ta-dah!'

Rachel's hands appeared from underneath the desk and Florrie was amazed to see she was also wearing fingerless gloves. 'It's the latest fashion craze and it's all thanks to you. You need to start your own merchandise; these will sell like hotcakes along with your flowers.'

'Wow!' Florrie was surprised. 'Maybe. I'll think about that.'

'And can I just say I love your flower van and your bouquets are beautiful? I *must* visit.' Rachel's friendly nature immediately put Florrie at ease.

'Thank you.' Florrie smiled. 'I'm already feeling very loved today.'

'How was your journey?' Rachel stood up, walked around the desk and shook Florrie's hand.

'Straightforward and I didn't hit any traffic at all.'

'But I bet you're in need of a warm drink and some light refreshments. Follow me and I'll show you to your dressing room. The bathroom is right next door and the Green Room is directly opposite. You can hang out in there and watch the guests that are on the show after you. Cathy and Ben can't wait to meet you. The story of your great-grandfather is so romantic. Honestly, it melted everyone's heart here in the studio and all the viewers are going to fall in love with you. You're so adorable.'

They walked towards a set of double doors, which Rachel opened with her security card. The long walkway with its high ceiling was lined with columns and the bright lighting lit up the navy walls, on which a long line of gold frames held photographs of famous people. Florrie glanced at every picture as she passed.

Just outside her dressing room was a round table with a large crystal vase full of pink roses. And then she saw it, her name in bold letters on the door – FLORRIE APPLETON.

'Here we are.' Rachel checked the schedule in her hand.

'You have a few minutes before Meg, the hair and make-up artist, collects you, so take a moment to relax. You can leave your personal belongings in your dressing room, as you're the only person who has access to it.' Rachel handed over a key card. 'This opens the bathroom and the door to the Green Room. It's full of refreshments, so do help yourself. Once your hair and make-up are done, you'll have a quick briefing with Cathy and Ben before you go live on air. Is there anything else you'd like to ask?'

'No, I think you've covered it all,' replied Florrie.

'I can't wait to see you live on air – I'll be watching it from my desk – and remember to try and enjoy it.'

As soon as Rachel was out of sight, Florrie whipped out her phone and took a photo of her name on the door. She felt giddy. What would it be like to be an actual celebrity? She put the key card against the fob, there was a click, and the light turned green. She pushed open the door and let out a low whistle. The dressing room was bigger than the living room at Rose Cottage! There were two oversized plush settees, a TV, a fridge full of bottled water, floor-to-ceiling mirrors and expensive art on the wall, not to mention the biggest basket of fruit she'd ever seen in her life. 'Wow!' she exclaimed, holding her arms out wide and spinning around, something she used to do as a little girl when she was excited. Falling on to the sofa she scrambled for her phone and FaceTimed Isla, who picked up immediately.

'Isla! Look at the dressing room.' Florrie gave her a virtual tour of the room. 'It's huge! The Green Room is next door and I'll be going for my hair and make-up very soon. I'm living the dream.'

'Look at you! Superstar! You're going to have a blast. This is the start of something, I can feel it in my bones!'

'My heart is beating so fast. I can't actually believe I'm here and about to appear on national TV.'

'You better believe it because we're all waiting. Look at us!' Isla turned the phone around. In front of her was a TV screen with rows of chairs occupied by the villagers. They let out a rapturous cheer and all waved madly towards the phone camera. 'We're all ready for you!'

'Oh my, look at all that support!'

'We'll leave you to enjoy superstardom and we'll all see you tonight.'

As soon as Florrie hung up the phone, she couldn't resist posing for a few selfies, which she immediately uploaded to her social media channels. Within seconds, her phone began to ping with notifications. Comments were flooding in. Her followers and lovers of The Vintage Flower Van were tuning into *Today's Scotland*.

The Green Room was just as impressive as her dressing room. There were comfortable-looking chairs and sofas with vibrant plush cushions to lounge on, and a fridge stocked with fresh water and juices. Bowls of fresh fruit were scattered around the room, and platters of food lined a buffet table. On one wall were oversized photos of the presenters, Cathy and Ben, and on another wall were photographs of past shows. The huge TV screen on the wall made her feel like she was in the cinema. Sinking onto one of the settees, she saw the morning show was about to go live and the presenters and production team were huddled around a script on screen. It was all becoming so real. Soon she would be with them on set, sitting on the settee in front of them, and their discussion would air all over Scotland. *Today's Scotland* had tremendous viewing figures and even though she knew Tom was unlikely to be watching, she wondered how soon he might find out about her TV interview.

Soon after, the door to the Green Room opened and a woman in her early thirties stepped into the room. She was wearing headphones and talking into a microphone. After looking at the clipboard she held in her hand she glanced towards Florrie. 'Hi, I'm Meg, you must be Florrie.'

Florrie smiled. 'I am.'

'How you feeling?'

'After watching the TV, more nervous than thirty minutes ago,' she admitted.

'Honestly, you don't need to be. I'm here to do your hair and make-up and get you ready for the show. But first, I'm going to take you through to the studio where you'll meet Cathy and Ben before they go live on air in twenty minutes' time. They'll explain what's going to happen and hopefully put you at ease. Come this way.'

Florrie followed Meg along a different corridor to the one she'd traversed with Rachel and suddenly the studio was there in front of them. The sign above the door, reading ON AIR, wasn't lit, but Florrie still felt her heart racing as she stepped inside the studio. The set resembled a living room. Two settees were positioned opposite each other with a coffee table between them. Four cameramen faced the set from different angles and behind the set was a window with a stunning backdrop that overlooked a lake. The presenters were sitting on one of the couches in the middle of the set and looked up as soon as they heard Florrie and Meg approaching.

'Good morning, Florrie!' Cathy said, getting quickly to her

feet and extending a hand. 'It's lovely to meet you and you're just as adorable in real life. I've been following your posts online and wow, you're an overnight sensation!'

Florrie had watched Cathy on TV many times and it was surreal to be standing next to her and talking to her in real life. 'I've just been saying to Ben we need to visit your van.'

'You do,' replied Florrie, shaking both of their hands. 'Lovely to meet you both.'

Cathy gestured for her to take a seat on the couch opposite them. 'It's going to be quite a straightforward interview – in fact, think of it more as a chat between friends over a cup of tea. We emailed you an outline of the questions that we are going to ask, are you okay with those?'

'Yes,' replied Florrie, knowing that she was going to set the cat amongst the pigeons when she added the possible demise of the gardens and the flower van.

'We'll introduce you, talk all things flowers and share your great-grandfather's story, and then we'll lead on to the gorgeous vintage flower van and, of course, how well the business has been doing since you've become a social media sensation, with visitors travelling from far and wide.'

'Is there anything you would like to ask us before we're on air?' added Ben.

'I don't think so,' replied Florrie.

'All we ask is that when you're talking keep looking at us, not at the cameras, and everything will run smoothly.'

Meg interrupted. 'I'm going to take Florrie through to hair and make-up and I'll bring her back in the break just before she goes live on air.' Meg touched Florrie's arm and after saying goodbye to Cathy and Ben they began walking towards the door.

Hearing the words 'live on air', Florrie's stomach began to churn. She took some deep breaths and hoped her face hadn't turned the same colour as the walls in the Green Room, because she was beginning to feel nauseous with nerves.

The hair and make-up room was just how she imagined it – white, bright and full of make-up, brushes and hair products. Florrie sat down and faced the mirror. Meg stood behind her.

'How would you like your hair styled today?' she asked, gently grabbing a handful of Florrie's long hair in both hands then letting it fall down her back.

For the first time in ages Florrie had to admit that her hair style didn't excite her anymore. Every day she twisted it up in a bun. She couldn't remember the last time it was cut or styled. 'I've always been useless at styling and looking in the mirror it appears my hair has lost the will to live.'

Meg smiled. 'We can trim it, or give it a good cut, it's up to you.'

'Could you?'

'Of course. Just a tidy-up or…'

Florrie looked at Meg's chic wavy bob.

'Maybe it's time for a change. I feel like this is the old me and it's at odds with who I am now.'

'What are you thinking?'

Florrie felt an intense desire to move on, and a sudden need for a different and new look. A dramatic change of hair was a great way to shed the past.

'I'm thinking I want something a little more classy, timeless, effortless. Like your hair.'

'We can do that, but are you sure?'

Florrie looked at her reflection in the mirror. 'Yes, let's go for it,' she said with utter conviction before she could change her mind.

Meg began to comb through Florrie's hair and then took hold of the long locks with her left hand and held the scissors up with her right.

'Are you definitely sure? Last chance to change your mind,' she said.

'I'm definitely sure.'

'All right then.' And without further ado, Meg made a cut straight across, just below Florrie's shoulder.

'Oh my...' Florrie exclaimed, looking at the mass of hair in Meg's hand before shaking her head from side to side. 'It already feels so light.'

'I think you've made the right choice. Now let's get it washed, trimmed, blow dried and maybe a few waves if you like, then we can apply your make-up.'

Once her hair was dry and styled, Florrie couldn't stop smiling. Her hair was so soft, wavy and free. It framed her face beautifully; Meg had done an amazing job.

'What a transformation!' exclaimed Florrie. 'I feel like a brand-new woman. I can't thank you enough. My hair looks vibrant and glossier.'

'It really suits you. You're going to light up that screen,' declared Meg, untying the cape from around Florrie's shoulders and brushing the loose strands of hair from her knees with a soft brush. 'Your make-up we'll keep minimal and natural.'

Florrie watched Meg set to work with a number of lotions and potions that smelled divine. A light tinted moisturiser was applied and set with a translucent powder that gave her a natural glow. After shaping and tinting Florrie's eyebrows, and a few light brushes of colour across her cheeks, Meg applied mascara and lipgloss, then stood back to let Florrie take a look at her reflection.

'Is that actually me?' she asked in wonder.

'It is. What do you think?'

'I look like a movie star.' Florrie edged forward on her chair to take a closer look. 'I can't believe that's actually me. I look… I'm actually lost for words.'

'Stunning,' replied Meg.

'I really like it, thank you.'

'You're very welcome.'

'Would it be possible for you to take a photo of me so I can post it online?'

'It'll be my pleasure.'

As soon as the photo was taken, Florrie uploaded it and captioned it 'New Hair, New Me'. A second later she heard a cheer coming from the open window. Swinging a glance that way, she could see the security gate she'd driven through earlier, and beyond it a large group of people.

'Look at all those people. What are they doing?' asked Florrie, thinking there must be a famous person arriving very soon.

'They're hoping to get sight of you.'

'Get away…'

'No, seriously, they are. They're some of your followers off social media.'

Florrie stared at the crowd. 'Are you sure you aren't winding me up?'

'As soon as you posted that picture, they let out a cheer. Post something else and see what happens.'

Florrie snapped a second selfie and captioned it '*Just about to be live on air on Today's Scotland'.* She uploaded it then looked towards the window.

Another cheer erupted.

'Who'd have thought The Vintage Flower Van in the village of Heartcross could create so much—'

'Joy and happiness,' interrupted Meg. 'Flowers are a wonderful thing.'

'I quite agree,' replied Florrie, still amazed at the crowd outside.

'Now, are you ready? Your audience awaits.'

Florrie held out her hand, which she could see was trembling slightly. 'I think so.'

Meg led the way to the studio floor.

Standing in the wings, Florrie watched as the programme went into the commercial break. Cathy looked up and did a double take. 'Look at your hair! You look amazing. Come and take a seat.'

'Thank you,' replied Florrie, swishing her hair from side to side. 'I love it.'

Meg touched her arm. 'I'm going to wait in the wings. Don't be nervous.'

Florrie slipped on to the couch and took a look around. The camera crew were positioned strategically around the set, capturing the interview from all angles.

'Just relax, we aren't going to ask any difficult questions,' reassured Ben. 'Just think of it as a chat between friends. That glass of water on the table in front of you is yours so feel free to take a drink if you need a moment during the chat.'

Florrie nodded. She suddenly felt her throat go dry and prayed that her voice sounded relatively normal. Her heart was beating nineteen to the dozen. She listened nervously to the director counting them in.

'We're going live in three, two...' He signalled the 'one' with his index finger and pointed to the hosts as the signature soundtrack concluded. Ben and Cathy turned towards camera three with beaming smiles.

'Welcome back to *Today's Scotland*! This morning on the couch we have been joined by new TikTok and Instagram sensation Florrie Appleton, who went viral this week when she started posting all about her vintage flower van in Heartcross, a charming village in the very heart of Scotland. The Vintage Flower Van has been a family business for decades and Florrie has recently taken over running it, following in her ancestors' footsteps. Welcome, Florrie!'

The camera spun towards her but thankfully Florrie remembered she was meant to look at the presenters rather than the lens. 'Thank you for inviting me to join you this morning.'

'Not only has your vintage flower van become an object of fascination for tourists and your followers, but the story of your great-grandfather has also captured the hearts of the nation. Tell us all about it,' Cathy encouraged.

Florrie began telling the story and within seconds her nerves had evaporated, she had relaxed and she was beginning to enjoy herself.

'My great-aunt Ada passed away recently and before she did, I made her a promise that I will keep The Vintage Flower Van in business and our family's floral traditions alive,' she concluded, 'and that my great-grandmother will never be without flowers on a Friday.' Florrie held up the photograph of her great-grandparents that she'd brought along.

'This is such a romantic story,' Cathy gushed, taking the picture and showing it to one of the cameras. 'Have you always been such a fan of flowers, Florrie?'

Florrie nodded. 'It was always my dream to become a florist, and growing up I worked alongside my great-aunt Ada in The Vintage Flower Van. She taught me everything I know, and there was nothing she didn't know when it came to flowers. She grew the majority of them herself in the gardens at her home, and created a landscape that is truly wonderful to behold.'

Ben turned towards the camera. 'Let's take a look at this transformation, as it is indeed spectacular.'

Florrie looked towards the camera and saw the reel that had been put together showing the gardens going from sparse and sad to their present spectacular life and colour.

'Now talk us through the different areas of this stunning garden,' said Cathy.

Florrie chatted happily about the different sections and about how Ada had staggered the growth of each to ensure that there were flowers available throughout the seasons.

'I feel like I'm looking at a garden that belongs to a palace or a stately home. The love and attention to detail that have gone into it over the years have created something so wonderful. Now, I believe that the garden will be open to the general public very soon. Can you tell us more about that?'

'That's right, every year the village of Heartcross holds a competition called Flowers in Bloom and anyone can buy a ticket and wander around all the gardens that have been entered. Each ticket-holder votes for their favourite garden – and Ada has won that competition for the past thirty years. Believe me when I say that the competition is fierce every year so it's quite an achievement! Tickets go on sale tomorrow. They can be purchased from The Vintage Flower Van at Rose Cottage. Anyone interested will need to be quick though, as there are only a limited number of tickets available. And can I just add that the ticket also includes refreshments from Bonnie's Teashop on Love Heart Lane.'

Cathy turned towards Ben. 'I think this is a date for the diary.'

'You're both more than welcome to visit Heartcross anytime.'

'We'll take you up on that! For now, what's next for Florrie Appleton and The Vintage Flower Van?'

It was the question she'd been waiting for and Florrie silently thanked Cathy for setting things up perfectly for her.

'I'm saddened to share with you that it's not good news.' Florrie noticed the two presenters exchanging a fleeting puzzled look.

'Just after my great-aunt Ada passed away, it came to light that she didn't own Rose Cottage as I had been led to believe, but instead had rented it all her life from a property company.' They have refused my request to transfer the lease to me, which means I am about to lose my family home, and as if that wasn't enough, they are also taking The Vintage Flower Van, as it was also rented. After sixty years in business, The Vintage Flower Van will cease trading at the end of the month. And if that wasn't enough of a shock for our beautiful village of Heartcross, the company that owns the cottage is proposing to flatten great-aunt Ada's beautiful garden in order to build new houses. It's absolutely devastating to me, to the memory of my family and to the community of Heartcross.'

There it was, all out in the open. Florrie knew by the looks on Cathy and Ben's faces that they were sympathetic by what she'd just revealed.

'These beautiful gardens are going to be demolished?' asked Cathy.

'Yes, that's what the developers are proposing, so this year's Flowers in Bloom will possibly be the last chance to enjoy everything Great-Aunt Ada created – and one of the last days you'll be able to buy your flowers from The Vintage Flower Van.'

'We're so sorry to hear this,' said Ben. 'What started as such a romantic and uplifting story has turned into a true tragedy. We never anticipated things might take a turn like this.'

'I, of course, will not be making it easy for the company, and will continue to appeal and fight for my business and the gardens.'

Cathy nodded. 'I think you may have the whole nation behind you, Florrie. Thank you for joining us today, and we wish you success in saving the iconic flower van and gardens of Rose Cottage.'

'Thank you for having me.'

The music played and the commercial break kicked in.

Cathy turned towards Florrie. 'We're off air. I'm so sorry to hear about this extremely sad development in your story.'

Florrie nodded her thanks. 'It's been a blow, but I'll keep fighting.'

'I think, after this appearance, the media will be fighting your corner alongside your ever-growing followers.'

'I really hope so.'

'We wish you lots of luck.' Cathy shook her hand. 'Meg will take you to collect your things. Thank you again for joining us and telling your story today.'

Ten minutes later, Florrie was sitting in her van in the car park outside the TV studios. She pulled her phone out of her bag. The text messages and notifications she'd received were in their hundreds! The first person she phoned was Isla.

'You were very natural and oh my gosh, your hair! Your make-up! You looked stunning! But more importantly you came across brilliantly.'

'At first I was nervous but then I have to say I rather enjoyed it.'

'Your story is out there now so let's see what impact it has. You'll definitely need to keep on top of the social media. Aidy is going to run a follow-up to his first story and include what you revealed today, so that will be circulated in the news asap.'

'That's great, Isla. I'm going to head home now and I'll see you later at the meeting.'

Just before she started the engine, she quickly uploaded a short video to her social media channels thanking Cathy and Ben for having her in the studio. By the time she was headed towards the barrier, her phone was pinging out of control. Slowing down as she reached the barrier, she wound down the window and handed back her lanyard and car park permit to the security guard.

'I was watching and I'm sorry to hear your news.' He nodded towards the crowd gathered outside the gate. 'You've got a lot of people who want to support you and help keep the flower van in your family. I've got all my fingers crossed for you.'

Florrie thanked him sincerely and drove out through the gate to where there was a gaggle of fans, who began to chant, 'Save The Vintage Flower Van, Save Rose Cottage!' Everyone was taking photos of Florrie as she drove slowly past. She waved at them, then beeped the horn as she headed off up the road.

'Let's see what you make of that, W. Houston Property Developers,' Florrie muttered, knowing she still had the ace that was Dolores up her sleeve.

Chapter Sixteen

F eeling invincible and cheerful knowing the interview had gone well, Florrie decided to take the scenic route home. Driving along the coastline with the radio turned up she began singing along. She had the glistening sea on one side, the spectacular view of mountainous terrain on the other, and the wide blue sky with its few scattered clouds above. A welcoming warmth came through the open window.

Still singing at the top of her lungs, she navigated the next narrow twist and turn on the coastal road. As she did so, she felt the van tilt and then there was a massive thud, followed by a grinding sound. The van hurtled onto the grass verge. Braking hard, Florrie felt her seat belt tighten. She squeezed her eyes shut until the van bumped to a stop.

Shaken, she unclipped her seatbelt and opened the door. Gulping fresh air, she attempted to calm her beating heart. She got out and walked unsteadily around to the front of the van to assess the damage. A tyre had blown – and there wasn't another car or soul in sight.

Florrie sighed, cursing the fact that she had no clue how to change a tyre. It had been on her to-do list at one point to take a short mechanics course, just in case anything like this ever happened to her, but she'd kept putting it off because what were the chances of that? Now she knew – the chances were very good indeed.

She needed to phone for help and was thinking to herself that maybe Drew or Fergus could bring the tow truck from the farm, when she suddenly heard a car engine in the distance.

Florrie spun around and hurried to the side of the road frantically waving her arms, hoping to attract the driver's attention. As soon as the car turned the corner, her arms stopped in mid-air. Heading towards her was Tom's Bugatti.

'No,' she breathed in dismay. Of all the cars on the road, of course *his* had to be the next one. Unfortunately, he'd spotted her and had begun to slow down. She dropped her arms and watched as he parked behind Rose.

As he stepped out of the car, she had to stifle a surprised – and delighted – gasp.

Tom was dressed in a kilt.

Perfectly sailing the fine line between handsome and downright sexy, his kilt was accompanied by a dirk and sporran, a three-button waistcoat, a white shirt and a bow tie.

Florrie was temporarily speechless but quickly pulled herself back into the moment, reminding herself where she had just been and why.

'We meet again,' he said, his eyes fixed on Rose's tyre. 'That's completely blown. You can't drive on it.'

'I know that,' she said, irritated.

Tom looked at her and his gaze intensified. For a second, he was silent as he took her in.

Eventually, he pointed to her hair. 'It's different. Your hair is … different. Have you been somewhere special?'

Florrie felt rooted to the spot. This probably wasn't the time to tell him she'd just been on national TV attempting to ruin his company's reputation.

'Very special,' she replied. 'Look, it's nice of you to stop but I need to get on with finding my way home.' She looked at her mobile and began to search for Drew's number.

'What are you doing?'

'Ringing for help.'

'Am I invisible? I've stopped to help you.'

Florrie was in a predicament. There was no denying that she needed help – she was hungry and just wanted to get home – but the longer she stayed in Tom's company the more likely it was that she would reveal where she'd just been and why.

Tom looked at her. 'I know you may have been spooked by my arrival in Heartcross, and you haven't made me feel welcome at all—'

'And why are you surprised by that?'

'Okay, I can sense you still have a bee in your bonnet about something and I'm sick of being spoken to in this way. Either we resolve this now or I get in my car and head to my hotel and pretend that you haven't come back into my life.'

Florrie raised an eyebrow.

'*I* haven't come back into *your* life? It's you who is turning up everywhere in mine!'

'How is that so? You're the one who damaged my car, you're the one with a flat tyre on the side of the road. And there's been not even a hint of an apology for the way you've treated me since I've arrived. I should have known you hadn't changed. In fact, I should have been done with you all those years ago.'

You could cut the tension with a knife.

But Florrie was also perplexed. He didn't have a right to be angry with her. Why would he be? And what did he mean by he 'should have been done with' her?

'Done with me? Done with *me*? We spent two whole weeks together at that private beach house.' She pointed in the direction of the sea. 'I had the best time of my life. You made me feel alive, happy and loved. I thought we had something special. Why would you do that, why would you give me false hope for the future?'

'I didn't. Everything I did and said was truly how I was feeling. I was hoping it was the start of something new.'

Florrie gave a strangled laugh. 'The start of something new. How could you start something new? You left me in the car park with an iPod full of songs to remind me of the wonderful time we shared—'

'For the record, it was more than wonderful,' Tom interrupted.

'And what happened right after that, Tom?' Florrie continued, undeterred. She blinked back frustrated tears.

'What happened was you disappeared out of my life and I've no idea why. How did you think I felt, sharing those two weeks with you then being cut dead? There was no way of contacting you,' Tom said, sharply.

'If it was that important to explain yourself you could have tracked me down. I mean, you're in Heartcross now, even if it is eight years too late.'

'Why would I track you down? You made it pretty damn clear you didn't want anything to do with me. You blocked my phone calls, cut ties with me on social media. Is that what you do, use people and then discard them once you've had your fun?'

'Use you? Are you kidding me?' Florrie was aghast. Was he actually trying to paint *her* as the bad guy in this whole situation?

Tom exhaled. 'Look, Florrie, I'll share this with you.' He took a breath. 'I liked you … a lot. In fact, spending those two weeks together … I've never felt more comfortable or more like myself in my life. You got me. We had fun and everything was so easy. Those two weeks were the best two weeks I've ever had. I was falling in love with you.'

The words took Florrie completely by surprise.

'Then you cut me off completely.'

'And you really have no idea why?' she asked.

'I'm afraid I don't,' he said, looking bewildered.

'Unbelievable. I've got two words for you: Sophia Henley. You left me and went directly to frolicking on your father's yacht in St Tropez with your childhood sweetheart. How do you think I felt seeing pictures of you together and reading that marriage was on the cards in the near future for you two? She obviously had a lucky escape and married someone else. Is that why you're still single? Did she break your heart the same way you broke mine?'

Tom raised an eyebrow. 'You seem to know a lot about Sophia.'

'Is that all you've got to say?' she asked, annoyed.

Tom looked like he was about to say something but changed his mind.

'You can't even tell me I'm wrong, can you?' Florrie persisted.

Tom's eyes flickered as he ran his hand through his hair.

'Have you got anything to say?' she demanded.

'Sometimes things aren't the way they seem.'

'That's it?' Florrie could feel her eyes burning as she stared at him.

They were at a stalemate.

Tom sighed. 'I'll change your tyre. I can't leave you stranded here.'

For a moment she hesitated and glanced at the screen of her phone. There was no signal. Damn. If she didn't let him help, she wasn't sure how long she would be stuck here, and with the community meeting planned for tonight at Rose Cottage, Florrie wanted to be home in plenty of time to prepare. Taking the keys from the ignition, she placed them in his outstretched hand. They held each other's gaze for a silent moment before Florrie pointed to the double doors at the back of the van. 'The spare tyre is in there.'

Sitting on a rock at the side of the road, Florrie quietly observed him as he took off his waistcoat and white shirt and hung them over the branch of a nearby tree. There was a heavy silence as he pushed his hair from his eyes, and they made eye contact for a second, but neither said a word.

She wasn't going to admit it to him but he'd captured her full attention with that half naked, sultry, damn-right sexy look he had going on as he effortlessly changed the tyre. He glanced back over his shoulder and she felt herself blush, having been caught looking.

Barely twenty minutes later Tom was putting the flat tyre into the back of the van and saying, 'You'll need to get that fixed, otherwise you'll be stuck if it happens again.'

Florrie nodded. 'Thank you.'

Tom locked the back of the van and handed the keys back to her. Then he put his shirt back on and held his waistcoat in his hand. 'And just for the record, I think about the time we spent together ... a lot.'

With that he turned and headed to his car, his open shirt flapping behind him as he walked.

Florrie watched as he drove off. She wanted to dislike that man so much, but her heart was telling her something totally different.

Chapter Seventeen

E very time Florrie pulled up outside Rose Cottage, she marvelled at the beauty of the place. It certainly lived up to its name with its cluster of pink roses decorating the oak-timbered porch. She parked the van and noticed Martha and Isla carrying a trestle table down the gravel path. As soon as they spotted her, their smiles grew and they put down the table and waved.

'Here, she is, our TV star with brand-new hair. Give us a twirl, you look gorgeous!'

Florrie laughed as Isla twirled her around.

'It really suits you. And you were amazing on TV. Your face has been plastered all across the news channels and no doubt the story will be in the newspapers tomorrow. Goodness knows what's been happening on your social media channels in the last couple of hours.'

'I've not had time to look just yet.'

'Why don't I put the kettle on and you girls can take the table through to the garden?' suggested Martha, and disappeared into the kitchen whilst Isla and Florrie positioned the table next to another that had already been set up. Florrie looked around. All the picnic blankets were laid out, ready for the meeting, and Rona had dropped off a container full of mugs, the tea urn and trays of home-baked delights.

'You've all been busy,' she observed.

'We have but let's get back to you. How did it feel being on TV? I honestly think if we all stick together, the planning department will have to take notice of us.'

Florrie smiled. 'Let's hope so and being on TV was amazing, though I was a little nervous at first. Would you believe there were followers outside the TV studio, calling my name? It was a little surreal.'

'No way! How was the journey? We thought you'd be back before now,' said Isla, draping paper tablecloths over the tables before beginning to lay the mugs out in rows. 'And by the way, I think we're expecting between fifty and sixty people tonight.'

'I hit a pothole on the way back, and the tyre blew.'

Isla stopped what she was doing. 'Are you okay? That must have been a bugger to change.'

'It wasn't as difficult as you might imagine… You probably won't believe me when I tell you the name of the driver of the next car to pass me on the road. It was none other than Tom Houston who came to my rescue.'

Isla's eyes widened in surprise.

Florrie blew out a breath. 'It was a little heated. I told him I knew about him and Sophia Henley.'

'And how did that go down?'

'He said something quite weird.'

'Which was?'

'That some things aren't quite what they seem.' Florrie

shrugged. 'I think that it was his way of deflecting from the fact that he'd been caught out cheating, as he didn't offer any other explanation.'

'Possibly. Seems a strange thing to say though. Why wouldn't he just accept responsibility for his behaviour?'

Florrie shrugged. 'It just shows the type of person he is.'

She was still thinking about Tom's words. If there was a reasonable explanation for what happened, then why didn't he take his chance and explain it to her? She felt so confused and just wanted the truth, some sort of closure, so it wasn't always preying on her mind.

'Did he know where you'd just been or have any inkling about the meeting tonight?'

'I don't think so, and even if he did, it wasn't mentioned.'

'Tea's ready,' shouted Martha from the kitchen.

'That's good news. I'm in need of a cuppa and I'm feeling rather peckish.'

'It's a good job I brought you a sandwich back from the pub along with a chocolate brownie then, isn't it?'

'You're just the best friend,' gushed Florrie, with a bright smile.

As they walked through the back door of the cottage, Florrie noticed a large number of boxes stacked up in the hallway. 'Where have all those come from?'

'Flynn dropped them off along with the picnic blankets. He thought they may come in handy when you start packing up the cottage. There's tissue paper and bubble wrap too.'

'That's really kind of him. I know I should be making a start but it's just so difficult to know where to begin, packing up someone's life.' Florrie sat down at the table.

Martha placed the sandwich and brownie in front of her. 'It

is difficult. If you like, I can pack up Ada's clothes and take them to the charity shop in Glensheil.'

Florrie blinked back the sudden tears. 'Would you? I don't think I can face it.'

Martha touched her arm. 'Of course I can. I can do it this weekend.'

'Thank you,' replied Florrie, before taking a bite of her sandwich.

'We expected you back earlier than this,' added Martha.

'Florrie had a flat tyre on the way back from the TV studios,' shared Isla. 'And guess who was on hand to help her out.'

'Go on,' replied Martha, looking between them.

'Tom Houston!'

'Does he know about your TV appearance?'

Florrie shook her head. 'I don't think so, he didn't mention anything.'

'He will soon enough, and wait until the world discovers that Dolores will be singing here during Flowers in Bloom.'

'It's very kind of Dolores to put herself out there to create that type of publicity for Ada,' said Florrie. 'I had a chat with her about William Houston, founder of W. Houston Property Developers, and apparently they were good friends.'

Martha nodded. 'We all were.'

'But Dolores wasn't keen on his son Edward. Do you know why?'

Martha raised her eyebrows, 'Something went on back then but I'm not sure exactly what. Whatever it was, Ada and Dolores kept it to themselves.'

'But you must know something?' pressed Florrie.

'All I know is just before Ada married Ewart and moved

196

into this place, I was somewhere I shouldn't have been and I think I witnessed something I shouldn't have witnessed, but I couldn't tell you what it was about. I'd sneaked into a party that was invite-only.'

'Whose party?' asked Isla.

'A masquerade ball on a private yacht anchored on the banks on the River Heart. That day, Dolores had been splashed all over the headlines because she'd been linked romantically to the prince. I was sitting in the pub when Dolores came in. She was livid about the story and wondered how they'd come up with such nonsense. Ada joined us a while later, after her hospital shift.'

'What hospital shift?' queried Florrie.

'Ada was a volunteer at the local hospital. She spent a lot of time chatting with patients who had no family, and would help dish out the meals on the wards.'

Isla put her hand on her heart. 'How lovely. I never knew that.'

'I didn't know that either,' added Florrie. 'How did I not know that?'

'I'm not sure, but she loved her work at the hospital. Ada had a heart of gold and such a caring nature. She would help anyone.'

'So true. I only recently discovered that she never charged anyone who lived in the village for funeral flowers,' added Florrie.

'That's because they're dead,' chuckled Martha, giving her a playful nudge of her elbow.

'Martha!'

'I'm only joking. Ada didn't charge because she didn't want to cause any extra stress for the families of the deceased.

Anyway, I remember Ada looked a little worried. She asked Dolores for a private word and they went outside. I didn't mind, in fact at the time I didn't think anything of it. I finished my drink and picked up the newspaper. Underneath was an invitation to the ball that night and curiosity got the better of me.'

'Gran! You didn't steal Dolores's invitation, did you?'

'I did. I wanted to go to the party and it wasn't as though anyone would recognise me, as I'd be wearing a mask and a costume. I'm not proud of it, but I had a golden ticket in my grasp and I didn't want to miss my chance. You should have seen the inside of that yacht. Everything was gold-plated, the champagne flowed and I've never tasted food like it. Anyway, cutting a long story short, just before midnight, when we had to reveal our identities and the masks would come off, I slipped off the yacht and took a breather on the rocks by The Little Blue Boathouse. I heard raised voices so I sneaked to take a look. No one saw me, but I saw them.'

'Who?'

'Dolores, Ada and Edward Houston.'

'What were they arguing about?'

'That I don't know. But Edward was clearly in turmoil, begging them for something. I slipped away, not wanting to be seen. All I know is that Dolores and Ada never had a good word to say about that man after that. They avoided him at all costs and snubbed him whenever they were in his company. In fact, they never spoke to him again.'

'Really? That is interesting . . . and they never mentioned to you what went on that night?' probed Florrie.

Martha shook her head. 'Nothing, but I've known Ada and Dolores a very long time and they've never snubbed anyone before or since. They're kind, genuine people. Whatever went on, it was big, and it's never been resolved.'

'Why did you never ask Dolores and Ada what went on that night?' asked Isla.

'Because if they wanted me to know they would have told me.'

'Do you think that if you asked Dolores now, she would tell you?'

'No. If she hasn't mentioned it to me in all these years, it's for one of two reasons.'

'Which are?'

'Firstly, that there's nothing much to tell or secondly, there's a huge secret with consequences.'

'And which do you honestly think it is?' asked Florrie.

'The latter,' replied Martha.

Florrie poured tea. 'All this is very interesting. I wish I could get to the bottom of it.'

'I don't think there is much chance of that,' admitted Martha.

'On a brighter note,' added Isla as she pointed to the TV on the wall, 'Gran recorded your TV debut so you can watch it back. Honestly, you were brilliant.'

'I'm not sure I want to watch myself.'

'You have to!' Isla picked up the remote control. 'Are you ready?'

The familiar image of the TV studio flashed up on the screen and Florrie realised it looked larger than in real life.

'Oh my, it's so surreal,' Florrie said as the camera flashed to her own face. 'It's so strange. Look at my hair and make-up! It looks fantastic!' She laughed, swishing her hair from side to side. 'But do I actually sound like that? I'm not sure I like my voice.'

'No one likes their own voice,' chipped in Martha. 'I'll go and cover the van until closing. Sales were a little slow this morning but I think that's just because everyone was watching you on TV.'

'There was a crowd gathered at the TV studio gates. I couldn't quite believe they had made a special trip to try and get a glimpse of me!'

'Famous you are. Everyone loves you and that van,' replied Martha before disappearing outside.

While she tucked into her sandwich, Florrie watched the rest of the interview.

'Ada would have been so proud of you.'

'Let's just hope it's enough and we can stop the planning permission from being approved.'

As soon as Florrie's appearance came to an end, Isla switched off the TV.

'I'll take a look at your socials now and see what the response is to your news.' Isla looked down at her phone just as Martha appeared at the door.

'Have you run out of flowers already?' asked Florrie, concerned by the look on Martha's face.

'Not quite,' she replied. 'I think you need to come and look at this.'

'What is it?' asked Isla, but Martha was already out the door.

'Gran looked quite serious.'

Florrie pushed her chair back. 'We'd better do as she says then and take a look.'

Hurrying after Martha they stopped short at the gate of the cottage.

'Oh my gosh.' Florrie looked at Isla then back at Martha, who was standing on the other side of the gate in front of a sea of people holding placards.

'Save The Vintage Flower Van,' they chanted. 'Save Rose Cottage Gardens.'

Florrie leaned towards Martha. 'Who are these people?'

'Environmentalists. They're a local group from Glensheil. They advocate for the protection of the environment and don't agree with harmful human activity – and by that I mean they don't agree with W. Houston Property Developers proposing to destroy the gardens. They visit Flowers in Bloom every year and couldn't believe the sad news you shared in your interview this morning.'

'Wow! I'm not sure what to do or say. This is a good thing, isn't it?'

'It's always good to have support, and these people are very influential when it comes to spreading the word. They have a huge success rate and a track record of saving land from building work.'

'And who is this?' Florrie pointed to a large van with blacked-out windows that had just turned into the top of the road.

They stayed where they were and watched as the van pulled up opposite the cottage. The driver cut the engine and a man jumped out of the passenger side, followed by the driver, who slid open the side door of the van and soon had a microphone in his hand.

'They're reporters,' whispered Isla, watching as one of them balanced a camera on his shoulder. 'It's TV News.'

Florrie's heart began to pound. Aidy was right, the media attention was escalating just as he'd anticipated! Everyone wanted a piece of her. She quickly turned towards Isla and grimaced.

'What are you doing?' asked Isla, looking confused.

'Check my teeth. Do I have chocolate brownie or any of my sandwich stuck anywhere?'

'All clear,' stated Isla with a chuckle.

'Florrie, can we have a moment of your time? I'm Ollie, from BBC Scotland News. We've seen your interview this morning and would like to chat with you if possible, and take a look around the gardens. Would that be okay?'

Florrie nodded. 'Yes, of course.'

'Great. Could we position you inside The Vintage Flower Van? It will be the perfect spot. And if we could have the protesters surrounding you?'

'I think you need to get used to this,' whispered Isla, opening the gate to let Florrie pass. Florrie walked with the reporter towards the van whilst Isla and Martha leaned against the garden gate and watched.

Fifteen minutes later they had finished filming. The crew began packing up their equipment, and the protesters with the placards were quietly walking away up the lane.

'How was that? Did you manage to hear much of the interview?' Florrie asked as she joined them again.

'You're on fire and the protesters gave it extra clout,' replied Martha.

Florrie glanced over her shoulder. 'They turned up at just the right time to show their support, didn't they? It was perfect for filming. They've also taken some of their own footage, which they're going to upload on their channels, and next week, once the community has sent in their opposition letters, they will protest outside the planning offices.'

'I've got a good feeling about this. I know it's difficult because you won't be able to live here, but at least we may be able to stop it being demolished,' Isla said kindly.

Florrie looked up at the cottage. 'If the new-builds don't go ahead, who knows what will happen to the cottage? Maybe they'll put it up for sale. If that's the case, I'm going to make sure I'm in a position to buy.'

'There's only one way you're going to make that happen,' replied Martha, 'and that's by selling those flowers!'

She pointed over Florrie's shoulder and Florrie turned to find another queue was forming outside The Vintage Flower Van. 'You're right. I'd best get back to doing what I do best, and that's selling flowers!'

Chapter Eighteen

After a busy day, Florrie was happily sitting in the garden of Rose Cottage with a gin and tonic in her hand. People were due to start arriving for the meeting in the next half an hour and Florrie was fully prepared, with notes and pointers written on her notepad to ensure everything was covered. With the power of social media and her TV appearance, Florrie felt a renewed sense of strength and belief that W. Houston Property Developers were not going to get their way.

She heard a car pull up outside the cottage, and Isla and Martha soon appeared around the corner.

'Rona and Felicity are just coming up the lane, along with Dolores and Hamish. We spotted Andrew and Grace heading this way from Heartcross Castle and Molly and Cam are leading the community from the bottom end of the village. And what a beautiful evening it is,' chirped Martha, in good spirits.

'Isn't it just? Oh, here they are now,' Florrie replied, standing up.

Rona and Felicity arrived carrying trays of refreshments and set them out on the long trestle tables. Felicity filled up the urns with water and placed jars of coffee, teabags, milk and sugar next to the mugs.

'I can't thank you enough,' said Florrie, overwhelmed by the effort they'd put in.

'You're very welcome. Look at this place, it feels like we're attending a garden party,' said Felicity, staring at the beauty that surrounded her.

'No one is going to destroy all this hard work,' declared Rona. 'Not on our watch.'

'You were marvellous on the show this morning and even made the six o'clock news too,' enthused Felicity.

'Ooh, I didn't see that,' said Florrie. 'I'm sure it'll be repeated later.'

'The nation has fallen in love with your great-grandfather's story and The Vintage Flower Van.' Rona smiled at her warmly. 'Everyone's arriving. Come on, let's grab some refreshments and sit down on a blanket.'

Florrie began to welcome her friends. Molly and Cam followed Dolores and Hamish along with Ben and Katie from Peony Practice, Allie and Rory from the Clover Cottage estate and Jinny and Gabe from Bumblebee Cottage. Earlier in the day, Florrie had spoken briefly with Dolores and they'd agreed she would share her birthday plans during the meeting tonight.

'I'm actually beginning to feel nervous now,' Florrie said, turning towards Isla.

'There's no need for that! Everyone knows why they're here and they're happy to help in any way they can.'

It wasn't long before everyone was settled on the picnic blankets and their attention was focused on Florrie.

'Thank you all for coming, and thank you to Rona and Felicity at Bonnie's Teashop, who have, as usual, pulled out all the stops and made sure we'll never go hungry. Thank you also to Flynn for providing the blankets. Now, we all know why we're here.' Florrie swooped her arm towards the stunning gardens around them. Suddenly feeling a tad emotional, she took a deep breath, thankful she was surrounded by her friends. She knew they would lift her up the second she started talking. 'It's been a little difficult since Ada's passing, and even more so when I discovered the cottage was rented and that W. Houston Property Developers plan to destroy everything Ada created here. She lives on in these flowers and I know I would find comfort watching them grow and bloom in the coming days, months and years, so I'm asking for your help. If we all oppose this development, or sign a petition, or make a fuss on social media – basically do anything and everything to try and put a spanner in the works – I really think we have a chance of saving Ada's legacy. Will you all join me?'

There was murmured agreement from the crowd and heads were being vigorously nodded.

'I'll get a petition circulated,' shouted Hamish. 'I can put it on the counter in the village shop.'

'Perfect,' replied Florrie.

'In fact, we can have several around the village. The Little Blue Boathouse is packed with tourists every day. We can even put one on the water taxis.' Bea looked at Roman, who agreed with a nod.

'One at The Lake House, too, and Starcross Manor,' added Flynn.

'We can also have one at the B&B,' suggested Julia.

'And we can have one at the vet's surgery,' chipped in Molly. Rory and Allie nodded their agreement.

'And I think you can safely count on each of us to write a letter to the council,' added Flynn. 'Probably more than one in some cases.'

Everyone agreed and a timescale was agreed to ensure that the letters would be written and posted by the end of the week.

'You may have also heard that The Vintage Flower Van also belongs to W. Houston Property Developers and will therefore be forced to cease trading at the end of the month.' Florrie swallowed. 'Again, another blow. This has been Aunt Ada's business for decades. I know most of you are aware but just so we're all on the same page, I recently started up several social media accounts for The Vintage Flower Van, and the followers and interaction they've accrued have been mind-blowing. My TV appearance this morning, has already brought even more attention to the van's plight. In short, we're making progress and I'm going to keep on creating havoc on social media in the hope that W. Houston Property Developers will change their minds. Anything you can do to support and amplify those efforts would be so appreciated. I'm not going to give up on this place or The Vintage Flower Van easily.'

Everyone cheered.

'Rose Cottage Gardens will be opening for one last time under my watch during this year's Flowers in Bloom. It meant a lot to Aunt Ada and she took great pleasure in showing you all what she was capable of achieving.' Florrie smiled. 'Tickets go on sale tomorrow, but this year I'm giving everyone gathered here this evening the first opportunity to purchase them – for two special reasons.'

Florrie took a sip of her drink, before turning back towards everyone. 'Now, what I'm about to share with you is for community ears only. Do not talk about this in a public place, and definitely do not share it on social media.'

'Ooh, this sounds exciting, very cloak and dagger. I love a secret,' remarked Julia, who was sitting at the front next to Flynn.

'W. Houston Property Developers has unknowingly booked their property inspection for the same day as Flowers in Bloom...'

There was chatter all around.

'...And I want them to be met with the whole of Heartcross, out in force. The second special reason is that this year Rose Cottage will have a little extra sparkle on the day – something that will have the media out in force and will catapult Rose Cottage Gardens and the plight of The Vintage Flower Van worldwide ... and Dolores is going to share with us exactly what that sparkle will be.'

Dolores stood up and walked towards Florrie with a heart-warming smile.

Everyone in the garden was silent, all eyes were on Dolores in eager expectation.

'Heartcross is just the best community and has been my safe haven for many, many years. My choice of career threw me into worldwide fame and over the years I've travelled and lived in many different countries but Heartcross has always been my home. Ada was one of my best friends – a loyal, genuine, honest friend, who often helped me to throw the paparazzi in a different direction when I wanted to escape unnoticed. Along with Martha and Bonnie, of course.' Dolores smiled at Rona and Martha. 'Which brings me to why I'm standing here. As I approach my one hundredth birthday the world press has already started to go mad, wanting to know what I'll be doing and how I'll be spending it. Between you and me, it was going to be a quiet one with Hamish and my friends in the pub, but after hearing what's happening here, I want to help.' Dolores took a breath and shot a brief look at Florrie.

'Each and every one of you sitting in front of me is invited to a special gig for my one hundredth birthday celebration, which will take place here in the Rose Cottage Gardens, in memory of Ada. Tickets will be selling fast due to Florrie's current press profile and her social media, so you all need to get your tickets soon. Who wants to come to a party?'

Everyone stood up and began clapping. Dolores hugged Florrie. 'We've got this,' she whispered.

'I take it that's a "yes" from everyone?' Dolores asked with a laugh as she turned back to the crowd. 'But...' She waved her arms in the air to quiet everyone down. 'This needs to stay between us for now. The press can't find out until the very last minute. Now, to make sure you all have a ticket' – she gestured to Hamish to come and join her – 'Hamish has got them here. I've paid for each and every one of them, and all the money will be donated to a charity of my and Ada's choosing, because I know exactly which one she would choose. But for now I'm going to keep that under wraps.'

As Hamish began to hand out tickets to everyone at the meeting, Florrie turned towards Dolores. 'Thank you for all this.'

'You don't need to thank me, I'd do anything for Ada,' she said as she touched Florrie's arm and gave a supportive squeeze. She walked off towards Martha, who handed her a cup of tea.

Isla joined Florrie, who was still looking in Dolores's direction. 'I'd love to take a trip to the past and see how life was when they were all young.'

'Wouldn't that be fun.'

Florrie smiled at Flynn, who was heading in their direction.

'Flowers in Bloom, Dolores's birthday party and inspection day all in one? The publicity is going to be huge! I really wouldn't like to be in the shoes of whoever is representing W. Houston Property Developers that day.'

'I wonder who they might send?' Isla pondered.

Florrie gave a small laugh and gave voice to something she'd been quietly wondering about for a few days now. 'I'm actually thinking it could possibly be Tom Houston. After all, he's in the village and staying at Starcross Manor.'

'Starcross Manor?' questioned Flynn.

'Yes, he's here for the charity event. He's representing the William Houston Foundation. It was on the email you sent over.'

Flynn took out his phone and swiped the screen, read something, and looked back at Florrie. 'I didn't make the connection, probably because the person I've got listed as presenting at the charity event is Sophia Henley.'

'Sophia's here, in Heartcross?'

Flynn nodded. 'She will be soon. I believe she's arriving just before the event,' he said, slipping his phone back into his pocket. 'I don't think the charity is linked to what's happening here, so don't worry about any potential crossover.'

'Mmm.' Isla glanced around at the community members

currently gathered in the garden. 'I'm not sure that the people of Heartcross will see it that way.'

'We need to make sure that the villagers realise that the charity and property business are separate,' Flynn continued. 'The charity is a fantastic charity supporting the NHS and I'm happy to support them alongside the other winners.'

'Unlike the property business, they are certainly not going about it the right way,' cut in Florrie.

'Morally, no, but from a business standpoint...' Flynn looked around the gardens. 'There's no denying that this is an easy source of profit for the company and that whatever they build here will be in high demand, as houses in Heartcross rarely come up for sale. I'm not opposed to development in the area, but not here. This place is just too beautiful to destroy.' Flynn bade them farewell before walking off to chat with Dolores.

'How do you feel about Sophia being in the village at some point?' Isla asked tentatively.

'I really don't know. She probably never knew that he spent two weeks with me before he spent the summer with her, or that for years I've blamed her just as much as I blamed Tom for my broken heart. It's probably best not to dwell on it. No, I've got to stay focused on saving these gardens and The Vintage Flower Van.'

'We will.' Isla linked her arm through Florrie's as Hamish walked towards them. 'Here you go, the last two community tickets for Flowers in Bloom.' He handed one to each of them. 'And here are the rest of the tickets that can be sold outside the community. You can drop off the takings to me at the end of each day and I can lock the money in the safe. Once they're all sold, we can transfer the money to Mum's chosen charity.'

'Perfect, thanks, Hamish. I can't believe your mum is going to be one hundred.'

'I can't believe all the energy she still has! I'm secretly pleased she's chosen to have her birthday here, surrounded by all her family and friends. We know how much she loves Heartcross but she also still loves performing, and this allows her to combine the two.'

'I've got a feeling it's going to be a day to remember,' said Isla.

'Without a doubt! We'll have never seen a frenzy quite like it when the press discovers where the celebrations are being held.'

'Or the general public who purchase a ticket for Flowers in Bloom; they won't believe it ether,' added Florrie.

'It'll definitely be a day to remember, that's for sure,' Hamish said happily.

Chapter Nineteen

T wo days after the successful community meeting, Florrie greeted the first customer of the day with a huge smile.

Anticipating a busy day ahead, she'd woken an hour earlier than usual, packed the buckets with flowers and then filmed a new reel, which she'd uploaded immediately. The post was simple, the video showing her standing on the steps of The Vintage Flower Van holding up a handful of tickets for Flowers in Bloom and giving all the details of where and how they could be purchased.

'Even though the village of Heartcross wishes all of you could come, there are only a very limited number of tickets so you'll need to be quick. The Vintage Flower Van and I are looking forward to meeting you all!'

The notifications were already pinging and Florrie smiled to herself. People who got their hands on a ticket would have no clue they were going to witness one of the greatest icons of all time performing on her birthday. Receiving a text from Martha, she read it quickly.

Don't forget it's Friday! And in other news, Jinny has decided not to enter Bumblebee Cottage in Flowers in Bloom and likewise Grace won't be entering Heartcross Castle. The community have decided that all focus should be on Rose Cottage and so no other gardens will be entered this year.

Florrie was touched that the other gardeners in the village were willing to sit out this year in order to allow the Rose Cottage Gardens to take centre stage. She could see their thinking behind the decision though, and as she read through the community chat WhatsApp messages she was buoyed by everyone's determination to put pressure on W. Houston Property Developers by making sure all emphasis was on Rose Cottage and The Vintage Flower Van.

Florrie quickly replied to Martha.

Everyone is so lovely! And not to worry, I've not forgotten it's Friday. I'm heading to the cemetery now before I open up the van.

It was a beautiful day. The sky was clear and blue with hardly a cloud to be seen. After making up the bouquet Florrie jumped into her van and made her way up the crest of the hill towards the impressive wrought-iron gates of the cemetery. The churchyard was awash with colour, the lawns had been recently cut and the hedgerows trimmed. Florrie glanced around the graveyard. It was deserted except for a woman on the far path, her tear-stained face saying it all. Florrie gave her a warm, gentle smile, knowing the pain she was likely going through.

After placing the bouquet on her great-grandmother's grave, Florrie laid a different bunch of flowers on Great-Aunt Ada's grave. 'You aren't going to believe what is going on here, Ada. Dolores is performing at Rose Cottage on her one hundredth birthday, and she's doing it for you.' Florrie took a breath. 'I miss you, Aunt Ada. Everything is a bit of a mess since…' She swallowed and took a moment before continuing. 'Anyway, I'll be back next week, if not sooner, but I have to go and open the flower van now.' Taking another deep breath, she followed the tree-lined path back towards where she'd parked Rose.

Florrie drove back to Rose Cottage to discover a queue of customers already stretching along the lane towards The Vintage Flower Van. As soon as she opened up the hatch, the blooms were flying from the buckets. Florrie posed for countless photos and the tickets were selling fast. By her reckoning, they would be sold out within the first forty-eight hours, or perhaps even less!

'Thank you so much, Florrie. Please could I grab a photograph?' A customer who'd just bought a bunch of tulips and a ticket waggled her phone in the air.

'Of course.'

'I love your TikToks and your great-grandfather's story,' she enthused as Florrie stepped from the van and joined the girl. She held up the phone and as Florrie smiled at the camera, she noticed a familiar figure standing behind them in the queue – Tom.

Florrie's heart began to race and she briefly wondered if he was here because he'd got wind of her TV interview or the community meeting. The girl snapped a couple more photos before Florrie returned to the counter.

Her heart was pounding as Tom stepped forward. 'I was out for a walk and wondered where everyone was going so I followed the crowd.'

His tone was friendly and Florrie didn't sense he was here for any reason other than the one he'd given.

'What a beautiful flower van.'

Florrie narrowed her eyes in confusion. She wasn't sure whether he was genuinely oblivious to what was going on or was simply choosing not to acknowledge it. 'Business is blooming, isn't it?' He swiftly glanced back over his shoulder at the queue. 'I remember all those years ago when that lecturer questioned you about your business model. If only he could see you now.'

'If only,' she replied, knowing there was a fair chance that their former professor might have seen and recognised her in the news in the past couple of days. Feeling nervous, she tried to keep her voice as calm as possible. 'Is there anything I can get you today? I don't mean to rush you but I do have people waiting.'

'Flowers,' he replied. 'I'd like a bunch of flowers.'

'Then it seems you've come to the right place.' She gestured towards the different varieties displayed in the buckets that stood on the grass in front of the van.

Tom glanced at the buckets. 'Those ones,' he replied, with a glint in his eye.

Florrie swallowed as she stared at the blooms he'd pointed to – red tulips. He knew they were her favourite flowers.

Her heart began to race and she hoped he couldn't tell by the look on her face that she was slightly flustered. Had he chosen those flowers to see how she reacted?

'Good choice,' she replied, sounding a lot calmer than she felt. 'She must be a lucky lady.'

'She is,' replied Tom.

Trying to act as normally as possible she looked away, knowing she had blushed slightly.

'How many would you like?'

'As many as you think would make a beautiful bouquet.'

Wanting to send him on his way as quickly as possible, Florrie set to work. Fourteen stems were gathered and she paired the tulips with roses, skimmia sprigs and mini pitto, which lent a delicate texture to the arrangement. She finished it off with eucalyptus foliage to give it a fresh, woodsy scent.

'That'll be twenty-five pounds please. Card or cash?'

'They're breathtaking.'

He flashed her a warm smile and his eyes skimmed her face briefly, the intensity of his gaze causing her to tingle. From where she was standing, she could feel the raw chemistry between them, and her heart was beating wildly.

'Card,' he replied, taking a card from his wallet and handing it over. 'And the tickets that everyone in the queue before me was buying? What are they for?'

'Heartcross's annual open garden day, Flowers in Bloom.'

She handed one to him and he scrutinised it for a second.

'Then I'll take one of these, too.'

'One ticket or two?' asked Florrie, with Sophia in the back of her mind.

'One,' he replied.

Florrie nodded. As she handed Tom back his debit card, she was close enough to take in his aroma and briefly closed her eyes. When she opened them, he had leaned towards her. 'I know this isn't the right time, but can we talk, clear the air?'

She hesitated. 'We can do that when you decide to be truthful with me.' She pointed to the flowers. 'Make sure whoever you give those to puts a two pence coin in the bottom of the vase.'

He looked at her, puzzled.

'Dropping a copper coin into the water keeps your tulips from drooping, so they last longer.'

'Okay,' he replied doubtfully.

'Trust me,' she replied, watching him walk away.

Florrie began serving the next customer but glanced back at Tom just as he reached the top of the lane. He looked back over his shoulder, catching her eye as he answered his phone. Still watching him, Florrie thought the conversation looked heated and he seemed to be speaking faster and faster, waving his free hand in the air, even though he was still holding the bouquet. Even from that distance, it was clear the conversation had riled him. Finally, he hung up and stuffed the phone back into his pocket, then for a brief second stared at Florrie. He seemed to be in turmoil, his face like thunder as he turned and walked away and finally disappeared from sight.

There was something about the way he'd stared at her that had unnerved Florrie. She didn't know why but her gut feeling was telling her that that phone call had had something to do with her. All she could do for now though was push it out of her mind, so she put on a smile and served the next customers.

As soon as the queue began to dwindle, Florrie rang Isla. The second she answered, Florrie announced, 'My gut is telling me that Tom may know about our campaign to save The Vintage Flower Van. He's been to the van this morning and bought flowers and a ticket for Flowers in Bloom, and he asked if we could talk.'

'He doesn't need a ticket.' Isla gave a chuckle.

'Don't joke! I have a bad feeling and I don't know why.'

'I wonder if it has anything to do with the local protesters outside the town hall today. Aidy made sure that they were featured on the news.'

'I don't know anything about that. I've been run off my feet ever since opening the van this morning. I've not had time to check anything.'

'Midday there was a large group of environmental protesters chanting outside the town hall. They had placards and were voicing their opposition to the plans for the demolition of the gardens at Rose Cottage. I'll send you the clip from the news.'

Isla hung up and as soon as the link pinged through Florrie clicked on it. She quickly counted at least thirty protesters. According to the accompanying news report they'd positioned themselves from the start of the work day to ensure maximum visible impact to the staff at the town hall.

As soon as the footage finished, she rang Isla back. 'There's no way he can't know after that.'

'Of course he'll know, the company is in his hands now. So, let's see what his next move will be.'

Florrie had an uneasy feeling in the pit of her stomach but all she could do was wait to see what impact, if any, the last couple of days would have on the planning application. Because by her reckoning the opposition letters would be starting to roll in at the council office any time now.

Chapter Twenty

It was late afternoon and after a busy day Florrie was cleaning out The Vintage Flower Van. She was exhausted yet happy, as today's flowers had sold out in record time and the Flowers in Bloom tickets had sold like hot cakes. As she was collecting the aluminium buckets and lining them up at the side of the cottage, Florrie heard a car pull up. She turned to see who it was and waved at Aidy as he climbed out of his car and began walking towards her.

'Aidy! I've never seen anything like today. All the flowers were sold out just after lunch yet still people queued in their droves just for a Flowers in Bloom ticket. We've already sold hundreds! Isn't it marvellous?'

Aidy smiled supportively but there was something uneasy about his countenance.

Florrie noticed he had his phone in his hand. 'What brings you to Rose Cottage? Is this about the protesters?'

'Not quite.'

Immediately, she got that sinking feeling in her stomach

once more.

He handed her the phone and she saw that a rival newspaper's website was showing on the screen. 'You need to read this.'

Florrie scrolled through to the article and couldn't believe her eyes when she read the bold headline '*University Friends in Tug-of-war Over Business That Has Traded for Sixty Years*'. Underneath were two photographs, one of Tom sitting on his father's yacht drinking champagne and one of herself serving a long line of customers outside The Vintage Flower Van.

'Why didn't you tell me that you and Tom Houston knew each other? Did you not think that was an important piece of information?' asked Aidy.

Florrie could sense Aidy was a little miffed that he'd been scooped by a rival reporter.

'I didn't think it was that important, to be honest. It was years ago that we knew one another and I wouldn't say we were friends exactly. Also, we haven't seen each other since, well … until he turned up in Heartcross. Apparently, his grandfather's charity is being featured at Flynn's charity event up at Starcross Manor.'

Florrie turned back to the phone and kept reading. The article hadn't left any stone unturned. Tom's professional reputation and moral standing were being questioned. The article suggested he was hell-bent on destroying her late great-aunt's business and leaving her homeless and penniless. Though some bits were accurate, it wasn't quite the whole truth, as Florrie was the owner of Buttercup Barn and lived in her rented home on Love Heart Lane. But it was the next line that really caught her eye.

When approached, Tom Houston from W. Houston Property

Developers refused to comment for this article.

'In journalistic terms, what does that mean, Aidy?' she asked as she pointed to the sentence.

'That the journalist asked Tom Houston to share his side of the story but he declined.'

Florrie's heart began to race. Tom was definitely fully aware of her campaign now!

'Do *you* have any comment on this?' Aidy asked, his pen poised over his notebook.

Florrie was unsure what to say. What she did know was that she didn't want anyone getting wind of the fact that she and Tom had spent two weeks wrapped up in one another's arms, as that could make a blooming good story considering they were now at loggerheads.

'There's nothing to say.'

'And there is no other link between you two?'

Telling a little white lie she said, 'No,' then quickly tried to change the subject. 'This article certainly puts Tom's company in a not so good light, doesn't it?'

'Yes, it's definitely in your favour. By the way, those appeal letters have started to land in the council offices but we need to keep the pressure on.'

'I think we can rely on Dolores for that.'

Aidy smiled. 'Yes, I've got an article detailing how she's planning to celebrate her centenary ready to run just as soon as she gives us the go-ahead. But my fellow journalists are already getting wind that something big is going to happen, because Dolores's media assistant has started to post cryptic clues on her social media that an announcement is coming. I'm confident that I'm going to be first with the full story though.'

'I'm sorry if you think I was keeping this from you,' Florrie said as she handed his phone back. 'It didn't cross my mind as it just didn't seem important.' It wasn't exactly true. Florrie couldn't shake Tom from her mind these days.

'If anything else comes to light do let me know. W. Houston Property Developers will be well aware of exactly what's going on here now so we'd best prepare ourselves.'

After such an up and down day, Florrie was at a loose end after she cleared away the dishes from dinner and took a walk around the gardens. The freshly mowed grass had an earthy, slightly sweet aroma, and the stripes and chequerboard patterns were a piece of horticultural art. Hector, the head gardener up at Heartcross Castle, had kindly offered his services to help get the gardens into tip-top condition before Flowers in Bloom.

Pausing and standing next to the fountain, Florrie stared at the coins scattered in the water. When she was a little girl, she'd walk down the garden with Aunt Ada every Friday night after school and throw in a coin and make a wish. All those coins still lay there, a constant reminder of those special times. Florrie leaned over the shallow water and lifted out a coin. Grasping it in her fist, she looked up at the sky and made a wish. Then she headed back indoors.

In the hallway were the cardboard boxes that Flynn had dropped off, still stacked up where he'd left them. Knowing she had to start packing up Aunt Ada's belongings, she made a cup of tea then grabbed a couple of binbags. First she pulled out a drawer from the dresser in the kitchen and placed it on the table. It was one of those drawers that housed anything and everything: old pens, balls of Blu-Tack, lots of faded receipts and a pile of bank statements. Florrie put those to one side and emptied the rest of the drawer into the bin bag.

The next drawer was full of placemats that only came out at Christmas and old takeaway menus. She put the placemats in a cardboard box, then began to make up another box, of things that could be dropped off at the local charity shop. She felt a little guilty at trespassing in Aunt Ada's personal life but she knew it had to be done and it wasn't long before the boxes were stacking up. Old plates and mugs had been packed for storage, and any pots and pans that hadn't been used in years, or odd glasses that had once belonged to a set, were put aside for the charity shop.

The pantry was packed with jars and spices that had been out of date for years. Florrie began to sort through them, separating those that were still good. She smiled. Aunt Ada had never believed in best-before dates, relying on what she'd called 'the sniff method'. She'd say that if it smelled all right then it was okay to use.

It didn't take long to clear the shelves and wipe them down. Florrie stopped to take a breather and glanced up at the clock. The time had flown by, and she was surprised to realise she'd been packing up and clearing out the kitchen for over two hours. She was just about to close the pantry door when she noticed what looked like a wicker hamper at the back of the top shelf. Standing on a chair, she retrieved it and placed it on the kitchen table. In all the years she'd lived here she couldn't recall ever seeing this box before. Lifting the lid, she found it was full of paperwork, and lying on top were newspaper cuttings and a lanyard. Turning the lanyard over, she saw it bore Aunt Ada's name along with the logo and address of Glensheil Hospital. Placing the lanyard on the table, Florrie took out a bundle of newspaper articles and photographs held together with string. Untying the knot, she found they were all clearly labelled. Every article was about Ada, highlighting all the awards and gardening competitions she'd won over the years, including Flowers in Bloom. Among them was the article and photograph that Aidy had shared with Florrie about The Vintage Flower Van opening for business. Florrie spread the articles out over the table. In each photograph Ada was holding a medal or a trophy and wearing a radiant smile. Florrie felt proud of her aunt and her achievements.

The next item in the box was a certificate in a clear plastic wallet along with another newspaper article. The headline read, *'Local Volunteer Wins Kindness Award'*.

Aunt Ada looked so young in the photograph. She was sitting on a hospital bed next to a patient. The article said that she had been nominated for a regional award by the patients at Glensheil Hospital for her kindness. Ada gave up ten hours of her own time every week to volunteer at the hospital, helping to serve the meals and chatting to patients to keep their spirits high. The photograph showed her wearing a medal around her neck, as well as the lanyard that was in the box. Florrie took a closer look at the lanyard and realised Aunt Ada must have been a volunteer before she was married, as her maiden name was printed on it, and in the photograph she was only wearing an engagement ring. She looked more closely at the caption to the photograph and was surprised to find that Ada's name was followed by that of William Houston. Looking at the date of the article Florrie realised it had been written a couple of months before William had passed away. She wondered why Aunt Ada had never mentioned her time at the hospital.

Rap, rap, rap.

Florrie looked down the hallway. Someone was standing

outside the front door. As the knocking continued she rushed to answer, calling out, 'I'm coming!'

Opening the door, she discovered an angry-looking Tom on the step. In one hand he was holding a newspaper and in the other the bouquet he'd purchased from The Vintage Flower Van earlier that day.

'I'm sorry but the flowers are non-refundable.'

'What the hell are you playing at?' Tom demanded.

'I'm a florist, I sell flowers for a living, that's what I do,' she replied facetiously, knowing that's not what he meant at all.

Tom raised his eyebrows and looked like he was about to burst a blood vessel. '*This* is what I'm talking about.' He flapped the newspaper in the air.

'All I'm doing is telling the truth.'

'You're spreading rumours, tarnishing my reputation—'

'I don't think you need much help with that,' cut in Florrie.

'Have you lost your mind?' He stared at her, his eyes darkening. 'Do you know what's happened to me this afternoon? I've been bombarded by press. Hordes of them were waiting up at Starcross Manor wanting to know my take on this story. I didn't have a clue what story they were talking about and so when they mentioned your name, I Googled and discovered just what's been going on behind my back. I found your social media appeals and apparently, you've even been on TV to garner public sympathy!'

'I didn't mention anyone's name when I was on TV.'

'It doesn't take long for journalists to dig out the details.'

'It's not my fault you've come here with an agenda to make money, without a thought of what the hell you're doing to other people and their memories.'

Tom looked puzzled. He stared at her.

Florrie launched her attack. 'Do you not think it's been hard enough to deal with my aunt Ada's passing, without the likes of you and your company serving me an eviction notice only days after she died? What about the fact that you didn't even give me an opportunity to argue my case? I guess you were too busy rushing to submit your application for planning permission to demolish the land and the cottage, just to make more money by building houses that don't even fit in with the character of Heartcross.' She took a breath. Tom was looking at the name of the cottage on the oak sign beside the door. 'It was a shock to find out that the cottage was rented, but then, as if that wasn't a big enough kick in the teeth, you take away a business that has been trading for over sixty years! What the hell is W. Houston Property Developers going to do with a vintage flower van? I promised Aunt Ada that her legacy would carry on and you' – Florrie pointed at him and Tom took a step back, but his eyes didn't leave hers – 'and you…' Her voice faltered. She briefly closed her eyes and lowered her voice. 'The gardens of this cottage are a gorgeous place of beauty that has taken decades to mature and cultivate. Those gardens have won awards and you're going to level them without a second thought. Shame on you.'

She took a deep breath, Tom looked a little stunned and had turned pale.

'It's not my intention to take anyone's home from them … or their business.'

'Well, you would say that, wouldn't you. The likes of you are always the same.'

'Florrie, I don't know anything about this.'

'You own the company that's causing all the upset. How do you not know?'

'You've had ample opportunity to come and have a conversation with me about all this, but instead you've decided to embroil me in a public fight. That might be your style but it certainly isn't mine,' Tom said, not answering her question. He exhaled. 'But for the record, and I'll say it again, I'm not trying to take away a business or leave you destitute and I've got no clue what you're talking about regarding plans to flatten the grounds.'

Leaving him on the doorstep, Florrie returned to the kitchen and picked up the letters from W. Houston Property Developers before returning to the front door and thrusting them against his chest. 'That's your logo on the letters, isn't it? And this one even has your signature on it.' She didn't hold back. She couldn't. Not now that the floodgates had been opened. 'I'm not sure how you can stand on my doorstep and even try to defend yourself.'

Tom took the letter she'd pointed to and quickly scanned it. He looked up at Florrie. 'You should have come to talk to me.'

'It's easy for you to say that now. You just don't want to have to deal with the aftermath of what you've done.'

'What about the aftermath of *your* actions?' he countered. 'Do you know what's happened to me today?'

Florrie didn't answer.

Tom's eyes were wide. 'Hamish wouldn't serve me in the shop, Rona and Felicity wouldn't serve me in the teashop. Some people have ignored me when I've walked past. Others began whispering and shooting me dirty looks. I thought I was going bonkers and only now am I finding out it's all because of this. But the worst part? I'm here in Heartcross to champion my grandfather's charity on the anniversary of his death, and now, thanks to the media circus going on up at Starcross

Manor, businesses that I've networked with and arranged meetings with to enhance the profile of his charity have cancelled on me. This was my grandfather's pet project and it has nothing to do with the property business. The foundation does really good work and makes a difference in people's lives – and now, because of you, no one wants to deal with me. The foundation desperately needed the exposure, not to mention the investment we were set to secure to build a unit that could help spinal cord injury survivors to walk again.'

Tom was visibly upset and Florrie immediately felt guilty. She hadn't thought about the possibility that her fight against the property business could affect the foundation. But she should have – the community of Heartcross were an unbreakable force that stuck together. Nevertheless, she didn't want any charity to miss out on vitally needed money. That really hadn't been her intention.

'Things are complicated at the moment – very complicated – and creating a false narrative in a newspaper isn't going to help. Please, promise me there will be no more talking to the media,' he pressed. His eyes glistened with urgency in the late afternoon sun.

'It's not a false narrative. It's actually happening to me.'

'Please just trust me.'

'Trust you?' Florrie shook her head.

Thrusting the bunch of tulips towards Florrie, he said, 'How did I get you so wrong?'

'Ditto,' she replied without hesitation, her hands firmly at her side.

Realising she wasn't going to take the bouquet, Tom lowered it, turned and walked down the path. He shut the gate behind him and didn't look back.

Chapter Twenty-One

F lorrie shut the front door. Her heart was beating fast. Frustrated and emotional, she didn't know what to think. None of it made any sense to her. She had every right to talk to the media if she wanted to.

Exhaling, she looked around her. The kitchen was in a mess, boxes scattered everywhere, and with Tom very much on her mind she began to tape them up, labelling the ones she was going to store in the barn and the others that she would drop at the charity shop sometime soon.

An hour later, Florrie was curled up in bed and still unable to get the altercation with Tom out of her head. She played the conversation over and over again in her mind and didn't know what to do. Maybe she should have spoken to him first before talking to the press, but there was nothing she could do about that now. She'd checked her social media on her phone, and the reel she'd posted today was still seeing a lot of engagement and bringing new followers to her account.

Texting Isla, even though she knew it was late, she told her she'd made a start on packing up Aunt Ada's belongings and had found a number of newspaper articles from the past. She didn't mention Tom turning up at the cottage, deciding she'd tell her that face to face. Whilst waiting for Isla to reply, Florrie Googled the history of Heartcross, wondering if anything about Aunt Ada's kindness award would come up. Immediately, she found numerous articles and photographs from the past which she had already seen before. Top of the search list were reports and photos of the worst winter in the history of Heartcross, when the bridge between the village and Glensheil had collapsed in a storm, leaving Heartcross cut off from the town. The community had worked together to look after each other during that difficult time. Felicity had almost immediately begun an online campaign to raise money to build a new bridge, and the power of social media had increased awareness of a situation that Heartcross hadn't ever imagined it would find itself in.

The internet was full of village history. There were old photographs of times gone by – Bonnie when she first opened the teashop at the foot of Heartcross Mountain, men on horseback in top hats on the cart track that ran over the bridge and passed Heartcross Castle, Hamish's village shop and the Grouse and Haggis, neither of which had changed a bit in decades. There were photos of bands that had played at the bandstand in Primrose Park, and of women wearing Victorian dress with bonnets, standing with parasols outside The Old Bakehouse. Florrie Googled 'The Vintage Flower Van, Heartcross' and straightaway a photo came up of Ada, along with an article that had featured in a national magazine. Aunt Ada's flower van had been declared the place to buy the best blooms in the Scottish Highlands. The feature had run in some newspapers, too.

'From Volunteer Hospital Carer to Award Winning Florist' read one bold headline. She smiled at the next photo, which was exactly the same as the one on the shelf across the room from where she sat. It showed Ada and Ewart standing at the garden gate outside Rose Cottage. Moving her laptop to one side, Florrie slid out of bed and picked up the photograph, then slipped back under the duvet. She felt emotional looking at it. They were just starting out their life together, the smiles on their faces saying it all. Anyone could see how in love they were. A date was written in pencil in one corner of the photograph – it was not long after the newspaper article that had reported Ada winning the kindness award. Placing the framed photograph on her bedside table, Florrie Googled 'Rose Cottage'. She laughed when the first image appeared on the screen. Ada, looking as if she was in her early twenties, was standing in front of The Vintage Flower Van, which was presented beautifully with a wide variety of flowers. She was standing next to a wheelbarrow, the same one she had often used to wheel the flowers from the back garden to the van. Her hair was tied up in a messy bun with flowers sticking out at every angle, and on the top of her head was her favourite pet chicken, Henrietta, who used to follow Aunt Ada everywhere and even joined them for dinner in the kitchen. Aunt Ada had told Florrie all about this photo. A gardening magazine had spent the morning at the cottage and Ada had talked them through her gardening tips for the summer. During the photo shoot Henrietta had stolen the show and she'd managed to photobomb every single shot. The photo was captioned 'Loving the Good Life'.

It was great to take a trip down memory lane. Growing up, Florrie had always realised how popular Aunt Ada was, and even though she'd seen the articles before, she felt proud that Aunt Ada was written about and described as an expert in her field. She must have lost count of all the awards she'd won in her lifetime. Florrie felt honoured to have been taught her own trade by such a wonderful person, so full of knowledge, so passionate about flowers, gardens and wildlife.

Florrie scrolled on to the next page and noticed a very old photo of Rose Cottage, one she hadn't seen before. There was a man standing at the gates she didn't instantly recognise so she zoomed in. Closer inspection set an alarm bell ringing in her head and she quickly clicked back to the photograph of Ada sitting on the hospital bed. She stared at William. It was definitely him in the photograph standing outside Rose Cottage.

Quickly typing 'William Houston', 'Rose Cottage' and 'Heartcross' into the search engine, she held her breath and waited for the results to load. And there it was in black and white: *Property Mogul Purchases the Oldest Cottage in Heartcross.*

Florrie wasn't sure if she was surprised. She'd assumed the cottage had been purchased through the family company at one time or another but according to the internet Rose Cottage was William's home. He was even quoted as saying that he couldn't wait to become part of the community and set up his life in Heartcross.

That confused Florrie.

Florrie Googled 'William Houston's Spouse' and hit enter. It pulled up his Wikipedia page, which said: *Spouse – Rose Houston.* There was no other information available.

Florrie's curiosity about William and the cottage and Ada

and how it all might fit together had increased tenfold since she first opened Google. She checked the time and was disappointed to see that it was too late in the day to ring Martha or Dolores. She couldn't understand why neither of them had ever mentioned that Rose Cottage had been William's family home. And did that mean that Edward had lived here as a child?

Switching off her laptop, she snuggled under the duvet. Her curiosity was unsatisfied but all she could do now was wait until tomorrow and then ask Dolores what she knew.

Chapter Twenty-Two

Florrie woke up to news of Dolores's birthday celebration being splashed all over the Sunday newspapers. Ada had always had her newspaper delivered on a Sunday and it wasn't something Florrie had got round to cancelling, and now she was glad. She picked it up off the mat before making herself a cup of tea. The sun was streaming through the window and she had already decided to embrace the gorgeous morning by taking a walk down by the river before heading over to Foxglove Farm.

Sitting down at the table, she read the front page. '*Global Superstar Dolores Henderson Prepares for Glitzy Party to Celebrate One Hundredth Birthday.*'

Florrie chuckled. The journalists were so far off the mark. As she read on she found they'd hinted at a number of outrageous possibilities, the frontrunner being that Dolores was hiring out a whole island in the Caribbean for her, her family and her showbiz pals. There were also rumours that she might hold a private concert at a royal palace, as Dolores had been a friend of members of the British Royal Family for most of her life. They were clutching at straws, but Florrie knew that now there would be numerous journalists milling around the village trying to break the true story, not knowing that Aidy had already written it and was just waiting for the right time to print it.

After closing the newspaper, Florrie checked her social media accounts. The Vintage Flower Van was still being tagged in many posts every day and the local protesters had created reels of their action outside the planning office. According to the village WhatsApp group, everyone had sent letters opposing the demolition of the gardens, and the petition sitting on Hamish's shop counter now had over a thousand signatures.

Finishing her tea, Florrie thought about Tom's visit last night. She hadn't agreed with him that she wouldn't post any more reels or create further publicity, and there was still a part of her that had wondered if she was being tricked when he'd asked her to trust him. Trust Tom Houston? Not likely! He was probably just trying to get her to back off so the planning permission would sail through, giving him and his company exactly what they wanted.

There were only a handful of unsold tickets left for Flowers in Bloom. Dolores was set to perform, and the whole community would be there in support of Florrie and Ada's legacy. Maybe she didn't have to do anything more.

After a shower, she headed down to the river and The Little Blue Boathouse, which was already busy renting out kayaks and rowing boats to tourists and locals alike. Across the river, she noticed a man in a wetsuit, and she realised she could still pick out Tom, even from a distance. Mother Nature had certainly dealt him a generously fair hand of cards.

He pressed the screen on his watch before he waded into the water and began swimming with the current towards a small sandy bay on the left-hand side of the river. She watched him for a moment then carried on along the river path.

Ten minutes later she was knocking on the door of Foxglove Farm.

'Here she is! I've just been trying to ring you. Drew is going to collect the first of Aunt Ada's boxes and store them in the barn. He could pick them up sometime this afternoon, if you're free?'

'Perfect, thank you.'

Isla opened the door wider. 'You look like you have the weight of the world on your shoulders. Was it difficult beginning to sort out Aunt Ada's stuff? I'd have come and helped, you know.'

'It was, but in a way it was quite comforting, too,' replied Florrie, taking off her jacket and slipping it over the back of the kitchen chair. 'I stumbled across some old newspaper articles and photos of Aunt Ada when she was younger, including a picture of Aunt Ada and Uncle Ewart standing outside Rose Cottage and...' Florrie pulled out the chair and sat down. 'And then I discovered some information that took me a little bit by surprise. Oh, and I had an awkward and heated visit from Tom.'

Isla raised her eyebrows. 'Let me put the kettle on and you can tell me all about it.'

'Is Martha home?'

Isla shook her head as she reached for two mugs from the

top cupboard. 'No, she's gone for a walk with Rona, though I suspect that's code for tea and a natter.'

'Last night I discovered William Houston, Tom's grandfather, owned Rose Cottage.'

'Surely that's not a huge surprise, given that it's owned by W. Houston Property Developers?'

'I know, but what I didn't realise was that he actually lived there – it was his family home. That's why he's buried at Heartcross Church; he was part of the community. So why hasn't that ever been mentioned before?'

Isla slid a mug of tea over towards Florrie. 'I'm not sure. You would have thought that would have come up in conversation sometime in the past couple of weeks, with all the news about your fight for the grounds and the van.'

'Exactly!' Florrie agreed.

'Would Gran know? Dolores certainly would. She's got twenty years on everyone in this village. Maybe she forgot? Or just thought it wasn't important or worth mentioning?'

'Maybe. Something I did discover was a photo of Aunt Ada and William when he was a patient at the hospital, just after suffering his heart attack.'

'We know that they all knew each other but we still don't know the history between Dolores and Edward, or what the serious falling out that Gran mentioned, between Dolores, Ada and Edward, was about.'

'There's only three people who knew that, and one of them has passed away. Do you think I should ask Dolores about it?'

Isla shook her head. 'It's between them and in the past. I think just focus on the here and now.'

It didn't sit right with Florrie to just leave it alone, but she understood Isla's point.

'And what went on with Tom?' Isla probed.

Florrie filled Isla in on what had happened last night. 'He swears blind he didn't know anything and… Damn. I've only just realised he walked off with the letters that were sent to me from W. Houston Property Developers.'

'So, what are you thinking? Was his asking you to trust him just a means of shutting you up so the planning approval goes through?'

'I don't know what to think. Changing the subject for now, did you see that Dolores is gracing the front page today?'

Isla rolled her eyes playfully. 'I assume you mean the article that suggests she's hiring out a whole island to celebrate her big birthday?'

Florrie nodded.

'Yes, I saw it. Did you also happen to see the article about a young man sneaking in and out of her flat?'

'What?' Florrie raised her eyebrows in shock.

'According to one tabloid, Dolores has a mystery toy boy who's keeping her young at heart.'

'Are you kidding me? Why on earth would anyone think that? She's ninety-nine.'

'It's laughable, isn't it? We all know Charlotte was the love of her life and Dolores has been broken-hearted since she passed away.'

'Honestly! The stories they print these days are ludicrous.'

'It *is* ridiculous but unfortunately some people believe every word. Apparently this man has been photographed entering the stairwell leading to her flat on a number of occasions.'

'He might just be Hamish's new tenant in one of the other flats. That seems more plausible,' argued Florrie.

'But that wouldn't create a story.'

'Do you have a copy of the newspaper you read it in?'

'Drew's taken it. He's fishing with the boys. Since finding his old fishing rod they've been attempting to catch our tea up at the fishing pond in Primrose Park almost every day. They've not caught anything yet, which I'm secretly chuffed about as I'm not sure I fancy eating anything from that pond.' Isla smiled. 'By the way, you're always more than welcome to stop by for tea. I know you used to eat with Ada most days.'

'Thanks for the offer,' Florrie gave a smile, 'but…'

'You really don't need to make an excuse.'

They both laughed.

'You can hang around for a bit though, can't you?' asked Isla.

'No, I'd better get back. I'm going to attempt to pack up another room at the cottage. Time is ticking and even if the gardens do stay as they are, I do need to get the cottage cleared out. First, though, I'm going to pop into Buttercup Barn and then home to grab the post and water the plant that's no doubt fighting for survival on my kitchen windowsill.'

'Do you want any help today packing up the boxes?'

'I think I'm going to be okay. It's a slow process but only because everything brings back memories. There are a few more personal boxes I need to go through and then I'll start to pack all the ornaments from the living room. Maybe if I have time I'll film a reel promoting Flowers in Bloom.'

'If you change your mind, just drop me a text.'

'I will, I promise.' Florrie smiled warmly at her friend. She really was lucky to have her.

After finishing her cup of tea, Florrie picked up the post from Buttercup Barn and her home on Love Heart Lane, then took the scenic route through Primrose Park. In the distance she spotted Drew and the boys huddled around the fishing rod, sitting on fabric stools at the water's edge. Taking the path to the woods, Florrie cut across the green in front of The Old Bakehouse. There were buttercups peppering the grass, so Florrie picked a handful, sat on a bench and began to make a buttercup chain. Before she knew it the chain had grown quite long and she decided to drape it over Aunt Ada's gravestone before she headed back to the cottage.

As she was about to cross the road, she heard raised voices ahead and looked towards the wrought-iron gates of the churchyard. She stopped in her tracks and then dived behind a tree, hoping the two people standing there hadn't spotted her – Tom and another man.

They were in the midst of a heated debate and as Florrie watched she recognised the older man as Edward Houston, Tom's father.

Edward raised his voice. 'You need to sort this. It will have lost your grandfather's foundation huge amounts of money. How could you be so stupid? You're meant to be here to build up trust. We need those houses to be built.'

Florrie's eyes widened and her heart began to race at the words she'd just overheard. She could feel anger slowly rising inside her. Tom *had* been playing her after all with his request for trust. Right at that moment all she felt towards him was contempt.

Tom didn't reply to his father's tirade and when it ended, he watched him stride towards an expensive-looking car with a personalised number plate that was parked nearby. As Edward opened the car door, he turned and glared at Tom, a glare that even unnerved Florrie.

'You'd be nothing without me' were his parting words before he climbed behind the wheel and drove off without another glance in Tom's direction.

As soon as Edward was out of sight, Tom took his phone out of his pocket. He spoke urgently but Florrie couldn't hear a word. The call was short and Tom began hurrying towards her.

'Shit,' she muttered as she slowly edged around the tree and into the overgrown bushes, the buttercup chain lost somewhere along the way.

Thankfully, he didn't see her as he passed her hiding place, and she decided to follow him. She shadowed him all the way to the high street, where she blended in amongst the tourists. Tom stopped outside Hamish's shop and looked around furtively before reaching into his pocket and taking out a key. Florrie came a little closer and watched with astonishment while he put the key in the lock of the door to the private stairwell. Opening the door he quickly stepped inside and closed it behind him.

There were only two reasons why Tom would have a key to that door: either he had rented a flat from Hamish, which she very much doubted if Hamish refused to even serve him, or Dolores had given him a key to let himself into her flat. Florrie crossed the road to the newspaper stand outside the village shop. She pulled out a newspaper from the metal rack and opened it to read the headlines. Isla had been right. The paper claimed that a young man had been photographed coming out of the stairwell to Dolores's private flat. The photograph accompanying the article was a little grainy, and the man had tried to cover his face with a cap, but there was no mistaking Tom Houston. Which led Florrie to just one question.

What the hell was going on?

Chapter Twenty-Three

C lutching the newspaper, Florrie decided to head straight
back to the cottage, hardly daring to wonder what
might be going on here. After pouring herself a glass of water
she sat down at the table and read the article slowly. The
mystery man had been spotted coming out of the apartment
four times in forty-eight hours. The images were all of the
same man – Tom. Why hadn't Dolores mentioned that she
knew him, and why would she suggest having her birthday
party at Rose Cottage and doing whatever it took to stop Tom's
company? It just didn't make sense and her mind was whirling
with numerous possibilities.

All Florrie wanted to do was to race over to Dolores's and
barge in on the pair of them to demand answers, but she knew
she needed to take a breath and calm her thoughts before she
took any action. Confronting Dolores could be humiliating, if
she refused to answer Florrie's questions, and it could also lead
Dolores to pull out of the performance at the cottage, which

they desperately needed in order to keep Florrie's battle in the news.

Florrie pushed the newspaper to one side. She needed to channel her energy in a different direction so, even though her mind was still racing, she picked up an empty cardboard box and made her way into the living room. She began to wrap the ornaments in tissue paper and carefully place them in the box. It wasn't long before everything was packed away and the box labelled and taped up securely. Placing it by the back door, ready for Drew to collect, she decided that next she would tackle the chest of drawers. She pulled out the first drawer, which was stuffed with instructions for electrical appliances. It seemed like Ada had kept them for every appliance she and Ewart had ever owned! Florrie scooped them all up and put them in the recycle bin, which was sitting just outside the living-room window.

In the next drawer were knitting patterns, old notebooks and magazines. Florrie laid everything out on the table. She smiled at the knitting pattern on the top. It was a jumper with a large multi-coloured flower in the centre. Aunt Ada had knitted this pattern for Florrie's eighth birthday and she had worn it with pride for many years, despite the gigantic neck hole and one arm being longer than the other. She put that knitting pattern to one side and placed the rest in the recycle bin.

The last drawer contained nothing but bank statements – hundreds of them, secured by elastic bands. Florrie picked up a pile dated over twenty years ago and opened the one on top. Anyone looking at these bank statements could easily see the standing orders that came out of the account at the start of the month. The same amount of cash was withdrawn on a Friday and along with the statement was a spends book. Aunt Ada had recorded what the cash had been spent on. She liked routine, as the entries were like clockwork. She shopped for food on a Monday, went to the pub every Tuesday, paid for the pop man on a Wednesday, paid the milkman on a Thursday, and Friday was a treat day, usually lunch at Bonnie's Teashop.

As she scanned the statements, a thought suddenly struck Florrie. She ran her finger down the standing orders. She knew exactly what she was looking for but she couldn't find it. She picked up another stack of statements and spends book. She scoured month after month and still there was no entry for W. Houston Property Developers. Aunt Ada had had the same bank account for years and there was not one rental payment for the cottage. Flummoxed, Florrie rang Isla.

'How are you? Is it all getting a little too much?' Isla asked as soon as she picked up the phone.

'Are you able to come over?' Florrie felt tearful. 'There's something I need to talk to you about.' Her voice quivered.

'Drew is just about to come over to you. The boys have had enough of catching anything but a fish, and Martha is back so she can mind them. I'll jump in with Drew, see you in ten.'

Florrie was so confused. If there were no transactions between Aunt Ada and W. Houston Property Developers then how had she been paying the rent for all these years? Leaving the bank statements spread out on the table Florrie looked around the room and began ransacking every drawer. She wasn't yet sure what she was looking for but she'd know it when she stumbled across it. Five minutes later the whole room was a mess, papers strewn everywhere. She blew out a breath and nearly jumped out of her skin when she saw Isla standing in the doorway.

'It looks like you've been burgled. What's going on?'

Florrie could feel the emotion brimming inside. Hearing a noise, she looked over Isla's shoulder.

'It's okay, it's just Drew, he's stacking the boxes onto the trailer to take to the farm. It'll only take him a minute. Shall I put the kettle on? Then you can tell me what's going on here.'

Florrie nodded. Numbly, she moved to the window, but there were a couple of tourists taking photos next to The Vintage Flower Van so she moved away again, not wanting to be spotted, and sat down on the settee.

She heard the slam of the trailer door and the engine of the tractor, which meant that Drew was leaving. She felt terrible for not having even said hello, but she was about to burst into tears.

'Here, a nice strong tea.' Isla gave Florrie a warm smile as she handed her a mug before sitting down next to her on the settee. 'So, what's all this?'

'You have to promise that this stays between us.'

'Of course.'

'Not even Martha can know.'

'Not even Gran,' reassured Isla.

'I feel like I'm going mad. After I left yours, I picked my post up from Buttercup Barn and Love Heart Lane and then went for a walk. For a while I sat on the bench on the green near The Old Bakehouse and then I decided to make a quick visit to Aunt Ada's grave. As I neared the cemetery, I heard raised voices and saw Tom arguing with his father at the gate.'

'Edward Houston is in town?'

'Yep, right here, in Heartcross.'

'Did you hear what they were arguing about?'

'I've been trying to remember exactly what I heard. I'm

sure it was something along the lines of "How could you be so stupid? You're meant to be building up trust. We need those houses to be built."'

'You're kidding me?' Isla raised an eyebrow.

Florrie shook her head. 'Unfortunately not. It suggests Tom has known all along what was going on, and when he asked me to "just trust" him he was simply hoping that he still might be able to sweet-talk me into not causing them any more trouble or negative publicity. He even had the cheek to come to The Vintage Flower Van and buy my favourite flowers.'

'Cheek indeed. What are you going to do now? I'm assuming you'll want to share this information with the community and expose their wrongdoing?'

'I can't.'

'Why not? This is the perfect opportunity to show them we'll not be walked over.'

Florrie had her hand on her heart; she was close to tears. 'Two reasons. The first is that they could have me over a barrel. I need to chat with Jaydon to find out my legal position.'

'What do you mean, they could have you over a barrel?'

'Isla, I feel sick to my stomach. These are Aunt Ada's bank statements and she recorded all cash transactions in what she called a spends book,' she said, gesturing to the pile of paperwork on the table in front of them. 'What do you make of them?'

Isla picked up a couple of the statements and then the spends book. She studied them carefully. 'Monday, she liked food shopping and Friday she always visited the teashop? I don't really know what I'm looking for but it's clear that she was a creature of habit.'

'Precisely. Those were my thoughts exactly. Aunt Ada was a

creature of habit. The same regular standing orders went out of her account on the same regular basis … all except one.'

'Which payment?'

'These statements go back years, and not one of them has a single rent payment to W. Houston Property Developers.'

Isla looked surprised, picked up a handful of bank statements and flicked through them to confirm what Florrie had said. 'You're absolutely right. I can't see one single payment.'

'Does that mean that Aunt Ada was living here rent-free? If so, I'm just not sure why that would be the case, unless…' She paused as an idea began to form in her mind. 'Isla, I've got a stupid notion going around in my head, and I don't even want to say the words out loud because as soon as I do, it could all become too real for my liking. But I have to say it. We all want to believe that Uncle Ewart was the love of Aunt Ada's life –' Florrie took a breath '– but do you think it might be possible that Aunt Ada had an affair with William … or even possibly Edward?'

Isla laughed loudly. 'Don't be ridiculous! Your imagination is running away with you. Ada and Ewart were solid as a rock.'

'I'm glad you said that.'

'Of course they were. Those two were made for each other and anyone who ever met them could clearly see it.'

'Then why has Aunt Ada not made a single rent payment on Rose Cottage for all these years? Do you think there could have been a blip in W. Houston Property Developers' computer system and somehow it didn't register that Aunt Ada lived here? But then, if that was the case, then surely Aunt Ada would have told them? She was scrupulously honest and wouldn't have been able to stand having it on her conscience if that had happened. And what if Tom finds out and they check and somehow I'm liable for payment as Ada's next of kin? I can't afford to pay it all back!' she said, growing increasingly worried.

'Let's not panic. There has to be a reasonable explanation for this.'

Florrie looked at Isla, hoping she might know what that reasonable explanation was.

'But I can't think of one right at this second,' Isla said, crushing Florrie's hope.

'Isla!'

'Actually, you know what? I can.' Isla took hold of both of Florrie's hands. 'I think there's only one person who might have all the answers we need.'

'Who?' replied Florrie.

'Dolores.'

Florrie shook her head. 'We can't say anything to Dolores.'

'Why not?'

'Because there's a possibility Dolores is in cahoots with W. Houston Property Developers.'

Isla laughed. 'For a moment there I thought you were serious.'

'I am being serious.' Florrie picked up the newspaper. 'The person in this photograph coming out of Dolores's flat is Tom Houston.'

Looking at the newspaper in disbelief, Isla asked, 'Are you sure?'

'Believe me, I'd know him anywhere.'

'What's the plan of action then?'

'I've absolutely no idea.'

Chapter Twenty-Four

Florrie and Isla spent the afternoon packing up another few rooms before they decided to call it a day. They'd sorted the boxes into ones for the charity shop and ones for storage, which Drew took back to the farm when he picked up Isla. They'd spent several hours talking about the situation before they decided that they couldn't keep second-guessing what was going on. Florrie needed answers and so tomorrow she was going to ask Dolores the questions she needed answering ... even if doing so could lead to consequences that were out of Florrie's control.

It was now a little after five o'clock and after picking some flowers from the garden Florrie tried to relax by taking a bath. Whilst the water was running into the tub, she squeezed in her favourite bubble bath and the gorgeous aroma of lavender filled the room. She placed the flowers she had just picked in jam jars scattered around the bathroom. After lighting tealight candles and grabbing a glass of lemonade, she slipped out of her clothes and into the bathtub, her shoulders sinking under the hot water. As she sipped her drink, she couldn't shake thoughts of Tom from her mind. She couldn't even begin to guess what his reaction might be if he discovered that no rent had been paid on this cottage for years – no, decades.

The thought had crossed Florrie's mind that there could be a rent book that was separate from Ada's other banking statements, or a statement letter from W. Houston Property Developers specifying the amount of rent that had been paid each year but the money would have still come out of the same bank account. After Isla had left, Florrie had searched high and low but couldn't find anything either.

Forty minutes later, she was out of the bath and dressed but she still couldn't calm her thoughts. The night was still young and she needed to clear her mind so she pulled on her trainers and jogged towards the track at the bottom of Love Heart Lane. Along the high street she saw a group of paparazzi camped outside the Grouse and Haggis, their lenses trained on the upstairs window of Dolores's flat. Florrie wondered what it would be like to be under constant scrutiny for so many years. Even at Dolores's advanced age it hadn't let up.

The bridge between Heartcross and Glensheil was busy with tourists enjoying a walk and Florrie stopped in the middle to catch her breath while looking out over the River Heart. The water sparkled in the fading early evening sunlight, the eddies and whitecaps creating constant movement. Multi-coloured kayaks and rowing boats still littered the river, and Florrie smiled at the kids swinging on a rope out over the water, something she'd done in her teens. She took a sip from her water bottle and as she turned she saw a group of people huddled together whispering and pointing in her direction.

'Excuse me, are you Florrie Appleton? Owner of The Vintage Flower Van?'

Florrie smiled. She was beginning to be recognised more and more but she still wasn't used to it – or totally comfortable with it. 'I am.'

'Please could we have a photo? We follow you online.'

'Of course.' Florrie posed for photos and noticed other people looking in her direction wondering what the commotion was about. As much as she wanted to create an awareness of what was going on in her life right now, she also wanted a peaceful run and to be lost in her thoughts, so after a few more selfies were taken, she headed on her way, following the road that ran by the river.

Taking a breather, she walked towards the water and hopped onto the river taxi that took her across the river to The Little Blue Boathouse, thankful for the light breeze cooling her down. In the last few years, a lifeboat centre and a café had been built on this stretch of the river, providing jobs for the community and making the area safer for the tourists.

Stepping from the water taxi, Florrie decided to enjoy a glass of wine overlooking the river before she ambled home. As she walked along the jetty, she noticed Tom sitting at one of the bistro tables outside the boathouse, enjoying a beer. He was handsome and mesmerising with a whole sexy look going on, the sleeves of his shirt rolled up to reveal his tanned and toned forearms. Tom was looking at his phone but must have sensed somebody was watching him because just then he lifted his gaze. His eyes fell on her and his whole body appeared to tense.

It wasn't in Florrie's nature to ignore anyone but it was clear he wouldn't welcome her intrusion, so she decided against the drink and walked on past the café. Feeling Tom's eyes burning into her back, she stopped and spun round. He was indeed still staring at her.

She walked back and stopped next to his table.

'Why can't you just tell the truth?'

'Look' – he held his hands up – 'I don't want any trouble. I just wanted a quiet drink by the river. It's been a hell of a day.'

Florrie was torn. Despite everything that was going on at the minute she didn't want to believe she'd gotten him so wrong, but still her gut wasn't one hundred per cent convinced that he was the bad guy he appeared to be in this whole thing.

'Can we call a truce for at least five minutes? This is a lovely part of the day,' he said, gesturing to the seat opposite him, 'and surely we can get along for one drink.'

Remembering the phrase 'keep your friends close and your enemies closer', Florrie decided two could play this game. He didn't know what she'd overheard, so sitting down and being friendly might lull him into a false sense of security. Perhaps she could discover something to her advantage.

The waiter came over to the table as Florrie took a seat opposite him and ordered herself a large glass of pinot grigio.

'I didn't know you were a runner,' he ventured.

'I dabble from time to time but not as much as I used to.'

'How are you?' he asked. 'And that's a genuine question.'

'It's been a difficult day,' she answered. 'I've been packing up my family home and putting Aunt Ada's things into boxes to make sure I'm out of the cottage by eviction day. And I'm not saying that to have a go. That's honestly what I've been doing, and it's one of the hardest things I've ever had to do.'

He nodded and closed his eyes for a moment.

'Look, I...' He paused as the waiter reappeared and placed

a glass of wine down in front of Florrie. As soon as the waiter was out of earshot, he carried on. 'I'm very sorry for your loss. Ada sounds like a remarkable woman; I know my grandfather thought so.'

'How do you know about Ada but I didn't know about William?'

'When he passed away, he left me a box of treasures ... well, that's what I've always called it. I didn't really appreciate what it was at the time but in recent years I've revisited it and come to value the fact that he shared it with me. There're all sorts in the box. It's around this big' – he gestured with his hands – 'and it's full of newspaper cuttings, articles, photographs, a watch he always wore, his favourite bow tie, his favourite book... One of the things I found was a photograph of my grandfather when he was in hospital. He's sitting with your aunt Ada.'

'I've seen that recently.'

'Attached to the photograph there was a journal of his thoughts. He said Ada had helped him immensely after his heart attack and kept his spirits high with her daily visits. He referred to her as one of his best friends and he ended the entry by writing he would always look out for her and Ewart, who I assumed was her husband.'

'But why did my aunt Ada never mention him?'

Tom shrugged. 'I don't know. Grief does funny things to people.'

'How did you end up at the funeral?'

'My grandfather also left a letter for me in the box. In it he told me that Heartcross would always hold a special place in his heart and that one day, if I had the chance, I should visit. He did warn me though, there's a local curse. Once you arrive in Heartcross...'

'You never want to leave,' Florrie finished for him. They gave each other a tentative smile.

'Exactly, and when I arrived here, I overheard Hamish in the village shop talking about the funeral and realised I'd arrived too late to meet Ada. I'd wanted to chat to her about my grandfather, but I'd left it too long and missed my chance.' He took a sip of his drink and looked out over the river before turning back towards Florrie. 'How did it come to this?'

'You hurt me,' she said simply.

It was finally out in the open. She felt vulnerable, but she needed this conversation to happen. Tom Houston still confused her and she really couldn't make up her mind whether he was a good guy or not.

Tom briefly closed his eyes. 'I'm sorry I hurt you. It really wasn't my intention.'

'I do know we were both consenting adults, but having all the facts about your situation would have led me to maybe make different choices.'

'I wanted you to make the choice you did. I had an amazing two weeks.'

'And so did I. But why didn't you just tell me you were spending the summer with Sophia Henley? How did you think it would make me feel to find that out from someone other than you?'

'It isn't what you think.'

Florrie could sense he was holding back. He looked like he wanted to say something but he didn't.

'So tell me what to think. Because what I think is that after being on an extreme high for two weeks you let me crash to the ground without so much as a parachute to soften the landing. One minute we're wrapped up in each other's arms, sleeping under the stars, and the next it's in the newspaper that you're all set to marry your childhood sweetheart that I knew nothing about.'

'I can see now why you blocked me.'

Florrie could feel the frustration rising inside her. She was getting nowhere. Maybe he'd decided it was no good raking over the past as it wouldn't achieve anything. All they would do was end up in another argument. But she couldn't just let it be. There was still something niggling away at her. Why couldn't he just be straight with her? He had at least apologised. Maybe that was all she could ask for. Maybe this was just something Florrie had to let go of.

'Why are you here, Tom? Why make your visit to Heartcross now and not sooner?' she asked, not taking her eyes off him. 'You must have opened that box from your grandfather and found out about Ada years ago.'

'Because the opportunity to increase awareness of my grandfather's foundation came up, and it felt like a sign that I should finally come and see the place he was so fond of. I didn't know whether you still lived in this area, but I admit that I was hoping you did.'

As much as Florrie wanted to believe every word that was coming out of his mouth, Tom was still technically the enemy, and it was clear that there was more going on at Rose Cottage than met the eye – but she just couldn't work out what that 'more' was.

Florrie wasn't ready to let him off lightly. 'I heard that Sophia is speaking at the event and is a huge part of your grandfather's charity.'

There was a fleeting flash of surprise on Tom's face that she would know that. 'Yes, our families have always been close.'

They sat in an awkward silence for a moment.

'I saw you,' she shared.

'Saw me what? When?'

'I saw you outside the church arguing with your father.' She watched his eyes flicker as the words registered. 'It sounded like it didn't end well,' Florrie said, wanting to make sure he knew that she knew exactly what his father's parting words had been. 'I think you've played me, Tom. Do you deny it?'

'Florrie, I can't talk about this.'

'Can't or won't? Why don't you want this conversation? What exactly are you hiding? Shall I tell you what I think?'

Tom's eyes were downcast as he looked up from under his fringe. 'I've got a feeling you're going to tell me whether I want you to or not.'

Florrie kept her voice calm. 'I think you're weak and a player.' She had his full attention now. 'I also think you knew you were leaving uni to go and work for your father and deliberately didn't tell me, because you wanted one last fling before you were forced to take over the family business and settle down with your childhood sweetheart. Then, to add insult to injury, you come back into my life eight years later and have the audacity to ask me to trust you, even though you knew you were taking my aunt's home and business away from me and destroying everything she worked for.'

'It's just not true.'

'I heard your father. "Make them trust you." Those were his words.'

'You think you have it all worked out, but you haven't.'

'Do you know how infuriating this conversation is? You're telling me nothing yet expecting me to be okay with that.' She got up to leave but Tom reached out to grab her hand. Florrie pulled away.

'I know it seems you have no reason to trust me but I need you to just hang in there for a little while longer. Please,' Tom pleaded. 'Please sit and finish your drink.'

Florrie hesitated for a moment before finally sitting back down. What did she have to lose?

'I'm here because my grandfather meant the world to me even though I was young when he passed away. I have the fondest memories of him and, from what I understand, a lot of other people do too. In the past few years, I've become increasingly interested in his legacy and charity work, and it's something I want to continue in tribute to him. Part of that was coming here to make connections and accept Flynn's charitable award.'

'That all sounds very commendable but it's not sitting right with me. I told you, I heard what your father said.'

'Things are never as black and white as they seem.' Tom blew out a breath and looked as though he had the weight of the world on his shoulders. 'Believe me when I say I do know the difference between right and wrong and what effect it can have on people.'

Florrie thought about interjecting here but she didn't want to antagonise Tom just now. He was finally talking and she didn't want to stop him.

'Yes, I'm privileged in the sense of having a flash car and a company handed to me on a platter, but it doesn't come without its challenges. It's not that easy being me. What I'm missing is a family and love.' Tom looked at her. 'Just by sitting here and hearing you talk about her I can see the love you have for your great-aunt Ada. On the day of her funeral the church was packed because she was well loved – a kind and genuine person, according to my grandfather. Whereas I'd be surprised if anyone at all will be at my father's funeral. I don't think I've ever heard a good word said about him.'

Florrie was taken aback. He seemed to be genuinely hurting. 'I've been very lucky. No matter what we faced, Ada and I always had each other and that's what mattered.'

'That's something I'm realising. There's no love lost between me and my father. The only love he has is for success and money. Yes, I've followed in his footsteps, but believe me, it's not been my choice…'

'Everyone has a choice.'

'Yes, but when you've grown up carrying the weight of other people's expectations and your path has been drummed into you from such an early age… It was never a real option for me to have my own career. It was just expected that I would take over the family business, whether that was my choice or not.'

His voice wavered. His eyes were awash with tears, but he didn't let them fall.

'My guess is that my grandfather would have been proud of me no matter what, unlike my father, who measures his love for me by my success and academic qualifications. I did actually finish uni, by the way. I did an online course to secure the credit I needed to graduate early, which is why I didn't return after that summer.'

'What do you mean, your father measures his love for you by your success?'

'My father is a difficult character and has never been a

warm person. In fact, I can't remember even one time he's told me he loves me. He pushed me to do well at school and from a young age I had tutors, not because I was struggling but because he wanted me to outshine everyone else. My school day didn't end when everyone's did. It went on for at least a few more hours. I didn't have any friends because he wouldn't let me mix with boys at school. I only had one escape route.'

'Which was?'

'I learned to swim. It was the only time I felt free and that I could be me, with no pressure from anyone. I could power through that water, lost in my own thoughts, with not a care in the world. At first, he said it was a waste of time because he didn't understand why I'd want to swim, but then when I started winning county races and competing in competitions, he got onboard with it. He would post online how proud he was of me, how amazing I was, and yet he would never say it directly to me, would never give me a call or send me a text. His support and praise for me were only ever for the public arena – for everyone else *but* me, really.'

'Why would he do that?'

'Simple, keeping up appearances. He wanted the whole world to think we had this great relationship when in reality we barely spoke. We have nothing in common except our bloodline.'

'That's very sad,' said Florrie. She thought about Aunt Ada and how she'd championed Florrie every single day. She would have supported her no matter what she did. '"Surround yourself with people who fight for you in rooms you're not in," Aunt Ada always said to me.'

'Aunt Ada was a wise woman.'

'She was and I'm lucky to have had her. And if your

relationship is so fractious, why do you do what your father tells you to do?'

'Because what would I have, if I didn't?'

'Self-worth,' came Florrie's instant reply. 'Happiness, a career you actually want…'

'You make it sound so easy.'

'It is. The only person you have to rely on in this world is yourself. I was one of the lucky ones, in that I also had a family around me who would support me no matter what. They did fight for me in rooms I wasn't in. Every single time.'

'You're the lucky one.'

'And your mother?'

Tom was silent for a moment.

'I'm sorry, I don't mean to pry.'

'You're not. She passed away when I was very small. It's just been me and my dad.'

'I'm sorry to hear that.'

'I know it's hard to believe but I don't want what he has.'

'Which is what?' she asked.

'A lonely life with no friends, and colleagues and workers who don't respect you and avoid you at all costs. And it's all his own doing. He craves money, it's like an addiction, and he forgets about the people he hurts to get what he wants.'

'I can't argue with that.'

The Tom that was sitting opposite her showed an endearing vulnerability and seemed to be the down-to-earth, genuine person she remembered – but now she could see the demons he'd been dealing with behind the scenes, and it gave her new insight into the man he'd become. Florrie understood that families could be difficult, but thankfully all she'd ever experienced was love.

For a moment he seemed lost in thought as he finished his drink. When he put the glass on the table, he looked at Florrie. 'See? We can get along without trying to rip each other apart.'

Florrie was still staring into his eyes, her gaze unfaltering. He took her hand and she felt her heart beginning to race. She wasn't going to let herself fall for his charms a second time but she didn't pull away either. 'All I wanted was for you to be genuine and honest with me.'

'I have been genuine and honest with you. After I left you that day, all I could think about was you and when I would see you again.'

'How can you say that?'

'It's true.'

Florrie was confused. 'Am I meant to be reading between the lines here?'

'I'm not here just for the charity conference. I also came because I was hoping to see you. Then, when I got here, all hell broke loose. Those two weeks we spent together were the best I'd ever had. Fun, carefree and wrapped in the arms of someone I'd found attractive for over two years. It was the first time in ages that I felt like myself.'

Florrie stared at him. 'Say that again.'

'It was the first time in ages I felt like myself.'

She swiped him playfully. 'Not that part.'

He laughed. 'Don't think I didn't see you sitting up on that sand dune every time I trained.'

'I'm not admitting to anything.'

'I found you attractive from the first moment I saw you, I just didn't have the courage to speak to you. You were cool, hip and trendy whereas I was stuffy and so not cool.' He grinned. 'I knew then there was something about you.'

In the last ten minutes Florrie had let down her guard and had begun to once again get caught up in the mesmerising web of Tom Houston. She shook herself out of it. There was a bigger picture to think about here.

'It's all very well taking a trip down memory lane but what matters is the here and now. The reality is that I'm losing Aunt Ada's home, Rose Cottage's gardens are going to be flattened and your family business is taking away everything that meant the world to my aunt Ada.' Florrie finished her drink and put money on the table for it. 'I'm sorry to hear about your troubles with your father, but you're your own person and this situation tells me that you're more like your father than your grandfather. William would never have allowed Rose Cottage to be demolished. Not when it clearly meant so much to him.' Florrie stood up and left him with one final blow.

'I'm going to be shouting about those gardens, and doing whatever it takes to create as much publicity as possible. The newspapers got it right, we're simply university friends in a tug of war. Actually, no, there is one part they got wrong … because we were never really friends, were we?'

Tom opened his wallet and placed some cash on the table for the drinks, handing Florrie her money back.

'What are you doing?' she asked.

'I can't carry on like this. This may backfire, but that's a risk I'm willing to take.'

Tom held out his hand to her.

'And where do you think we're going?'

'To see Dolores. You need to know the truth.'

Chapter Twenty-Five

izarrely, they walked hand in hand to Dolores's apartment. Tom's grip was firm and Florrie couldn't work out if it was because he actually wanted to hold her hand or because he was scared she might break free and run away. He needn't have worried. Whatever Dolores was going to share was already weighing heavily on her mind and she wasn't going to miss it for the world.

They crossed the road and walked towards the door leading up to Dolores's apartment. Tom unlocked it and ushered Florrie quickly inside.

'Why do you have your own key?' she asked. He didn't reply.

They climbed the stairs to the front door. Tom knocked and pushed down the handle. 'It's only me,' he shouted before stepping inside.

Wide-eyed, Florrie followed him into the hallway. 'Do not think the worst when you walk into the room,' Tom cautioned her.

Florrie didn't have time to question him because Tom was already walking away. She'd heard about the inside of Dolores's apartment from Aunt Ada and had thought she'd exaggerated a little, but now she realised Ada had described it exactly how it was. The walls were lined with faded photos and magazine articles about Dolly Parton, along with photos of Dolores with royalty, pop stars and her closest friends in Heartcross. 'I knew she was a huge fan of Dolly but this is on another scale… I don't have any words.'

Tom looked over his shoulder. 'It's something else, isn't it?'

'And there's Ada and Martha. They look so young,' Florrie observed, wondering – and a little frightened of – what was on the other side of the door.

Passing an old-fashioned olive-green telephone on a small round table with a brown velvet stool tucked underneath it, Florrie followed Tom as he opened the living-room door.

The living room was cosy, with two armchairs, a sofa and a coffee table facing a pretty tiled fireplace. To the left of the fireplace was a bookcase loaded with books and to the right was an old record player with a number of vinyl records stacked next to it. The carpet was a vision of brown paisley swirls, and the walls were decorated in red and gold stripes and covered in photographs of yet more famous people.

Dolores, wearing a black feather boa around her neck and animal-print kitten-heel slippers, was bent over the dining table, where there were three laptops open and a mound of paperwork. She had company. Florrie froze. Tom must have sensed her apprehension as he grabbed her hand with a firm grip.

Standing next to Dolores was Sophia Henley.

They both looked in Florrie's direction, then glanced between her and Tom, questions clear in their eyes.

Tom held up his hands in a surrender stance. 'I know you're going to say that we were trying to keep this between ourselves but it's getting a little difficult to manage. I think it's only fair that Florrie knows what's going on.'

Slowly Dolores nodded. 'I agree.'

Tom touched Florrie's arm. 'Let me introduce you to Sophia. Her grandparents were friends of my grandfather and also knew Dolores very well.'

'Sophia's grandmother was my personal assistant for many years. Sophia's mum was my god-daughter,' shared Dolores.

'The reason we're all here is because we're working together, undercover, to expose my fraudulent father. We hope we can trust you with that information,' Tom said hesitantly.

Shock must have been written all over Florrie's face. Sophia stepped forward with an outstretched hand. 'It's so good to finally meet you. Over the years you've popped up in conversation quite a lot.'

Florrie's heart was beating fast as she shook Sophia's hand.

'And just for the record, though we've been friends since we could talk, Sophia and I have never been romantically connected, despite what the press might have suggested many years ago,' Tom said kindly.

'Tom is more like an annoying older brother than anything else,' added Sophia.

'Hey, less of the annoying!' he pressed, pretending to look hurt.

'You're just a little annoying, and a bit bossy, too.'

'I'll give you annoying, not bossy!' He smiled and turned to Florrie. 'I know what it must have seemed like back then, but it

271

really wasn't what you thought. My father had long hoped that we would marry to bring the wealth of the two families together and he would often sell stories about us to the newspaper in an attempt to make that happen, as it would have made him look good to have that connection. It was also a means of making himself more popular with the press so they would write flattering stories about him.'

Florrie felt like a complete idiot. Eight years ago, she'd seen red and blocked him with no explanation, and now she knew the truth she felt awful. Tom had been genuine in his feelings towards her. 'Is this where I should be apologising?'

Tom smiled and touched her arm. 'I should be apologising too. I should have come to find you but back then I was a little stubborn.'

'Oh, he can be very stubborn,' chipped in Sophia.

'And the reason I didn't want to talk about it when I arrived in Heartcross was because we had to keep all this under wraps,' he gestured towards the computers and paperwork. The reason Sophia is here is because she has been involved with charities for a number of years and she's married to a lawyer, which is very helpful as it's given us access to free legal advice. The bottom line is that my father has been using Grandfather's foundation money for his own gain for years, and has been executing fraudulent behaviour within W. Houston Property Developers.'

'I'll put the kettle on.' Sophia disappeared into the kitchen whilst Dolores pointed towards the settee with her walking stick, saying, 'Take no notice of Cary. He'll start chirping as soon as you sit next to him.'

Next to the settee was a large birdcage housing a yellow canary. In her flustered state Florrie hadn't even noticed it.

Dolores was right and as soon as Florrie sat next to him, he started chirping.

'I thought your canary was called Fred, after Astaire?' she asked.

Dolores gave a little chuckle. 'That was my previous canary. He stopped dancing. This is Cary.'

'As in Cary Grant?' asked Florrie.

'The very one. He starred in one of my favourite films, *To Catch a Thief*, and hopefully that's exactly what we're about to do this afternoon.' Dolores pointed to the laptops, their screens full of numbers and columns.

'What is all that?' asked Florrie.

Sophia brought in a tray with a pot of tea, four China teacups and saucers and a plate of chocolate Hobnob biscuits. After placing it down on the coffee table she took a seat in the armchair next to Dolores.

'Those are the confidential accounts of the William Houston Foundation, which has always been Edward's domain ... until now.'

'We think that the money raised for the charity is not finding its way to the right causes,' said Tom. 'And this has been going on a very long time.'

'I think we need to start this story right at the beginning, which was over sixty years ago. If that's okay with you, Tom?' suggested Dolores.

Tom nodded, and gestured to Dolores to go ahead.

Florrie didn't have an inkling about what she was about to hear but she could see that there must be parts of this story that were upsetting for Tom, as he suddenly looked sad. She placed a comforting hand on his knee and he gave her a warm smile of appreciation.

'Sophia, would you pass me that photograph?' Dolores pointed to a framed photograph on the bookshelf. She smiled at the image before passing it on to Florrie. 'Do you recognise anyone?'

'There's no mistaking you and Aunt Ada, you haven't changed a bit. But I've no idea who the other two women are,' Florrie answered honestly.

'That's Rose, William's wife,' Dolores said, pointing her out, 'and this is Elsie, Sophia's grandmother like I said, my personal assistant. She travelled with me everywhere.

'The four of us were good friends, very good friends.' Dolores swallowed and Florrie could see her eyes were suddenly glistening with unshed tears. 'We lost Rose way too young, just like William. She was killed in a boating accident in the south of France. Edward was swimming in the sea and Rose was sunbathing on the deck when she looked up and saw a speedboat heading towards him. Instinctively, Rose jumped into the water to push her son out of the way, and though she saved Edward's life, she lost hers.'

Florrie felt a sudden sadness bleeding through the room. 'I don't know what to say. That is so awful.'

'A complete tragedy. It broke all our hearts, especially William's. To be candid, I don't think he ever truly recovered from her loss. For the rest of his days, there was never anyone else because no one could even come close. Instead he surrounded himself with his closest friends, and we did everything possible to support him.'

Florrie turned towards Tom. 'I'm so sorry to hear this.'

'It's okay, I wasn't even born when it happened but I know how deep their love was. There were love letters that they'd written to each other, and old diary entries, in the box my grandfather left me. It was the purest kind of true love.' He held Florrie's gaze as he said those last words and she bitterly regretted how she'd reacted eight years ago. She should have let him explain but back then she could only go with how she felt at the time. Tom gave her a heart-warming look and she put her hand back on his knee, already feeling they were becoming closer to each other.

Dolores continued. 'Before she passed, William and Rose lived here in Heartcross, in the oldest cottage in the village.'

'Rose Cottage,' said Florrie, thinking out loud. 'Oh my, was it named after Rose?'

Dolores smiled. 'It certainly was. William's business started when he bought his first rundown property and spent most of his time renovating it with his own two hands. He flipped that property within the space of six months and made a hefty profit, which he used to build another house, which he flipped in turn. He did this several times in a row. At first everyone thought he was mad, including Rose, but he proved us all wrong and within a couple of years they had enough money to purchase their dream home – which they called Rose Cottage. Rose had great plans for transforming the land around it into a special place but not long after, tragedy struck and Rose was killed. William found it difficult being in the cottage without her and so he spent more and more time in an apartment in Edinburgh. Edward went to boarding school, and William threw himself into helping others less fortunate than himself.'

Tom cut in. 'He had a heart of gold.'

'He was always about the people. Such a decent man,' added Sophia, pouring everyone a mug of tea now that it had had time to steep.

'Unlike his son.' The smile had dropped from Dolores's face

and she looked at Tom, who held up his hands in surrender again.

'I agree with you. You know my feelings about my father. You're not saying anything I don't know.'

'Ada promised William she would turn the gardens into something wonderful,' Dolores went on, 'even suggesting a rose garden in memory of our beloved Rose.'

'Forgive me for interrupting,' said Florrie, 'but I don't understand why Edward would want to bulldoze the gardens to build houses if they have all these family memories, and that special garden was planted specifically in memory of his mother.'

'Revenge,' said Dolores, before dunking a biscuit into her tea and taking a bite. 'Edward had always been a difficult child, driven by his own self-importance. He believed, and still does –' Dolores gave a Tom a knowing look ' – that he deserves privileges and recognition for things he did not earn. He acts as if the world owes him something in exchange for nothing. As a child his attitude was challenging but everyone cut him some slack after Rose's tragic death. But it was to his detriment and he became a man who cared nothing for limits or consequences. He used William's success to get into the upper echelons of society, whether into clubs or onto the guest lists of exclusive parties where he would mix with the rich and famous. I know for a fact that it was Edward who sold stories about me to the press – including the story that I was dating royalty.'

Florrie raised an eyebrow.

'William was at his wits' end but then things started to calm down a little and Edward met Lucille.'

'My mother,' added Tom.

'But sadly, Lucille passed away from breast cancer and Edward went back to his unruly ways. William stepped in to look after young Tom, as Edward's behaviour began to spiral out of control. It was only when William hinted that he was going to strike Edward from his will unless he began to change his ways that Edward began to toe the line ... or at least that's what we thought.'

'My grandfather at that point gave my father a role in the business and the charity foundation he'd set up.'

'During this time, Ada became a volunteer at the hospital. I always said that if she hadn't ended up as a florist, she would have made a fantastic nurse. Ada always wanted to give back, make someone's life easier by having a chat, bringing in magazines and so on. She did as much as she could alongside her own job.

'As I mentioned, William had moved into his apartment in the city and Rose Cottage was lying empty. Everything was overgrown, the gardens were neglected and the cottage was falling to rack and ruin. Ada asked if there was any possibility she and Ewart could rent it after the wedding and of course William said yes. Ada quickly began to turn the cottage around. She worked so hard in the gardens, created her gorgeous blooms and the stunning rose garden for Rose. The bonus that came with the cottage was The Vintage Flower Van, which – would you believe? – was William's original building truck. He felt it was a lucky omen, so when Ada wanted to open up a flower business, it was included in the arrangement, which gave Ada instant business premises. She never looked back.

'When William had his heart attack we thought we were going to lose him. Ada visited him on every shift and sat with him for hours. William was weak, and worried about the future, so he asked us to keep his charity foundation alive, wanting his legacy to live on. This was when I decided to perform at the bandstand in Primrose Park and I was able to donate all the money raised to his charity. While William was in hospital, Edward stepped in on the financial side of things to make sure all the donations were collected and deposited into the foundation.'

'But the money never made it to the foundation?' Florrie asked, looking around them all.

'Yes. And we know this because William secretly asked Ada to keep an eye on the charity bank account.'

'Do you think that was because he didn't fully trust Edward?' asked Florrie.

'He was right not to. Only a quarter of the total money collected went into the charity pot. Edward didn't know about Ada keeping an eye on the bank account and so Ada was faced with the dilemma of whether to tell William, while he was still in recovery, that his son was a thief.'

'What did she do?'

'She told him, because William had enlisted her help for that very reason. But we did give Edward the option to come clean first.'

'Is that what you were arguing about on the night of the masquerade ball, outside the boathouse?'

Dolores narrowed her eyes. 'How do you know about that?'

Florrie didn't want to throw Martha under the bus but she had to be honest. She hoped Dolores would see the funny side of it. 'Aunt Martha was there. She saw you.'

'No, Martha wasn't there. I took Ada as my plus one. I

might be a little forgetful these days but I remember that party well because that's where she first told me that Edward had siphoned off the charity money that I raised. I was livid and confronted him.'

'She was there. She found your ticket inside a newspaper that you'd left at the pub and took the chance she wouldn't be recognised.'

Dolores playfully rolled her eyes. 'All these years she's kept that from me.'

'But my father didn't come clean,' said Tom, trying to steer them back to the matter at hand. 'He thought he was above everything and everyone, so he called Ada and Dolores's bluff.'

'What happened?' asked Florrie.

Tom gestured for Dolores to carry on with the story.

'Ada went to the hospital the next night. It wasn't her usual shift but she wanted to check in on William. He was getting stronger and it was rumoured he might be allowed out of hospital sometime in the following few days ... but all hell broke loose when she got there.'

'What do you mean?' asked Florrie.

'William had his own private room, and when Ada arrived there was something wedged behind the door. The light in his room was switched off, too, which was unusual. Ada was just about to leave when she saw movement through the glass window of the door. She gave the door an almighty push and discovered Edward holding a pillow over William's face.'

Florrie gasped. 'He was trying to suffocate him.'

'He was,' confirmed Dolores. 'There was some sort of altercation between Ada and Edward, then Edward fled.'

'He tried to kill William for his money?' Florrie asked, dumbfounded.

'It would appear so,' Dolores said sadly.

'That's terrible.'

'Isn't it just,' said Tom. 'Sadly, my grandfather passed away a few weeks later – his heart stopped when he was sleeping – before he could take my father out of the will, which meant everything was left to him – the company and the foundation.'

'All except one thing – and this is the part you're going to be most interested in,' Dolores shared.

Florrie couldn't believe there was more to this story.

'One of the biggest assets in William's portfolio was Rose Cottage, with its acres of sought-after land. William knew the property's value would only increase over the years but he didn't care about the money. What was important to him was that the person who lived there would love it as much as Rose had. So, in the weeks before he passed away, he gave Ada a life interest in the cottage.'

Florrie was puzzled. 'I don't understand. What exactly does that mean?'

Sophia chipped in. 'A life interest trust is an arrangement whereby your assets – or, in this case, one asset, i.e., Rose Cottage – is transferred to someone of your choosing. It means you can provide future security for a particular individual. Ada saved his life, and so, to repay her, William wanted her to never have to worry about financial security. So he gave Ada a life interest in the cottage up until her death, but with one condition.'

'Which was?' asked Florrie.

'Ada had to promise to turn the gardens into something

quite spectacular, create the rose garden in memory of Rose and keep The Vintage Flower Van bursting with blooms.'

'Out of interest,' Florrie said nervously, 'is there any kind of financial transaction involved with a life interest trust?'

'What do you mean?' asked Tom.

'Well, there's something I may need to come clean about, especially after you've shared all this with me,' Florrie confessed. 'Whilst I was sorting through Aunt Ada's personal documents, I found piles and piles of bank statements that suggest she … never paid rent.'

'We know,' chorused Dolores and Tom. Tom pointed to the laptops on the table.

'I stumbled across that very fact only recently. But Ada didn't need to pay rent. William had given her the life interest which meant she had a legal right to live there free of charge. That was the point of my grandfather's gift – it provided Ada and Ewart with financial security and ensured Ada had a roof over her head for as long as she lived.'

Florrie was astonished. 'That's one hell of a gift.'

'It is. Now, let's fast forward many years to a few weeks back. My father has never fully retired from the company or completely handed over the reins of the foundation and he mentioned to me in passing that he was handling a brand-new development. His take on it was that it was the last job he wanted to do before he retired. I had no involvement in it at all and didn't think anything about it. At the same time Sophia confided in me that she'd discovered some anomalies within the charity's finances and that's when I began to delve discreetly into the workings of the company and the foundation a lot more.'

Sophia took up the story. 'My mother always told me how

good William had been to our family and as a family we would always take part in the fundraisers for his foundation. I wanted to get more involved, which was why I started working for the charity and became familiar with the financial side of things. I then noticed in the charity's newsletter that the amount we'd raised in the most recent fundraising drive was significantly less than the actual amount I knew we'd brought in. I happened to mention it to Dolores one day when we were catching up and that's when she shared her suspicions that Edward might be using the foundation's profits to fund his own lifestyle, and that it had likely been going on for years. For instance, I discovered that he'd built an extension on his estate, claiming it was offices for the charity, when what was actually built was a state-of-the-art gym. Tom has been my friend for many years and I knew he needed to know what was going on so we started to dig around. Edward trusted me because I'd been a friend of the family for years and he was happy to have me come on the board as a trustee, which gave me the perfect opportunity to ensure the charity's money was used for legitimate charitable purposes ... and I discovered it wasn't.'

Florrie exhaled. 'Does Edward know you're on to him?'

'Not yet,' Tom replied. 'But he recently called a meeting with me out of the blue and told me about the planning proposal for the land Rose Cottage sits on. Straightaway, something about it didn't sit right with me. He told me that there was some opposition in the village and that I needed to smooth the way. The next thing I knew, I was being bombarded by journalists. That's when I discovered your posts and TV appearance. I couldn't believe my father had made an application to flatten the land and put in new-builds, destroying such beauty, especially when there are so many other places to build property. I began to do some digging and discovered that Rose Cottage had only appeared on the W. Houston Property Developers' computer system the day Ada passed away. Sophia and I decided to approach Dolores, knowing she was a lifelong friend of William, to see if she could help us make sense of it all.'

'I was just happy I could shed some light on the situation,' Dolores said modestly. 'I knew about the life interest and everything that had gone on.'

'It's been a lot to discover that my father attempted to end my grandfather's life for his fortune,' said Tom. 'I know he was a greedy man but that's on a different level. It must have been a huge blow to my father to discover my grandfather had given Ada a life interest in the cottage and he couldn't get his hands on it. The fact he wants to destroy it now – seemingly just for revenge – shows the man he is.'

Florrie wasn't quite sure what to say. She could see the hurt in Tom's eyes.

'I don't want any more to do with him,' Tom continued, 'and I would love to stop him from getting his hands on Rose Cottage and its land, but we need to tread carefully until we have a little more evidence.'

Florrie was confused again. 'Who actually owns the cottage now?'

'That's the question all of us around this table have been trying to answer,' offered Dolores. 'There was a document signed between William and Ada – I know this because I was the witness – which William told Ada to keep safe, but we have no clue where it is. To solve this whole thing, and to hopefully save your great-aunt's legacy, we need to find that piece of paper.'

'Surely there's a copy with a solicitor?'

'That solicitor is no longer living and the firm closed down.'

'Are we actually saying there's a small chance that W. Houston Property Developers doesn't own the cottage?'

'That's exactly what we're saying. It belonged to my grandfather, not the company,' said Tom.

'So how can Edward apply for planning permission if he doesn't own the property?'

'He can't. He waited for Ada to pass away and fraudulently prepared whatever paperwork he needed to make money from the cottage. He's waited a long time to get his hands on that land, but he's underestimated us all. He clearly doesn't know about the agreement William and Ada signed.'

'We need to find that document,' Dolores repeated. 'Without it we can't do anything to stop him.'

Florrie stood up. 'Then there's only one thing for it.'

'Where are you going?' asked Tom.

'Back to the cottage. We need to search every nook and cranny until we find that piece of paper!'

Chapter Twenty-Six

As they walked back to Rose Cottage, Tom slipped his hand into Florrie's. Taking a sideward glance, she caught him watching her with a smile on his face.

'Why are you smiling at me like that?' Her heart gave a tiny leap as she bumped her shoulder against his.

'You know why. I told you to trust me and you're trusting me.'

Florrie felt a pink blush springing to her cheeks.

'We've had a lot of misunderstandings, haven't we? Let's not let that happen again, eh?'

'Most definitely not. What's the plan after we've found this document?'

'Sophia will report him to the charity commission to investigate and we'll just step away, letting him take the consequences that are heading his way.'

'It's going to be an interesting week. I dare not ask what your father thought about my campaign to save the cottage and gardens.'

'Think of those cartoon characters that get angry and have steam coming out of their ears. He resembled something like that. Whereas me? I thought, there's Florrie Appleton, standing up for what's right and still as passionate and as beautiful as ever.'

Tom's words gave her a warm feeling all over.

'And then there's The Vintage Flower Van; it was a little extreme he wanted that too, don't you think?'

'I honestly have no words. My father must have brooded about this for years, just waiting to take everything back.'

'Even after everything that happened, I didn't hate you, you know.'

'I realised that when I saw you still had my number in your phone.'

Florrie gave a chuckle. 'I tried to delete it, believe me, but my heart overruled my head every time. It was always going to fight for what was right.'

'And that goes for me, too. We're in this together. On the same side, the same team.'

Florrie could feel the warmth towards him rising up through her body. 'Team,' she repeated. She liked the sound of that. 'And when we save The Vintage Flower Van and the gardens, we'll be the most liked people in Heartcross.'

'Just like my grandfather and your wonderful role model, your great-aunt Ada.'

'I wish you could have met her.'

'Me too. I know I've already told you this, but I think it's worth saying again – our two weeks together were very special to me. Maybe we could … do it again some time? After all, we have a lot of catching up to do.'

'I think that's possible.'

Tom slipped his arm around her waist and pulled her in close.

She pressed a hand against his chest, over his heart. 'But first we need to find that document.'

'Spoilsport.'

He stared deeply into her eyes.

'I want to kiss you, Florrie Appleton.'

'I want to kiss you too, Tom—'

Tom bent his head and kissed her mid-sentence.

'I've been waiting to do that since the moment I saw you again,' he said once he'd pulled away.

'Ditto,' she whispered. 'But now we need to find out who the cottage belongs to and I'm hoping it's not your father.'

'I'm hoping that too. But are you sure I can't have another one of those kisses first?' Tom asked as he leaned in again.

Florrie had never been so attracted to anyone before. Tom kissed her again, taking her breath away. It was some minutes before she pulled away slowly. Hand in hand they walked back to Rose Cottage.

Standing outside the gate, Tom looked around. 'I can't believe anyone would want to destroy the beauty of this place.'

'In the next week all of this is going to come to a head.'

'It is, and it won't be pretty. I've got a huge fight on my hands.'

Florrie bumped his shoulder. 'You said we were a team.'

With a lopsided grin Tom squeezed her hand tight. 'We're definitely a team,' he said.

'And if he does cut you off?'

Tom stretched out his arms and tilted his head towards the sky. 'The world is my oyster. I'll still have a share in the business – my grandfather made sure that was protected for me – so I'd need to make a decision on what I want to do with my life. I'm sure I could find some work in The Vintage Flower Van in the meantime.'

Florrie opened the garden gate. 'Ha ha. Come on, let me show you around.'

They took the gravel path around the side of the cottage and stood in the courtyard, taking in the view. 'Wow! This place is stunning. Just look at it.' He pointed towards the river and the mountain in the distance. 'What a special place.'

'Isn't it just? Do you want to come and see the rose garden?'

Tom nodded. 'That would be good.'

They walked side by side through the archway to the rose garden. The central circular area was enclosed by a yew hedge, and the roses were mixed with herbaceous planting, creating rich, seasonal flower beds. 'The best time to see the roses in full bloom is round about now, but they do continue to flower through to the first frosts. Aunt Ada planted twice a year with spring and summer displays, so, regardless of the time of year, there's always a rose to see.'

'It's magnificent. I can see why Ada won awards and why this place kept winning Flowers in Bloom.' Tom walked up to the rose garden. 'This whole place is tranquil. I feel truly at peace here, there's such a good feel about it.' He turned and looked at the rest of the property. 'I had a look at the plans that my father submitted.' He pointed. 'All of this would be destroyed.'

'It might still be if the document states that the cottage goes to Edward.'

Tom shook his head. 'If my grandfather went to such great lengths to give Ada a life interest, I'm sure he would have put measures in place to keep Edward from ever owning the cottage.'

'Aunt Ada would have kept that document in a safe place, I just know it. There were always two things that were very close to her heart, this garden and The Vintage Flower Van. You don't think she would have buried it, do you?'

Tom raised his eyebrows. 'We can't go digging up acres of land in search of a document hidden inside a rust-proof tin. It would take for ever.'

'You're right,' she replied, wondering where the hell it could be. She thought for a moment. 'Aunt Ada loved the glasshouses. I know there's a set of drawers in there. Maybe we should take a look in them.'

'Lead the way.'

They ambled along the stone path, which was laced with lavender, towards the row of glasshouses.

'These are impressive,' said Tom.

'Aunt Ada loved being out here.' Florrie opened the door of the first glasshouse. All the windows were currently lodged open, letting in a lovely breeze.

'It certainly does capture your eyes.'

'This is the hub of the business.'

There were rows and rows of seedling trays on wire racks with new shoots poking out, and shelving units holding a variety of pots with tags sticking out to identify which seedling was which flower and which section of the garden they would be planted in. The handheld broom and dustpan were still hanging off the wall, and intertwined vines ran along the dirt underfoot.

'This place, along with The Vintage Flower Van, pretty much ruled every aspect of Aunt Ada's life.' Florrie turned towards one of the workstations, where Aunt Ada's favourite gardening gloves were still lying on the wooden top along with her spare pair of glasses. As soon as Florrie saw them, she picked them up, feeling emotional.

'Hey, come here.' Tom stretched out his arms and Florrie stepped into them.

'I'm sorry, I didn't mean to come across all maudlin.'

'You don't need to apologise for missing Ada. It's the most natural thing in the world.'

Tom hugged her tight and she felt safe resting against his chest, taking in the aroma of his aftershave.

'I can't imagine anyone else living here. Look at the hard work that goes into this business.'

'It does look a bit like a military operation.'

Florrie pulled away slowly. 'The flower business needs lots of love and dedication.'

'And that's exactly what you're going to give it.'

'I am.' She hesitated. 'But what if we don't find that document?'

'We will. Have faith.'

She nodded and pointed to the cabinets in the adjoining glasshouse. They went through to them, took a drawer each and sifted through the paperwork.

'This is mainly invoices from the wholesalers, lists of gardening equipment bought, etc. There's nothing out of the ordinary. Have you found anything?' Florrie asked.

'Gardening diaries, photographs of The Vintage Flower Van and an old Valentine's Day card.'

'No way, let's have a look.'

Tom passed Florrie the card and she read the words inside. *My Dearest Ada,*

My valentine forever.

Yours always,

Ewart X

'Aww, how sweet. They certainly had a special love.'

'A rarity,' Tom added.

They continued to look through the rest of the drawers but found nothing of importance.

'It's getting late,' said Florrie, looking at her watch. 'Would you like to stay and have a drink?'

'That would be good,' he replied.

They began to walk towards the back door of the cottage. 'If you had to keep an important document safe, where would you keep it?' Florrie pondered.

'Maybe give it to a friend? A safety deposit box? Under the mattress?'

'I think Aunt Ada would have given it to either Dolores or Martha, but they haven't got it. A safety deposit box is a possibility, but surely she would have mentioned it in her will? And as for under the mattress...' She chuckled.

'Hey, you never know, people used to hide all manner of things under the mattress in case they got burgled.'

'And wouldn't that be the first place a burglar would look?'

'Fair point.'

As soon as they were in the kitchen Florrie opened the fridge door and pulled out a chilled bottle of wine. She poured two glasses and placed them on the table. As she went to sit in the chair next to Tom, he reached out and pulled her on to his knee.

'What is it about you that makes me so nervous?' Florrie could feel her pulse beginning to race.

'Is that a good thing?'

'It is.' She paused and looked over his shoulder.

'What are you thinking about? You suddenly look all worried.'

She sighed. 'I've got something on my mind.'

'Go on.'

'I'm worried about Flowers in Bloom.'

'Why?'

'Because I don't want any trouble. It's happening on the same day the cottage is being inspected by W. Houston Property Developers.'

'I think you're forgetting that's my company and I can change the date for that sort of thing.'

'But not if Edward doesn't know you're on to him by then. The idea was for you to be faced with all the community who would be here along with Dolores and the press. But I don't want that anymore. I don't want the day to be spoilt in any way whatsoever. Aunt Ada enjoyed this day for many years and as it's more than likely going to be the last one to be held here, I want to remember all those good years by making it a celebration of Aunt Ada's life and Dolores's birthday. The people who bought tickets will be here because they love Ada, or Rose Cottage or The Vintage Flower Van. I don't want protesters or conflict.'

'Look, we can make this day about anything you want. And I can cancel that appointment, no problem. My gut feeling is that's it's a ploy on my father's part to come and have a look at the cottage before he takes it. I'm sure he'd get some sort of sadistic pleasure out of seeing everything he's going to destroy out of spite.'

'But if you cancel that appointment, he might know you're on to him.'

'He might, but there's no guarantee of that, and what you want is more important: to celebrate the memory of your great-aunt Ada, Flowers in Bloom and Dolores's birthday. It *should* be a celebration, so we'll make it a day to remember.'

'Thank you.'

'You don't need to thank me,' he replied, entwining his fingers around hers. 'And what about us?'

'Us?' Florrie said with a smile.

'Yes, us. I don't know about you, but I'd like to pick up right where we left off when I dropped you back in the university car park eight years ago.'

'That's exactly what I want too.'

They stared into each other's eyes for a moment before Florrie leaned forward and pressed her lips against his. He kissed her back, and her whole body erupted in goosebumps. Getting slowly to his feet, he hugged her tight then glanced towards the door. 'Which way are we going?'

She nodded towards the hallway. 'That way, and then up the stairs to the first room on the right.'

Without hesitation they made their way up the stairs hand in hand and he laid her down gently on the bed. She pulled him on top of her. She had never wanted anyone as much as she wanted Tom right at that moment. Feeling the touch of his lips on hers, she gasped with desire.

But then she froze.

And pushed him away.

'What's the matter? Is it too soon…' Tom asked, looking concerned.

'The document,' she blurted. 'I think I know where it is! Oh my gosh, why didn't I think of it before?' Rolling out from underneath him, she was up on her feet in an instant and grabbing his hand.

'You pick your moments!' His trousers were around his ankles and he attempted to pull them up as he hurriedly followed Florrie down the stairs.

She flung open the back door.

'Where are we going?'

'Aunt Ada told me to never let it out of my sight when the business became mine.' Florrie sprinted outside and stopped right outside The Vintage Flower Van.

Tom was right behind her. 'I'm not sure I'm following.'

Unlocking the door, she stepped inside and pointed to the photograph of her great-grandfather. 'I think this photograph has something to do with this.' Florrie unhooked it from the wall and laid it face-down on the counter. She bent the small metal pins back and removed the back of the frame. They both stared down in excitement.

Hidden behind the photograph was a folded piece of paper.

'Woah! I think you could possibly be right.'

With a trembling hand, Florrie carefully unfolded the paper. 'It's definitely a document.' With a beating heart she scanned the legal jargon. 'This is what we needed. Look!' She held it out so they could both read it.

'You're right, this is it! There's Dolores's signature.'

Florrie carried on reading and gave a tiny gasp. She read aloud, 'In the event of Ada's death, the life interest will cease and Rose Cottage and all of its assets will be transferred to *Thomas Houston*.'

Florrie looked at Tom, who was still staring at the

document, but now in disbelief. 'It belongs to you. The cottage belongs to you!'

Tom exhaled and raked his hand through his hair. 'I don't quite believe it.'

'It's there in black and white. How do you feel?'

Tom held Florrie's gaze. 'Shocked. But more importantly, how do you feel about it?' His eyes were earnest.

Florrie gave him a heart-warming smile. 'I'd already prepared myself to lose this place. I'm happy for you.'

'I feel like I've stolen your home.'

She shook her head and swallowed. 'I will always be grateful for what your grandfather did for Aunt Ada and Uncle Ewart. He gave them lifelong security with no financial worries. But this cottage is your inheritance now and after you've dealt with the fallout from your father's misdeeds, this will be your fresh start too. I'm just thankful that we have the evidence we need to stop the planning application from going ahead. Now that we know these gardens are going to live on, we can focus on exposing your father. And hopefully we can strike up a deal.'

'A deal?'

'It was Aunt Ada's wish that no matter what, The Vintage Flower Van lived for ever.'

'It goes without saying that the van is yours and you can keep using the gardens and the glasshouses to build up your flower empire.'

'That's very much appreciated.'

Florrie pointed towards the back of the photograph. 'Look, there's another piece of paper in here.' She picked it up and unfolded it. 'It's a letter.'

Dear Ada and Ewart,

Sometimes in life you're lucky enough to cross paths with someone who becomes a friend and is there for you no matter what. They encourage your dreams and celebrate your wins without an ounce of jealousy. They want what's best for you, and you for them, and there isn't much more to it.

Thank you both for being that kind of friend to me over the years, supporting me unconditionally throughout the heartache of losing Rose and always looking out for my best interests. I will always be grateful our paths crossed.

Your friend,

William

As Florrie finished reading the letter, she swallowed a lump and tears began running down her face. 'Aunt Ada always told me to find friends who were there for you no matter what. I'm so happy to know she had those kinds of people in her life – people like your grandfather. This is so beautiful.' She put her hand on her heart. 'Look at me, I've come over all emotional.' Glancing up at Tom she saw that he had tears in his eyes too.

'They looked after each other for the time they were in each other's lives and that's exactly what we're going to do. We'll look after Rose Cottage and The Vintage Flower Van, and we'll honour the memories of those we've lost while we live on and make new ones.' Tom pulled Florrie in for a hug, wrapping his arms tightly around her. 'This is the beginning, Florrie,' he whispered, kissing the top of her head.

She held on tight, her heart swelling with happiness at his words.

Chapter Twenty-Seven

A couple of weeks later

It was early morning and Florrie was standing at the back door holding a mug of tea. The sun had only just risen and the gorgeous colours of the sky complemented the stunning apricot roses that had just come into bloom. She felt Tom's arm slide around her waist and she looked over her shoulder, pressing a kiss to his lips.

'Look at those roses. Aunt Ada always said they bloom just in time for Flowers in Bloom and here they are, right on time. They couldn't look any more stunning if they tried.'

'Roses for Rose Cottage,' Tom said, smiling. 'I'm not sure whether you've seen yet but all hell has broken out on social media. Dolores has announced that she'll be holding her one hundredth birthday celebrations in the grounds of Rose Cottage in honour of her good friends Ada and William. It's splashed all over every news channel.'

'We're in for an amazing day. I can't wait.'

'Flynn is bringing over a number of crowd barriers that he uses for events at Starcross Manor, and they'll be set up from the top of the lane all the way to the cottage gate. No one can get in without a ticket.'

'I hope Aunt Ada, Ewart, William and Rose are all looking down on us and smiling.'

'They will be and they'll be so proud.' Tom gave her a squeeze.

'How are you feeling about being the main speaker at Flynn's charity event with the brand-new charity you've set up?'

'Privileged, and glad that my new charity in honour of my grandfather will get the recognition it properly deserves. No money will ever go missing from it on my watch. And it gets better. I'm proud to say that the charity Dolores has chosen for this year's Flowers in Bloom is the brand-new William Houston charity, with the first donations going to the hospital and ward where Ada volunteered.'

'She would be over the moon to hear that.'

It had been a hell of a couple of weeks. As soon as the letter had been discovered, Tom had taken legal advice from Jaydon, as he had known and worked with Ada in the past. He confirmed that the document was indeed legitimate and the cottage was now Tom's property. Jaydon had also immediately prepared a letter to the council stating that the planning permission Edward had submitted couldn't be granted as he didn't have a legal right to the land. To add to Edward's misfortune, Sophia had reported his charity for a number of fraudulent claims. As expected, it had quickly turned ugly. Edward was livid and had cut all ties with Tom.

'What needs doing first today?' asked Tom.

Florrie pointed to the table. 'We have a list and not much time,' she replied, glancing at the clock. 'Firstly, we need to prepare The Vintage Flower Van and decorate the front of the cottage with balloons and bunting. The Vintage Flower Van is going to be bursting at the seams with roses, including on the roof, and with bucketloads in front of it. Hector is arriving from Heartcross Castle in the next twenty minutes to mow the lawns one last time. Flynn is arriving not long after that with the barriers and seating. Drew and Fergus are almost done erecting the makeshift stage in front of the fountain. Rona and Felicity are already organising the tent for refreshments and Dolores's team will be arriving with her band's instruments and setting up the microphones in about an hour.'

'And breathe,' Tom smiled. 'What would you like me to do?'

'Mmm,' she replied with a wicked glint in her eye. 'I've got a spare twenty minutes to spend wrapped up in the arms of a gorgeous man. What do you say?'

'I say, your every wish is my command.'

Placing her mug on the table, Florrie took Tom's hand and led him straight back up the stairs.

Exactly twenty minutes later, Florrie looked through the cottage window to see a hive of activity outside. The Flowers in Bloom event was due to begin in a little over an hour, with Dolores performing at midday.

'You get yourself ready. I'll make sure everything is running smoothly downstairs.'

'Thank you,' replied Florrie, kissing Tom one last time before she jumped in the shower.

After applying her make-up and blow-drying her hair, Florrie put on her favourite summer dress and stood in front of the mirror. She smiled at her reflection. She'd come a long way in the last month. Her eyes sparkled and her skin looked radiant, as she'd caught the sun while prepping the garden for today's event, and she noticed a lone line of russet freckles dotting her nose. She checked her appearance one last time, then she walked downstairs, where Tom was making drinks in the kitchen.

'Here she is. You look gorgeous,' he said as he leaned in towards her. 'And you smell divine. Are you sure you don't have any more minutes free?' He jokingly looked back towards the stairs.

Florrie laughed and then gave him a firm no. 'How's everything going out there?'

'Running like clockwork. Martha and Isla are currently out front, and the wholesalers have just arrived with all the roses. We have over five hundred to decorate The Vintage Flower Van.'

'Perfect. I'll go and take a look.'

'I'll be with you in a minute. I'm just making drinks for Drew and Fergus, who have just finished erecting the stage.'

Florrie couldn't believe her eyes when she walked around to the front of the cottage. The barriers were in place leading the queue towards The Vintage Flower Van, Isla and Martha had hung bunting between the street lamps, and clusters of colourful balloons were tied from every tree.

'It looks magnificent!' she exclaimed.

'The question now is what exactly would you like us to do with these five hundred roses?' asked Martha.

'I'm going to use them to decorate The Vintage Flower Van.

We're going to tie them into bunches and cover the roof and have them bursting out of the milk churns in barrels of colour leading the way to the gate.' She shouted towards Tom who was making his way around the side of the cottage. 'Tom, could you possibly bring me the step ladders?'

He acknowledged the request with a wave and disappeared.

'And what did I tell you?' Martha pointed first in Tom's direction and then towards the van. 'Your future love had something to do with The Vintage Flower Van after all. Tell me I was wrong.'

'Look at you being all smug!' Florrie laughed. 'Yes, Martha, you were right as usual!'

'And are you going to be staying here with Tom?'

Tom had suggested Florrie move into Rose Cottage but she'd declined. It wasn't because she didn't want to – she wanted that more than ever, and was anticipating it happening in the not too distant future – but for the here and now, she wanted them to enjoy the getting-to-know-each-other stage, the first flush of love, while still having their own spaces. Florrie was very happy with how things stood and very much looking forward to the next chapter in her life.

'Not yet.'

'I like the use of the word "yet",' Isla teased.

It took them over thirty minutes to decorate The Vintage Flower Van and when they stood back they admired their work. 'It's beautiful,' exclaimed Florrie. 'Utterly breathtaking.'

'It certainly is,' replied Martha, pointing to the paparazzi cars that were heading up the lane at speed. 'Here we go. The word is out! Are we ready to get this show on the road? There're people already walking up the lane clutching their tickets.' As soon as the press stepped out of their cars their cameras began to click. 'They'll get the shot they're looking for soon enough. Dolores is due to arrive any moment. She wouldn't miss the opening.'

There was excitement in the air as all the villagers began to gather outside the gates and Florrie, Tom, Isla and Martha stood at the front of the barrier. Martha had tied a red ribbon between The Vintage Flower Van and the garden gate and she handed Florrie a pair of scissors to cut the ribbon and officially open Flowers in Bloom.

Looking out over the sea of people, Florrie saw everyone who meant the world to her. The turnout was truly amazing. She smiled at Tom, who slipped his hand into hers. She stood in silence for a moment taking in the view. Aunt Ada had stood in this very spot for the last sixty years welcoming everyone to enjoy her garden, and Florrie felt honoured to be taking over the reins.

'This is quite surreal,' she whispered to Tom.

'Enjoy every second.' He nodded towards the top of the lane. 'Here she comes.'

Florrie noticed the TV cameras beginning to roll as a black limousine glided towards the cottage.

In her usual flamboyant style Dolores, helped by Hamish, stepped out the car to the sound of rapturous applause. They were joined by Sophia, who stepped out of the other passenger door. In a frenzy the cameras began to click as Dolores made her way towards Florrie and Tom.

'Before we kick this off...' Dolores said, taking Florrie's hands and pressing something cold into them. Florrie looked down to see a bunch of keys.

'What are these for?'

Dolores winked at Tom. 'A private beach house I co-owned with William while he was alive. I want you to have it.'

Florrie put her hand on her chest, her heart racing. 'Is this *our* private beach house?' she asked Tom.

Tom smiled. 'It is.'

'And you own it?' She looked towards Dolores.

'I did, but now I want you to have it. William made sure Ada and her family were financially secure, now it's my turn.'

'Aunt Dolores, I don't know what to say.'

'Say yes.' She winked.

'Yes! Thank you!' Florrie flung her arms around her, then Tom. 'Thank you! Thank you!'

With a wide smile on her face, Florrie felt a rush of adrenalin. Flynn had ushered the community and ticket-holders into a semi-circle in front of The Vintage Flower Van and now passed Florrie a microphone. She took it and the crowd hushed.

Tom was standing on one side of her and Dolores on the other, and Martha and Isla had positioned themselves at the front of the crowd. Glancing at Dolores, Florrie took a breath to compose herself.

'Thank you all for coming to this year's Flowers in Bloom.' She was thankful her voice sounded calmer than she felt. Her heart was beating nineteen to the dozen. 'For the last thirty years Flowers in Bloom has been an open day where ticket-holders could wander through all the spectacular gardens in the village of Heartcross. This year, to celebrate the memory of my aunt Ada, who lived here in Rose Cottage for over sixty years, and whose gardens won Flowers in Bloom more times than anyone can remember, we have only one garden open to the public today, together with a very special guest. Please let me introduce you to Dolores Henderson. You may all know her as a global superstar, but Dolores was also my great-aunt Ada's best friend for many decades.'

The crowd began to clap and Florrie felt tears spring to her eyes. She dared to look at Tom, who gave her a heart-warming smile and squeezed her hand.

As the applause began to simmer down Dolores took the microphone, Hamish and Sophia standing next to her.

'What is a true friend? A true friend isn't always the person you've known the longest – though in Ada's case it's that as well – a true friend is the person who walks into your life and says, "I'm here for you." They're like stars, always shining bright in the darkest of times. They're the ones who laugh with you, cry with you, and stick around through every chapter of your life. They see you at your best, they see you at your worst. They're the source of the greatest treasure chest of memories because every moment you share with them is a priceless gem. And they're the ones who see pain behind your smile and stay to wipe your tears away and stick around through your highs and lows. Ada Jones was my true friend and that's why I've chosen to celebrate her life with her family, who are now my family, today on my one hundredth birthday, here at Rose Cottage with all our friends.'

The crowd began to clap again and when Florrie looked out over the sea of people standing in front of her, there wasn't a dry eye in the place. In true diva style, Dolores waved her walking stick in the air and the crowd soon quieted down. 'Whilst others are starting out on their new journeys of life and love –' Dolores looked towards Florrie and Tom '– my own time of life is coming to an end and I want to share with you all that I've had a complete blast. Despite my worldwide fame,

Heartcross has always been my home, just like it was Ada's home and is Florrie's home, because this is where we all belong. Once you arrive in Heartcross, you never want to leave. It's a place where friends are there for you, no matter what.' Dolores's voice faltered as the emotion took over and she couldn't say any more.

Florrie couldn't say any more either. She was doing everything in her power just to stop the tears rolling down her cheeks. Taking a deep breath, she held the scissors out in front of her. 'Without further ado, I declare Flowers in Bloom officially open!' She snipped the ribbon.

As the queue began to pass through the barrier towards The Vintage Flower Van, Florrie and Tom stepped inside, ready to collect tickets and greet their guests. Florrie looked up at the photo of her great-grandfather, which was now hanging next to a framed photo of Aunt Ada. 'We're one hell of a family,' she murmured, overcome with emotion.

'It is true what Dolores said, isn't it?' Tom mused. 'Once you arrive in Heartcross you never want to leave.'

'You tell me.'

'I'm going nowhere. It's me, you and The Vintage Flower Van forever.'

Florrie smiled. 'That sounds perfect to me.' She leaned across and kissed him. 'Now we best start collecting these tickets as we don't want to miss the show!'

Florrie already knew she was falling in love with Tom. He was her happy ever after, and she couldn't wait to see what the future held for them.

Epilogue

Twenty-Five Years Later

Winter

The morning was cold, freezing in fact, the temperature having dropped to minus one. The sky was dark and it threatened snow again.

'I can't believe the amount of snow we've seen this year...' Isla was standing in the window of Foxglove Farm looking out over the rolling hills, Heartcross Mountain towering in the distance.

'Twenty-five years ago today, the weather was just the same – and by the end of the day we were cut off from civilisation when the bridge collapsed, leaving us all stranded,' said Drew, handing her a mug of tea before slipping his arm around her waist.

'This tiny village of Heartcross became worldwide news

that day and our lives were never the same again, were they?' added Isla. 'I can remember it so vividly, even now. Felicity had returned to the village following her grandmother's passing...'

'And had to get straight into rescuing her ex who'd fallen in the river,' Drew finished.

Isla chuckled. 'That's right, Fergus was rescuing that Shetland pony! And now look at them both: happily married for the past twenty years, Fergus a partner in the Heart of the Village shopping estate and Felicity running the coffee shop with their daughter Esme.'

'Rona and Bonnie would be so proud that the family teashop is still thriving.' Drew smiled. 'We've all done well for ourselves over the years. I mean, look at our boys, they're successful, what with Finn running the alpaca farm and Angus farming full-time. And us grandparents!'

Isla nodded warmly. 'More boys. I was hoping for a splash of pink around the place, but you never know, maybe one day...'

'As you say, you never know.' Drew kissed the top of her head.

'How are you feeling about the speech today?' Isla asked, shaking them out of their wistfulness.

'All good, but I have to admit I'm looking forward to the moment it's over and we can go and have food and drinks up at Heartcross Castle. Grace and Andrew certainly know how to host and he's not a bad cook.'

Isla laughed. 'He's a world-famous chef. I think he's a little better than "not bad"! I'm so happy they've joined us in the grandparents' club.'

'Twins again for their family!'

'That's probably because their boys, Freddie and Joey, were twins. Little Billy – who is not so little anymore, given he's a fighter pilot in the RAF! – is doing so well. And to think, Billy's career choice was all down to Andrew taking him up in his plane when they first arrived at Heartcross Castle.'

They both sipped their tea whilst watching the alpacas lollop over the snow, the comical pom-poms on top of the animals' heads making them both smile.

'Martha would have loved to see the unveiling of the new bridge and the plaque being erected in memory of all the old-timers that made the village of Heartcross what it is today.'

'Gran would be turning in her grave if she heard you calling her an old timer!' Isla chuckled. 'Who'd have thought that the "temporary bridge" would last twenty-five years? I'm glad they're keeping it and pedestrianising it now that the new bridge will finally be open.'

'Twenty-five years,' Drew repeated. 'Think of everything we've gone through in that time. Farming has certainly changed so much with the rising cost of, well … everything. It was a smart move of yours to set up Foxglove Camping. It's been quite lucrative for us and helped the Heart of the Village go from strength to strength.'

'We have been lucky, haven't we? All the businesses from the original Heart of the Village complex have flourished, especially Buttercup Barn. Florrie now has her own chain of florists dotted all over Scotland!'

'And each one run by the Houston-Appleton clan. Ada would be so proud of what Florrie's accomplished, and so happy she was true to her word,' Drew added.

Isla nodded. 'Ada's legacy lives on in The Vintage Flower

Van, and Rose Cottage has been the perfect family home for Florrie, Tom and their two children.'

'It is goddamn special, this place, isn't it?'

'It is, we are very lucky to live here, and I wouldn't change it for the world. This place captures hearts and mends broken ones. The village of Heartcross is known for its "curse" for good reason – because we've seen time and time again that once you arrive in Heartcross, you never want to leave. I hope that's in your speech today.'

'Of course it is.' Drew smiled then looked at his watch. 'We need to get our coats on. The unveiling is in half an hour and Allie and Rory, and Felicity and Fergus, are meeting us at the bottom of the drive so we can all head over together.'

After finishing their drinks, they walked into the boot room and grabbed their coats from the racks. Isla glanced around. 'I remember when this room was packed with the boys' coats and wellingtons, and we could never find a thing. It feels so quiet now everyone has left home.'

'Left home? They are still here all the time, eating us out of house and home! We should enjoy this feeling while we have it, because once those grandchildren start walking, you'll be wanting a little peace again.' Drew pressed a swift kiss to Isla's lips, then held her coat open so she could slip her arms into it.

She smiled, looking over her shoulder. 'You are probably right.'

Once they were wrapped up in their scarves and gloves they stepped outside onto the fresh snowy ground. Huddled inside their parkas, and hand in hand, they followed the path of snowy footprints along the drive towards Love Heart Lane as oversized confetti began to fall lightly. Even though there was an icy chill in the air, the unspoilt late morning view was stunning. Snow-covered, heather-clad, mist-filled hollows sloped over the mountainous terrain, and unspoilt blankets of snow across the fields.

'Can you believe we've lived here for over thirty years?' said Drew. 'It seems like only yesterday that we took over the farm from my father.'

'Time flies.' Isla linked her arm through Drew's. 'And I'm delighted for you that the boys followed in your footsteps.'

'I'm pleased about that, too.' Drew held his hand up and waved. 'There they are.'

Waiting at the bottom of the drive were Allie and Rory with their clan of four black Labradors.

'Morning,' said Allie, as the dogs gave welcoming barks.

'We thought we'd bring the kids,' joked Rory. 'Here come Fergus and Felicity.' He nodded towards Heartwood Cottage as Fergus and Felicity stepped outside and soon joined them at the bottom of the lane.

'Can you believe it was twenty-five years ago today that the bridge collapsed?' Felicity asked. 'I was just saying to Fergus, it's amazing how none of us have moved away from the village in all that time, and we're all still the best of friends.'

'I think there will be a lot of proud former residents looking down on us today,' Isla said, thinking particularly of her gran, Martha.

As they walked along the track at the bottom of Love Heart Lane, they could see lots of activity. Both the temporary bridge and the new one that ran alongside were cordoned off, ready for the grand unveiling.

'I have to say, I'm kind of grateful for the original bridge collapsing all those years ago. Because if it wasn't for that storm, you would have sneaked in and out of Heartcross without anyone knowing. But when you couldn't escape...' Fergus took hold of Felicity's hand.

'I'm thankful for that storm, too,' she replied, her emotions clear on her face.

'And if it wasn't for you, we would never have raised funds for the temporary bridge,' added Rory.

'And look at everyone, what a turnout! It's lovely seeing the next generation of Heartcross all here.' Drew pointed to their boys, and Fergus and Felicity's daughter Esme, who were standing with Grace and Andrew's boys. The group was soon joined by Flynn and Julia's son and daughter.

The TV crews had already set up their equipment to film the opening of the bridge, and as the group of friends began to walk towards the huddle of people, the press began to snap photos.

Drew had been elected speaker for the event by the villagers. He stepped up to the microphone on the small raised platform and looked out over the familiar faces. The whole community was smiling towards him: Jinny and Gabe from Bumblebee Cottage, Molly and Cam from The Old Bakehouse, Katie and Ben from Peony Practice, Flynn and Julia from Starcross Manor, Bea and Nolan from The Little Blue Boathouse and Roman, the skipper of the water taxis. Grace and Andrew had just arrived from Heartcross Castle and were standing next to Felicity and Fergus.

When Aidy Redfern, who was in charge of the news crew, put his hand in the air, everyone hushed.

'Going live in five, four, three, two, one...'

Drew brought the microphone up to his mouth. 'This morning we are live from the village of Heartcross, where, twenty-five years ago today, disaster struck when the Grade II listed bridge that linked Heartcross to the town of Glensheil collapsed in the ferocious storms. Our friend and local villager, Felicity Simons, whom I'm inviting to join me now, took matters into her own hands with a community appeal that went viral, and the funds to construct the temporary bridge were raised in a matter of days.' Drew handed the microphone over to Felicity, who had stepped up onto the stage next to him.

'I can remember that day so clearly. The bridge collapsing was a shock to the whole community, with potential devastating effects on local businesses and the livelihoods of many Heartcross inhabitants. But as a community we came together to make sure everyone in the village had food, water and enough heat to see them through the storm. But as anyone who has lived here in Heartcross will tell you, the residents are used to banding together and always looking out for one another. I think you'll agree when I say our community is a special one, and has been for generations. We are here today to open the new bridge but also to remember those who have gone before us, and the ways in which each of those wonderful individuals shaped Heartcross into the place it is today.' Felicity took a breath and pointed to the plaque that had been erected at the side of the new bridge. She handed the microphone back to Drew.

Drew read from the plaque: '"This bridge is dedicated to those who will never be forgotten in the village of Heartcross: Dolores Henderson, Hamish Henderson, Martha Gray, Aggie Campbell, Bonnie Stewart, Rona Simons, Stuart and Alana Scott, Fraser McDonald, Ada and Ewart Jones, William and Rose Houston, Dr Taylor, Wilbur Carter, Marley Power and Hector Bedford." These truly special individuals will always have a place in the hearts of our community and their legacies will live on in our village forever.'

Aidy passed Felicity a pair of scissors. 'Felicity, you opened the temporary bridge twenty-five years ago, and we'd be so pleased if you'd be kind enough to do the honours again.'

Felicity turned towards the new bridge. 'We – finally – declare the new bridge, and the new permanent walkway for pedestrians that the old temporary bridge has been turned into, open!' She proudly snipped the ribbon and the sound of clapping echoed all around.

As the whole community walked across the new bridge towards Heartcross Castle, the new generation following the old, each and every one of them knew how lucky they were to be a part of this wonderful community.

Love Heart Lane, where friends are there for you no matter what.

Because once you arrive in Heartcross, you never want to leave...

Acknowledgements

It's incredible to think it was four years ago when I took you all on your first trip to Love Heart Lane. The initial three book series expanded to fourteen books thanks to the wonderful readers who wanted more. I have without a doubt enjoyed my daily trips to the Scottish Highlands and I am extremely proud of the series I've created. As the saying goes, once you arrive in Heartcross you never want to leave.

As always, writing a book is a collaborative effort and thank you to the amazing team at One More Chapter, especially Charlotte Ledger, who is an absolute joy to work with, and I still can't quite believe you turn my stories into books. Much love to my wonderful editor, Laura McCallen. I am incredibly grateful to have you by my side during the Love Heart Lane series and I am excited for what we will be creating together next.

Special thanks to my children, Emily, Jack, Ruby and Tilly. I love you and am proud of you all.

Writing the Love Heart Lane series has been a huge part of my life. This series was created during a very difficult period of my life when everything I believed in came crashing down all around me. At the time, there were people in my life who I thought I could count on forever, but unfortunately, they didn't fight for me in rooms I wasn't in, but, luckily for me, I had friends that were there for me no matter what. That's when the concept of Love Heart Lane was born. Those friends I consider my family, Anita, Aidy, Jenna and Kimberley Redfern.

Big love to Julie Wetherill. You make me laugh a little louder, make my smile a little brighter and you make my life a whole lot better, not to mention keeping me entertained with the hundreds of hilarious TikToks you send me in the early hours of the morning! You are the best!

Bella Osborne, everyone needs an author friend like you! Thank you for taking my emergency phone calls, usually two weeks before my deadline is due, when I'm panicking that I still don't have a story! I'm very grateful I've not been blocked yet!

A special mention to Tom and Elaine Houston, Natalie, Ian and Sienna Appleton. The idea of this story was sparked whilst swimming in thirty-five-degree heat whilst enjoying the odd cocktail or two with you all! Thank you for the summer holiday of 2023 and to Tom who kindly allowed me to use his name as the main character in this book. Obviously, the storyline is completely fictional and doesn't bear any resemblance to Tom's personal life except that his name is Tom Houston!

All that remains for me to do is thank all my wonderful readers, the bloggers, reviewers, retailers, librarians and fellow authors who champion all my books. I couldn't do the job I love without you all.

I really do have the best job in the world.

Lots of love,

Christie x

ONE MORE CHAPTER

The author and One More Chapter would like to thank everyone
who contributed to the publication of this story...

Analytics
Abigail Fryer
Maria Osa

Audio
Fionnuala Barrett
Ciara Briggs

Contracts
Sasha Duszynska
Lewis

Design
Lucy Bennett
Fiona Greenway
Liane Payne
Dean Russell

Digital Sales
Hannah Lismore
Emily Scorer

Editorial
Jan Adkins
Kate Elton
Arsalan Isa
Charlotte Ledger
Bonnie Macleod
Laura McCallen
Jennie Rothwell
Tony Russell

Harper360
Emily Gerbner
Jean Marie Kelly
emma sullivan
Sophia Walker

International Sales
Bethan Moore

Marketing & Publicity
Chloe Cummings
Emma Petfield

Operations
Melissa Okusanya
Hannah Stamp

Production
Emily Chan
Denis Manson
Simon Moore
Francesca Tuzzeo

Rights
Rachel McCarron
Hany Sheikh
Mohamed
Zoe Shine

**The HarperCollins
Distribution Team**

**The HarperCollins
Finance & Royalties
Team**

**The HarperCollins
Legal Team**

**The HarperCollins
Technology Team**

Trade Marketing
Ben Hurd

UK Sales
Laura Carpenter
Isabel Coburn
Jay Cochrane
Sabina Lewis
Holly Martin
Erin White
Harriet Williams
Leah Woods

**And every other
essential link in the
chain from delivery
drivers to booksellers
to librarians and
beyond!**

Love Heart Lane Series

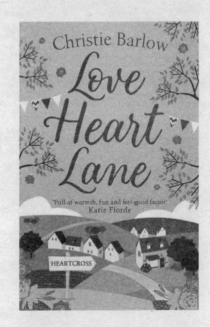

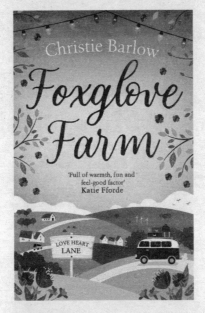

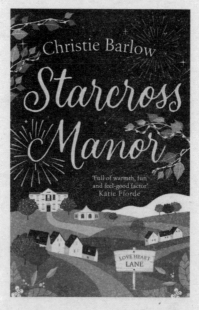

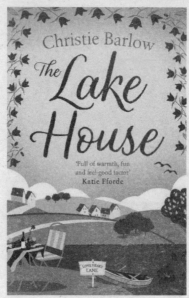

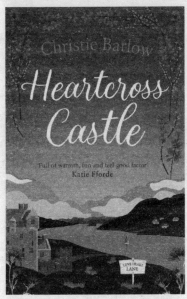

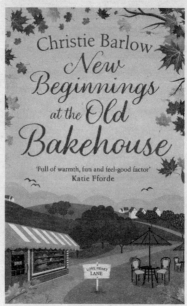

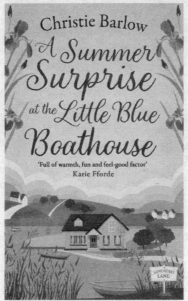

ONE MORE CHAPTER

One More Chapter is an
award-winning global
division of HarperCollins.

Sign up to our newsletter to get our
latest eBook deals and stay up to date
with our weekly Book Club!
<u>Subscribe here.</u>

Meet the team at
<u>www.onemorechapter.com</u>

Follow us!
🐦 <u>@OneMoreChapter_</u>
👤 <u>@OneMoreChapter</u>
📷 <u>@onemorechapterhc</u>

Do you write unputdownable fiction?
We love to hear from new voices.
Find out how to submit your novel at
<u>www.onemorechapter.com/submissions</u>